REIGNING CATS AND DOGS

Also by Tanith Lee

Heart-Beast
Elephantasm
Nightshades
Eva Fairdeath
A Heroine of the World

REIGNING CATS AND DOGS

Tanith Lee

HEADLINE
FEATURE

Copyright © 1995 Tanith Lee

The right of Tanith Lee to be identified as the Author of
the Work has been asserted by her in accordance with
the Copyright, Designs and Patents Act 1988.

First published in 1995 by
HEADLINE BOOK PUBLISHING

A HEADLINE FEATURE hardback

10 9 8 7 6 5 4 3 2 1

All rights reserved. No part of this publication may be
reproduced, stored in a retrieval system, or transmitted,
in any form or by any means without the prior written
permission of the publisher, nor be otherwise circulated
in any form of binding or cover other than that in which
it is published and without a similar condition being
imposed on the subsequent purchaser.

All characters in this publication are fictitious and any
resemblance to real persons, living or dead, is purely coincidental.

British Library Cataloguing in Publication Data

Lee, Tanith
Reigning Cats and Dogs
I. Title
823.914 [F]

ISBN 0-7472-1431-X

Typeset by Avon Dataset Ltd, Bidford-on-Avon, B50 4JH

Printed and bound in Great Britain by
Mackays of Chatham PLC, Chatham, Kent

HEADLINE BOOK PUBLISHING
A division of Hodder Headline PLC
338 Euston Road
London NW1 3BH

Dedicated to the memory of my mother, Hylda Lee, whose short story, *Jade Cat*, provided the seed of this novel.

The author would like to acknowledge the help and inspiration gained from the fascinating book: *Victorian Inventions* by Leonard de Vries, published by John Murray Ltd.

CONTENTS

Prologue:	Time and the Essence	1
Chapter 1:	Grace	5
Chapter 2:	Saul	13
Chapter 3:	Anger	23
Chapter 4:	The Society	35
Chapter 5:	White Cat	43
Chapter 6:	Jade Cat	49
Chapter 7:	The Apparition	57
Chapter 8:	A Visit, and After	63
Chapter 9:	The Runaway Carriage	71
Chapter 10:	On Reflection	79
Chapter 11:	Jackal's Hide	85
Chapter 12:	Love	95
Chapter 13:	Night Work	101
Chapter 14:	Grace and Anger	107
Chapter 15:	Hatred	117
Chapter 16:	Buskit at the Biscuit	125
Chapter 17:	The Courtesan	133
Chapter 18:	Once More, A Funeral	141
Chapter 19:	Lead Hearts and Feathers	147
Chapter 20:	Opium	153
Chapter 21:	Downriver	159
Chapter 22:	Anoxberus the Golden	171
Chapter 23:	The Black Church Terror	175
Chapter 24:	Green Witch	185
Chapter 25:	The Moon Into Blood	193
Chapter 26:	In the Pit	199
Epilogue:	At Home	205

Cave Canem.
> *Petronius*

The night has teeth.
> *John Kaiine* (FOSSIL CIRCUS)

They fought like cat and dog.
> *Traditional*

PROLOGUE

Time and the Essence

A quarter to midnight, and the City lies still.

The moon stands high above the river, among the tangled spars of ships in the docks. The moon is the silver cog of the wheel of night. And the river is stained with silver like a blade.

The buildings hold up their shapes into the darkness, and here and there a dull red window smoulders, but mostly the panoply of spires and hovels, domes and tenements lean black on black.

By the embankment the gas lamps run like a necklace of green pearls.

Not a sound beyond the whisper of ten thousand breaths.

A peaceful and a silent night.

The great clock, the Time Piece, bold above the river, showed ten minutes to the hour, as the keeper's assistant climbed upwards into its skull. Up there the machinery of the clock went round, its brass and iron, the huge levers. And the big bell, the voice of the clock, gleaming in the dark, as the workings prepared its tongue to strike.

The keeper's assistant knew all this very well. He had been years in the learning. He knew that to stand anywhere in the chamber of the clock and the bell, at the hour of the stroke, might be fatal, its noise cramming the brain and bursting it.

But tonight that was all part of his plan.

He had been in love, this little crooked man, for seven months. And she, of course, had never looked at him, except in disdainful pity. He had cursed himself for being what he was. Had he been otherwise, he might, he knew, have won her. Her golden hair shone in his mind like a searing flame. She, not yet the big bell, scorched out his brain.

Tomorrow she was to marry, a tall and upright man, a lawyer with good prospects. And the keeper's assistant, who had had seven months to understand that life was nothing now, only an aching dismal dream, climbed up the stairs of the Time Piece, with the thick cord trailing in his hand.

At five minutes to midnight, he reached the upper chamber, and put into the lock the iron key, and opened the door.

The fantastic chamber yawned before him. Enormous wheels turning so slowly and inexorably, weights, coils, the massive levers with their hulls of brass.

The clock made a sound, a deep strong thudding, which any way could be heard from the roots of the tower.

In the dim gaslight, the keeper's assistant ascended to the platform, and threw his rope, with the mathematical care that had marked his life, over one great lever.

The noose was already fashioned.

Calmly, the man climbed up now into the viscera of the clock. So finely balanced, yet his slight weight did not disturb it. It allowed him to scramble out upon a metal edge, and perch there, knotting his cord securely to the rod above, placing the noose securely about his throat.

It would not take much to break him. A slight girl of eighteen had already done so.

He felt no fear, no questioning, only tired. He poised, waiting, and heard the scratching of the mechanism as the clockwork moved to grip the tongue of the bell.

A pause then, as if night held its breath. The pointer of the clock slid on to the numeral of the twelve.

Midnight.

The first stroke.

The man groaned, but it was almost a noise of delight. Of satisfaction.

He trembled on his ledge and let his arms fall limp. The noose was reassuringly close about his neck, like two joined loving hands.

The second stroke. The third, the fourth.

He swayed and a thrumming vertigo whirled him away from himself so that for a moment he believed he had already fallen and could not understand why the rope did not tighten.

The fifth stroke, the sixth.

The voice of the bell burst his head and stars scattered through his eyes.

On the seventh stroke he fell.

The rope was effective. His neck was squeezed then snapped, and his legs kicked out only once.

But something else had happened.

Love had so cruelly cheated him. He was full of the fluids of love, which now, as in the prison over the river they could have told him, spurted from his loins at the pressure of the hanging rope.

Semen, the water of life, sprayed in the moment of death, and struck the face of time, struck through garments and air, to jewel the rotating valves and coils.

The eighth stroke came, and the night turned over like a page.

The man on the flycycle pedalled hard above the river. Behind him, from the gas-bag, a thin vapour trail curled out and crossed the moon. Above, the bat-like sail creaked and bloomed, full of air.

He was making for the large stables on Dogs Island, where the landing place was on the roof, signified by coloured flags.

He had no cares. He had come from the arms of a jaunty mistress and was going home to a cosy, unsuspecting wife. The flycycle and its airborne method were his pride and joy, and a sign of his wealth. No qualms for him, he had flown this way so many nights.

Below, the river gleamed like a mirror, and he saw his vague shadow pass there – a giant bat with a pod and pedals.

Strapped in his seat, he scanned the sky. No clouds tonight for advertisements to be projected on to, although generally in any case, this show ceased at eleven o'clock.

Dim strokes of the Time Piece wafted by, parting the atmosphere. The ninth stroke, the tenth and eleventh. And last, the sonorous omnipotent clang of twelve.

Downriver, the Island appeared with its gracious park and the pale dome of the Observatory.

Without a misgiving in the world, the man on the flycycle leant back and let impetus and the air currents carry him for a moment.

And in that moment, coming from the eastern horizon, he saw a strange boiling.

What was it? Some factory chimney uttering? A fire – no, it was not smoke.

A cloud was roiling in the sky and all at once, it gave way.

The flycyclist gave a cry.

Out of the cloud stretched a vast black thing. It was in the form of some sort of lean, long-snouted dog.

An advertisement after all, played up on a manufactured cloud.

But its eyes glittered, black stars, and round its muzzle was a frost of fire.

It stood gigantic over Dogs Island, and opening its jaws, let out a sound. This was not a bark. More a rush of cindery wind.

The heat of it, desert-like, caught the flycycle, and suddenly the machine was toppling, its sail bent askew and the gas-bag belching.

The flycyclist screamed. He clutched the bar and pedalled furiously, but the gas was burping and whistling away. In terror, he forgot the dog in the sky, which was, after all, fading like a mist.

More real, Dogs Island flared towards him, the garlands of the trees, old timbers with great boughs, rushing up at him in a wave of leaves.

Like a shooting star, the flycyclist tumbled.

Beneath the fish were rising in the river in silver rings, so all the water seemed on fire, and eels wove like ribbons of flame or skeins of spangled weed. At the docks the rats stood upright and squealed.

In a million yards and hovels dogs growled, howled and whimpered. The night was noisy now.

In despair the flycyclist saw the lighted roof of the conservatory atop the Observatory dome, a fantastic green jewel of ferns, in the second his machine cracked its roof and, plunging on, rolled over into the vast crowns of beeches, under which kings had ridden centuries before.

The boughs in fact had saved him, breaking the fall. Bruised and wailing, he dropped on to a gravel path of the park, the flycycle wrapped round him like a balloon in ruins.

As he scrambled free of the seat, the gas-bag exploded with a peony flash and loud bang, quickening the trees as if for a carnival. Illuminated, sobbing and singed, the man lay in the grass. The dog had been an illusion, one port too many. His clever air-machine had betrayed him. What in life could be trusted now?

CHAPTER ONE

Grace

She was so young and beautiful that she tempted him beyond endurance, and he gave in. He told himself he had not come there for that, it was forbidden. But she caught his senses. It was a golden afternoon, not so many whores on the streets as yet. He stole glance after glance as they walked along, and although she had not taken his arm, he felt they were together.

About eighteen, perhaps. Not long, surely, in her trade. Skin of milk crystal, green eyes, pale yellow-green like a cat's. And blonde hair so light it had no colour, only sheen, piled under her little netted hat with the white violets of cloth.

As they turned into the street of tall shabby houses, he said to her, 'What's your name?'

'Grace,' she replied, not hesitating.

Then she led him up steps and opened a door, and they passed into a carpeted hall and over a flight of stairs. This was not her home, but some address to which she brought certain clients. He had come across such things before. A rush of rage went over him. Probably her prettiness was all a sham. He was bemused, and had not seen her properly in the dusty summer light. A diseased bitch, no doubt of it, another monster of the streets.

The bedroom had a worn floor-covering, and a four-poster with a crimson coverlet, stained but not unwholesome. A broad gilt mirror framed the room, its wickedness.

Evidently seeing him hold back, the girl came forward and took his hands. She leaned up lightly and kissed his lips, decorous, like a young secretive maiden at some party.

He got hold of her, feeling her slim body in its tight boned corset, the swell of her bosom.

'Take off your clothes,' he said, 'all of them.'

'Of course,' said the girl called Grace.

She undressed without haste or delay, not sensuously, not even provocatively, more as if she went about some pleasant and familiar task.

Perhaps it was. Perhaps she liked it, catering to men.

He watched. And at the sight of her white breasts with their rosy centres rising from the lace petticoat, he became hard, and with the hardness his rage deepened.

He wanted to strike her, dishevel her, her lovely blonde hair that now cascaded round her white shoulders.

When she drew off her lace-trimmed nether garments, and he saw the blonde tinsel at her groin, he started to cry.

'I can't,' he said.

She watched him quietly. She said nothing.

He put his hand over his hard and urgent core.

'I had another one like you. No, she wasn't like you. But a harlot. And she gave me something. An illness. If I touch you, you too – riddled with the filth. It will kill me. Syphilis.'

The girl called Grace watched him still. She said softly, 'There's no need to be afraid.'

'No? There's every need. I'll go now.'

'Don't go,' she said. 'Come here.'

He thought she was insane, but even so the look of her drove him mad, and he went to her.

He filled his hands with her breasts that were like satin. He rubbed his face against her and she held him, and presently drew him down.

She was diseased. She had it already, and need fear nothing more. He pierced her strawberry velvet with his putrid member, cursing himself, and her.

He surged inside her body and felt his soul gush out. He had never climaxed so powerfully and now he was empty, sore and wrecked. All honour gone.

She said gently, 'You'll be better soon.'

'You stupid bitch. You don't know.'

'Yes.'

She wiped his fresh tears with her hair.

He gave her three gold pieces and she took them, smiling. And afterwards, when he was on the street, he thought himself a dupe and a fool.

REIGNING CATS AND DOGS

* * *

When she was a child, about six, her mother dead, her father had put her on the streets.

She was a pretty thing, so white, even under her grime, clean-looking, and she never smelled – her body, her breath. Always fresh, like roses and mint. Some of them did not like her cat's eyes, but many did not mind. By seven years of age, she was a prostitute, and knew how to run after gentlemen on the road, and pluck their sleeves.

Some would turn with an oath and shake her off, and once one hit her and her face was livid for a week. But often as not, even if they did not succumb, they gave her a coin for her beauty.

The forcing of her should have destroyed her, but did not. She never cried or complained. Late at night she sat in the hovel, tending the meagre fire, while her father drank himself into a delirium.

When she was ten he died, but she knew by then perfectly well what to do. She did not starve, and others in her way of business knew whom to come to if they were in distress. She would share her crust or her jug of gin, would Grace. Sodden whores of twelve, weeping in Grace's lap, got to their feet much better. When Lizzie burned her neck, and when Sarey caught her fingers in the mangle, it was Grace who comforted them, and in later years they told the tale, and no one believed them, for they had no scars.

About thirteen, Grace came to live in the Rookery, on Rotwalk Lane.

It was a fearful tenement, a canted house of three floors and fifteen rooms, inhabited by about a hundred persons. However, in the attics, about ten girls had each secured a cubicle which was her own, and since sometimes they took their clients there, this privacy was respected.

The house leaked, and lurched in the wind. It stank, and by night its overused chimneys let out a hug of smoke that matched the styxy vapours from all the adjoining buildings, which were each one another rookery. The lane below was choked with filth and dead creatures and sewage. It was dangerous to pass into this place at any hour unless you were one, or with one, of its own.

Grace was.

She moved without nervousness along the thoroughfare, in a louring sunset the colour of broken plums, and came to the house door, where three loungers in rags and battered hats made way for her, with a greeting.

'I'll see you presently, Gracie,' said one.

And Grace smiled at him and nodded, as if he had promised her flowers.

In the big kitchen of the house it was the usual scene. About forty people were squashed into the room, along the benches and the floor, and sitting on the table. At the fire two old women were toasting herrings, and a jug of gin was going round.

The room smelled of terrible things. Of dirt inches thick, poverty inches thicker.

Men gambled in a corner with two half-bald dogs snarling in attendance. Babies cried.

Kitty Stockings, one of the upstairs girls, came to Grace and offered her the gin jug. Grace took a mouthful, and passed the jug on.

Kitty was a thin, dark, raddled, pretty girl, looking about thirty, who was seventeen, one year younger than Grace.

'Any good today, Grace?'

'Yes, very good.'

A woman, fat with bad food, clutched Grace's arm. 'You've got some money? Give me some. The baby's almost dead.'

Grace turned and put a gold coin into the woman's hand.

At once there was a general pushing and shoving. The woman screamed as one of the men tried to take her prize.

'No,' said Grace, 'let her have it. Her baby's sick.'

The man said, 'Then give one to me.'

Grace did as he demanded.

She set the last coin on the table, where it was briefly fought over.

They were quite decorous when Grace was there. She withheld only enough from them to see to her own small wants. Besides she was a talisman. A man had broken his leg and Grace had taken the pain away, and later the leg was straight. And Grace had spoken to the policemen when they came, and they had gone off without trouble. And she was always ready to open her creamy body to them, to soothe them with her moon-white hair.

Grace sat by the fire with Kitty Stockings, and they ate a herring and drank the gin when it came by.

'Not one would go with me today,' said Kitty, 'I've got so ugly.'

Grace laughed. 'No.'

Kitty laughed too. 'Shall we go out tonight, up the lamp streets, and see what we can get?'

Grace said that she would.

REIGNING CATS AND DOGS

Night had already come down, and greasy candles burned in the kitchen.

Grace next went upstairs, to keep her appointment with the lout from below.

He was waiting at her cubicle, and when she had opened the door, he pushed her quickly in.

He had no money, and offered her nothing, for this was how she paid for her lodging.

Against the wall was where he had her, brutish and slobbering, but afterwards he was shamefaced, and thanked her.

Alone in the tiny room, Grace poured water into her basin, and washed herself by the light of a single surprising lamp.

Her room was rather different from those of the other girls.

A curtain of torn green brocade covered her narrow window – half a window, divided from the room next door. Her mattress was heaped with rugs and pillows, musty, once beautiful things, embroidered and thin as the wings of butterflies. She had no fireplace, but in the winter the amalgamated heat of the stifling house kept the worst of the cold at bay. Her lamp she had been given by a patron long ago, the same man who, between bouts of sex, had taught her to read and write when she was fourteen.

Grace's things were never stolen. Even her cake of soap and jar of toothpowder were let alone.

The Rookery was proud of her. She moved in it like the moon in a fog.

After washing, and dressing again in her grey frock, Grace combed up her hair and fixed on her little hat. She did not look like a whore, except that her skirt showed her ankles. She took business by offering herself sweetly and frankly. Most turned in astonishment. Sometimes they begged her to seek another life. Then she laughed and explained that she knew no other.

Indeed, no other was open to her. And besides she found no awfulness in what she did. Like pure water, rather than be sullied when dirt dipped into her, she made clean. She knew this in herself without marvel. Little things made her happy. The flowers that thrust up in the yard, the colour of an evening sky, rain on her windows, silence.

Kitty, on the other hand, was clad in red and pink, and on her hat a poor red bird was tilted, clinging precariously by one leg.

They went out into the dark, arm in arm.

On Rotwalk Lane they were not accosted, and went up and down a series of dire streets, lit only by the occasional murky door or window.

Here and there a wooden bridge ran over the thoroughfare, and in many places men lurked in the shadows. But two street-walkers on their way did not alarm or alert them.

Finally the grisly alleys and swervings led into the outskirt of the City, and all at once they were on a street lit by gas lamps, burning up on their poles like cats' eyes.

Here carriages rattled by, and at the corner one of the dangerous new vehicles, drawn, not by horses, but by metal animals, and bustling steam. No sooner had this passed, to the general consternation of the pedestrians, than gangs of little boys were swarming in the road to mop up the spillage of oil with rags.

The lighted streets gave one on another, growing broader and more pleasant. It was the upper area of Black Church, where so many of their profession plied their trade.

Grace and Kitty walked as if idly, and perambulating others of the sisterhood now and then called out a greeting.

Men too there were, sauntering by, and occasionally a carriage on the roadway, its occupant looking out.

But there were no takers for Grace and Kitty, this ill-assorted couple. The moon rose above the roofs and stood, pale and full, behind the spine of a church.

'Look there,' said Kitty. 'What must it be to live up there? Apple pie every day and no work to do.'

The street was now empty but for a costermonger with a barrow, and Kitty said, 'I'm starved.'

They went to the barrow and bought a pint of winkles, which they shared. A carriage went by and did not stop. Kitty said, 'There, they don't like to see you eating. You have to be good only for one thing.'

She was sad, because at fifteen she had been bought suppers, and sometimes even champagne.

Above them the street lights hissed and guttered, and the moon flowed over.

Then came a peculiar cry. In their own warren of streets it would not have been so strange, a shriek like an owl's, redolent of fear and perhaps pain. But on these walks it was bizarre.

The costermonger had put his arm protectively about his barrow. Otherwise the byway was empty.

'What was that?' said Kitty.

Grace said nothing. She had had a terrible feeling, as though her blood had stopped moving in her, and then begun again too cold, too hot.

'Something horrible happened,' she said.

'Where? What was it?'

The Rookery saw Grace as a seeress, and in some ways she was.

But Grace had no answer now.

In her heart there was an image. A dark shadow and a spattering of blood. Instinctively she, a healer, turned herself away. And yet it seemed she could not escape. Something hunted her. Something hunted the streets. Never in her life had she felt terror, but now, faintly, coldly, she did. She longed to take Kitty in her arms and shield the fragile body from the night, the costermonger too. Some deep new passion woke in Grace.

'Let's,' said Kitty, 'go home.'

CHAPTER TWO

Saul

'No,' he said. It was final and very cold.

His man knew better than to argue. He said, 'I told her it wouldn't be wanted.'

'Thank her for me, any way,' said the dark man at the table, 'but she should know by now. I take my food plainly.'

The offending sauce was removed, leaving only the hot soup and chill fowl of the normal dinner. The cook was a fool and perhaps would leave soon, tired of the boring routine of the plain food, the lack of company to be given dinners, the gloomy noiselessness of the big house.

The dining room was panelled in darkest oak, filled by heavy furniture of black and mulberry. A painting of a knight, almost a black mirror, hung above the fireplace, which for the summer night had been filled by an ebony screen. Two doors set with ponds of dark red and green glass let on to a conservatory, strangely dominated by ancient ferns, and tall palm trees, the bases of whose urns were filled by white sand. From here, high windows looked down into the City.

Having finished his dinner, the man at the table poured himself a second glass of the claret. The goblet was extremely fine, of prismatic crystal. He used it with a sort of care, as if it were not habitual, as if perhaps none of it was, the gold-streaked service, the white napkin, the fruit knife of silver.

A sip at the wine, and then a cigarette lit at a candle – he never used a match.

He had dressed for dinner, as he always did, it had always been the custom of this house. In his black and white he too was black and white. A black wealth of hair, black eyes leaded in by black lashes and brows. A pale handsome face that had no expression on it. A still face, like a shell left behind by some earlier sea. It had nothing to say. It wanted nothing. It was not at peace but yet it was engrossed with quietness.

Smoking, he rose and went into the conservatory of ferns and palms, which was kept very hot. He crossed to the windows and looked down and down the slopes of opulent streets, crenellated by towerlets and scaled by tiles, in their wreaths of glowing lamps. A hundred windows burned merrily, faint laughter or pianos, or mandolins daintily plucked, might echo out across the opened summer night.

He had no quarrel with that, no liking for it either.

He stared down beyond the frosted cakes of rich men's houses, down to where the warren of Black Church swelled, trailing to the river, on which the moon hung round and cool.

But other things were in the sky. The vapour trails of two flycycles, one going from east to west, and one from north to south. And there, a bank of cloud, probably fashioned on purpose by a smoking rocket. An advertisement played on the cloud. A girl toying with a kitten. Over and over, the girl's hand petted, and over and over the cat's paw tapped at a ball. Above in emerald letters the words: *Tiny Tiger Tea.*

The man turned his back upon this manifestation with a pale disgust. He walked from the conservatory into a mahogany study, and there drew shut the sombre curtains against this impure night.

He had been born in the workhouse, and as the screams of his mother died away, she went with them.

They named him Saul from the Bible, he was a dark child from the very beginning, and they did things in this way, there. They were very concerned with religion. Before every meal, which consisted of gruel, sometimes with an under-cooked potato or onion, a grace was said. Twice a day on Sunday, there was a service. They were told to be humble and grateful to a terrible God who had already, for their sins, these children of two and five and seven, cast them down into a grey hell.

But something else went on in this house of work, beyond hard labour, religion and gruel. Mr Lylch, the overseer, had organized a little band of girls, the prettier ones of about fourteen and fifteen, to go out begging, the proceeds of course to come to him. And for the assistance of these girls, babies and infants were sent out with them. In his earliest years, Saul was one of these. Wrapped in a threadbare shawl, he was toted from corner to corner, and sometimes swapped over into another shawl, or even a girl's dress, that another beggar might employ him again.

His first memory, one which haunted him after and recurred in various form in dreams, was of being tossed across the pavement from one pair of thin dirty hands to another. A miracle he was caught. But perhaps not, for a smashed baby that had been useful would have annoyed Mr Lylch.

Lylch was a red beery man, much given to pious utterance. He grew up into Saul's awareness as the years passed, big and grotesque, clown-like and dangerous. He had a jolly laugh, which frequently came bubbling from him in the seconds before he struck out with lash or fist.

At seven Saul was put forth again into a small sooty room, where in company with three other boys, as skinny and grim as he, he was set to making matchboxes.

These awful boxes too were to stay in Saul's mind. The make had the name of Three Flames, and on the front of the box was inscribed a fiery torch of three points. Their novelty was their flat but triangular shape, very difficult to fit together perfectly, so to start with there were many mistakes and many thrashings. The three sides of the box were one red, one white, and one black, and long after the day's work was over, the shape of them would be imprinted behind Saul's sunken eyes.

At dinner time, about twelve, he and the other boys were let out to seek some food, and Saul would go into a baker's for a little roll, and after that to a public house for a half tankard of sour beer. For this sumptuous lunch he received weekly just enough pennies.

One noon, as he leaned on a wall munching his roll, a man came strolling by.

He was dressed, this man, in a weird parody of high fashion, with a soaring hat and silken neckerchief, even a pocket-watch. But all was slovenly and tawdry, and indeed, the pocket-watch did not go.

'Good-day to you, my young sir,' said the apparition, pausing beside Saul as if to inspect the view, which was of the back of the grimy warehouses and a slimy alley or two.

Saul, who had had courtesy smitten into him, and knew no better – he was then nine years of age – replied in kind.

Pleased apparently, the man in the high hat next asked Saul if this was not a very unsatisfying meal he had, and would he not like a chop or something of that sort.

Saul knew no better, knew nothing in fact save how to slot together

Three Flames matchboxes, but his life had made him, along with polite, and fearful, also wary.

He thanked the man and turned his shoulder, aiming now for the ale-house.

Nothing deterred, High Hat went with him.

Companionably he said, 'Now, I could show you a very nice house, where you'd be well taken care of. Dressed like a little gentleman, and given wine with your beef.'

Saul did not now reply, but he wanted his drink – it filled him as the roll never did – and did not know how to shake off this odd friend.

They entered the public house, and here High Hat bought Saul a pint of strong ale, and sat with him as he drank it. When Saul was drunk, High Hat took him by the arm but, drunk or not, Saul was agile, and he gave the man the slip and ran off down the alleys to his employment.

Low and behold, High Hat was next seen there, lurking in the outer cubby, in converse with the manager of the sooty room. He did not again, however, approach Saul.

That night, in the house of work, after the supper of gruel, Saul was ordered to the parlour of Mr Lylch. Saul went in horror, for only when some punishment of special merit was to be meted out did the girls and boys of that place receive such an invitation.

Having knocked on the door, he was admitted by Lylch himself, and so passed into the one comfortable room of the establishment. A fire burned lovingly on the hearth, a jar of tobacco stood ready, and a jug of gin by a bowl of sugar.

'Well, well,' said Lylch, 'and here the beauty is.'

Saul did not look round for the 'beauty', although he had never before been so spoken of. His eyes instead were fixed on High Hat who, with glass of gin, was seated by the fire, smoking a long pipe.

'Here the beauty is indeed. I must say, you've kept him very thin, Lylch. But we can feed him up.'

'Thin is healthy for a lad,' said Lylch, 'as it says in the Good Book, Know when you have taken enough.'

'His eyes alone,' said High Hat, 'are worth some coin. Who could resist them?'

'I will say,' said Lylch, 'I've never seen much in this boy, but then I'm not that way inclined. However, you'll have to make it worth my while. He's canny with his boxes and brings in a regular wage.'

'Not a penny more than I've already offered,' said High Hat. 'Such boys are worth fifty a pound on the street. And without care, he'd be nothing.' Rather changing his tune.

Saul stood puzzled, only dimly aware he was not to be chained up or beaten, and so in a type of stupor of relief.

Lylch and High Hat though soon concluded a deal over their gin.

'Give the boy a nip,' said High Hat. 'It's a cold night outside.'

And so reluctantly Mr Lylch poured his workhouse orphan a tiny glass of liquor, which Saul drank coughing, his gin-worth eyes streaming.

Then High Hat bundled a blanket about him and took him out into the street.

There in the wide night, up against the workhouse bricks, which were all the home he had known, Saul was afraid, but High Hat quickly bounced him into a shabby carriage, and they were off.

'You'll thank me,' said High Hat, filling the coach with pipe smoke. 'It will be the making of you. A life of luxury. Lucky boy.'

'Where are you taking me?' asked Saul. He did not truly care. All places were potentially alike to him. What, despite the fulsome words, could he hope for?

'That nice house I spoke of,' said High Hat. 'Now don't chatter. They can't abide boys that chat.'

Thus in silence they drove on through the rumbling City night, and off over the river, that great clock, the Time Piece, groaned out the hour of eight.

After a while longer, they stopped, and High Hat left the carriage with Saul in a firm grip.

They had halted in a poor, curving street, with old houses lined up like cardboard pictures, leaning, and only a pair of street lamps, one at either end of the avenue. Above, however, was a house that had a lamp to itself standing by its steps, and up these steps the pair ascended.

A rap on the door, and a little portal opened, and an exchange of words. Then the door swinging back, and Saul looked into a wide hallway hung with scarlet velvets and long yellow tassels, with an awful plant like a huge stiff black spider craning from a pot.

'This way at once,' said High Hat, taking Saul through this hallway and into a back apartment, which was got up rather in the same way. A statue stood in one corner. It was of white stone, and showed two youths embracing. Saul looked at it in wonder. And then there came in a very curious being.

This was a man in a red velvet dressing-gown, with short black leather hair. His face was painted brightly, blue above the eyes, black under them, pink for the cheeks and cherry colour on the lips. From one ear dangled a golden earring like a chandelier.

'Ah, and here he is. What a treasure you are,' said the being to High Hat. 'I've never known you fail me.' And then to Saul the being said, 'Come here, little boy. There. What a lovely child. How old are you?'

'Nine, I think, sir,' said Saul.

'Now, don't call me sir. I am to be called Guinevere. There. But we can pass you off for seven, so slim and slight. What pretty bones. Now, then, you'll be a good boy and do what Guinevere tells you, and you'll have a beautiful life of ease and joy. Sit down now on the sofa, and you shall have a glass of sweet red wine.'

Then a dream began, which lasted one whole fortnight.

There was upstairs a porcelain bath of hot water in which essences were sprinkled, and an indoor easement with a smooth wooden seat. There was also upstairs a small bed, rather ordinary, not like the rest of the house, but piled with blankets and rugs, and its sheets very clean and white and without any lice. There were four meals a day. A great breakfast of kidneys and eggs and smoked fish, and a dinner of pies and greens, a tea of cake, and a supper of toasts and cold meats and oysters and jelly. There was white milk with the cream thick on it, and custards, and wine with every meal but breakfast, and strong tea, and brown oily coffee, and boxes of sweets.

There were new clothes, crisp soft linen, and a silk cravat, and a warm coat, and proper britches, and even a little hat to be worn when one of the servants of the house, who were all unfailingly helpful if not exactly kind, took Saul to walk on a wild green common behind the house, up paths where men rode by on horses, and birds sang.

He had been told he must on no account speak to anyone, except the servants or Guinevere, when Guinevere saw him. And every two or three days, Guinevere would have Saul come into the velvet room, by a back stair now, and Guinevere would admire Saul, and say that he, Guinevere, was delighted.

Saul did not ask himself what in return would be wanted of him. In the past everything had been demanded of him without recompense, and usually without explanation. He had been slapped, thrashed, put to work, starved, all without a true word said as to why. Therefore, now this wonder had occurred, *why* did not present itself. Things were. And he was only nine, and all he knew was matchboxes.

REIGNING CATS AND DOGS

At the end of the fortnight a blue evening came, when the usual discrete busy-ness of the house began, as it always did, comings and goings, the sound of steps and shutting doors, laughter, and once a noise like a beating, which had frightened Saul – strange hoarse cries, muffled in the depths of the house, went with it. But the servants had told Saul it was only someone playing a game, having fun, he must not mind.

Tonight, as they lit the lamps, one of the men drew Saul down to the room of Guinevere, as had happened so regularly, and Saul went blithely, used to it.

There on the sofa Guinevere sat, playing with a fur muff he liked to stroke. In a velvet chair was a gentleman, very upright and stern, in evening dress.

'Now here is a friend of mine,' said Guinevere of the gentleman. 'A very close friend. And I want you to please him. You'll do that for me, won't you, dear?'

Saul, not understanding any of this, nodded.

Then Guinevere gave Saul a large glass of the sweet wine, and Saul drank it, and the gentleman looked at him in a curious fierce way, that troubled Saul, but perhaps it was only his manner.

'Be gentle, dearie,' said Guinevere, as the gentleman rose and Saul was asked to get up and go with him. 'His first time, as I promised you.'

The gentleman and Saul came out together now into the house, and for the first Saul glimpsed into a big low room hung with purple, and full of statues of naked young men. Some of the men in the room were also in a state of undress, but it occurred to Saul that maybe they were making ready for some event.

Up a broad stair the gentleman now guided Saul by a curt quick touch on his arm.

It seemed to Saul the gentleman did not like him very much. What must he do to make the gentleman happy?

They reached a corridor of doors that Saul had never seen before. In an open one, a boy was lounging, a handsome boy without a stitch on him, and a man with a beard had his arm about the boy and was whispering in his ear.

This sight amazed but did not alert Saul. How could he know? He knew matchboxes.

The gentleman opened a door into a vacant bedroom. The wallpaper was thickly raised and coined by gilt. The posts of the great bed were gilded too. Guinevere had given of his best for this important occasion.

The gentleman told Saul to go over to the bed, and then to take off all his clothes.

Saul was surprised, and now he began to be afraid – of nothing specific, but this had somehow the ring of chainings and beatings. Nevertheless, it had never been possible to say no, and even in the dream of this house, there was no margin for no at all.

So Saul stripped, and the gentleman watched him, with slotted burning mindless eyes.

'Have you been bathed?' he asked at length in a slurred and drawling way.

Saul, embarrassed, assured him that he had.

Then the gentleman came and kneeled down by Saul on the carpet.

He began to feel Saul over, rapidly and jerkily, rough and hot, and his breath smelled of spirits and of something else, acid and unpleasant. Presently he put down this mouth and, to Saul's astonishment, took the boy's small penis between his lips.

Saul was afraid of being bitten, and indeed the gentleman's teeth grazed him, if not very hard.

Saul made a little sound.

'Like it, do you? That's right, that's right.'

Then the gentleman kissed Saul and stuck his bulging tongue into Saul's startled parted mouth. The taste of this tongue made Saul gag, but the gentleman did not seem to notice. He went on sucking and pushing, until suddenly he pulled away and, lifting Saul up on to the plushy bed, thrust him down face foremost.

Saul lay stunned, not knowing quite what had happened to him. So that when the next thing happened, he was utterly defenceless, both bodily and mentally.

A terrible, unspeakable thing was being perpetrated on him. A ram of fire was wedged between his buttocks and before he could even scream, forced through into his tight and virgin anus.

As Guinevere was to assure him in later days, the gentleman had been chosen not only for his gold, but for the reported smallness of his member, it could have been far worse. But to the riven child, held down in agony and terror on that bed of plush, while a demon forced and lunged and blood soaked out like wine, nothing in the world could console him, nothing in the world had meaning any more, but pain, defilement, and the pit of fear.

REIGNING CATS AND DOGS

He did shriek, and then the gentleman cuffed him. 'Be quiet, you little slut.' He arched in a paroxysm of pleasure and shouted aloud, deafening Saul as he lay, rent and crying, in a pool of velvet and blood.

'You must learn to be nicer,' said the gentleman, as he was putting on his coat. 'You'll grow to like it. They all do, all the sluts.'

Later someone came and took Saul away and wiped him, and bathed him, and put him to bed with a supper of anchovy toast and strawberries that he could not eat.

After this, after the dream, there was the nightmare.

Guinevere came with a striped stick of candy, and told Saul he had been very good and clever. But Saul knew this was nothing to do with it. Still he did not understand what was to become of him. He thought Guinevere's words were a fee, like the pennies he got out of his wage for the boxes. But he did not suppose such a fearsome thing would happen again.

It did.

Time and again, it did. Until, as they foretold, he should be used to it.

'My little star of the house,' said Guinevere.

At first he had struggled, kicked and bitten and struggled, until a blow – familiarity at last – made him realize he had no choice. And gradually the pain was less, though never entirely absent. He feared it less, also, for each time he survived beyond it.

They made much of him, when he was 'good', when he was docile, and smiled and went willingly.

In rooms of velvet and silk, red and mauve and orange, he was had. Sodomized to the core. Some brutal and some coaxing. Some old, some young. Some stupid and some – intelligent, even apologizing. One weeping after, as *he* had wept the first time.

This then, his new life.

Saul began to fill out a little from the plentiful food of Guinevere's house, but not to any great extent. Some of the little boys were plump and had curled hair. Some of the young men had the fat breasts of women. The huge black man, with his vast weapon, mocked and reviled, swore at the others as he feasted on rice pudding.

Saul saw them all now, all his peers, in the new red hell of that house. None befriended him, he was drawn to none. They were all slaves. He was alone. And now he must live this life for ever.

Two years passed, and now they said that he was nine, but he was eleven. Never was he completely unsupervised. They did not quite trust him.

A handful of new male children were brought to the house, and one died, and it was all kept hushed, the small coffin carried out by night.

Saul dreamed of the matchboxes. Those flat triangles with one white, one black and one red side. They stood in his dreams like a wall against which he could not prevail. He did not dream of the onslaught of men.

CHAPTER THREE

Anger

When he was twelve, he made up his mind to run away. The thought came to him quite simply, for although he was still watched, accompanied, they had grown lax of late. They thought him happy or resigned, because he never complained, did all that was asked. Besides, he was growing older, and might soon be trained also to other ways of the house, to take as well as to be taken. For this he needed to be allowed more boldness. They let him walk the common and the servant fell back. They let him lie in his room and eat pastry and drink wine, and no one came near, not even Guinevere's other disciples. Guinevere himself paid Saul scant attention; there were now other, younger, more toothsome apprentices, some even seeming eager.

He laid his plans with a breathless care. He stored up cold meat and cheese and a bottle of wine, and put them in a cloth bag he had acquired, and had sometimes been taking on the common, as if for no reason.

He waited for the day the one-eyed servant was to go with him for his walk.

First he engaged the man in mild conversation, talking of two or three of the patrons disparagingly, so the servant laughed.

Then, when a man rode down the path, Saul slipped away among the trees. He heard the servant calling him excitedly – he would be whipped – but Saul had no care for him. In Saul's world now and for so long, there had been only himself.

He ran deep into the woods, and lost himself, and was sure he had lost pursuit. He had.

That night he sat in the dark of the wood, and two roughs came by and stole his food and wine from him, knocking him flat for good measure. He did not grieve. He was free.

In the morning, he made his way down from the open land, and came among the slums of the City.

He had, he thought, no fear. It was as if fear had been used up. What else could be done to him? And he was still too young to dread death.

He begged at street corners along the better thoroughfares, and gained a shilling, which he spent on ale, for the house had given him a taste for liquor.

In the dawn, he woke rather ill in a gutter, and children younger than he pelted him with mud.

He roamed, suddenly in a no-man's land, not caring. At last he fell in with thieves, who wished to use him for squinnying in at narrow windows. But these too he escaped, and one night in late summer, when the heat of the day sank into the sudden breath of coming cold, he sat by the bank of the river at one of its lowest stretches.

Reeds grew up from the jetsam of the bank, and the last murky bottle-green had faded from the water with the sun. A boat with torches and huffing funnel went down the race, and the men who were there, setting their crab pots for the morning, cursed it and all bright shining things.

Saul was melancholy. Why had he waited for so long before he left the house of Sodom? And what should he do now among these trails of darkness? It seemed to him he would be glad to do ill, and yet he did not want to do it at anyone's order. In the half-light before the night had fully come, he wondered what it would be like to slit the throats of men and get at their pockets.

Then the moon rose in an indigo sky, and Saul went along the strand to the tavern he had been frequenting. It had its rickety struts in the river and all its walls were green by day with rot. It stank of fish and mildew, and here it was possible to drink all night for a few coppers.

Saul sank into his accustomed seat. And after half an hour, looked up to find a shadowy stranger had seated himself opposite.

'Are you the boatman's lad?' inquired this man.

Saul said, 'No.' He was no longer polite or fawning.

'Then, are you the youth goes by the name of "Saul"?'

Saul partly rose. After all it was feasible to fear.

The man showed him a silver coin.

Saul relapsed.

'My master has been searching for you high and low,' said the stranger.

'I won't go back,' said Saul. 'Don't try to make me. I've got a knife.'

'No, you have none. You've only got the pennies for drink. You ate three days ago and not since. Your mother died bearing you in the workhouse. Your father you don't know. But know this. Your father had a brother, and that brother has sought you out.'

Saul did not take this in. All lures were tricks, and this a singularly foolish one. He felt no affinity with any parents, both vanished before even he opened his eyes.

'If you will come with me,' said the man, who had a long, lean face and a battered black hat, 'it will be to your advantage.'

'Oh, you've some client, have you,' said Saul, 'who wants to bugger me?'

'Yes, we've learned of your years in that house,' said the man. 'There's nothing like that. But unless you take the risk, you'll never know. What life have you now? It will soon be over. Come with me. My master is rich. Your uncle. It's taken him years to catch up with you.'

'All a lie,' said Saul.

'Then,' said the man, 'he has offered to meet you here. What have you to fear? He's a gentleman and will come into this slough, in order to offer his good will.'

'Why does he want me?'

'You are all he has.'

'Let him come then,' said Saul, idly, deep in drink and far beyond concern.

The following night, Saul watched under the pylons of the tavern, up to his knees in the ooze.

About nine – for he heard the Time Piece strike miles away – a carriage drew up on the road above, and then the lean-faced stranger brought an old man down, leaning on him, to the tavern door. They went in.

Curiosity compelled Saul to go in after them. The old man would be easy to subdue if there were trouble, and the younger one was nothing.

They sat at the table where Saul had normally come to sit, and all the roomful of criminals and drunkards gave them a wide berth.

Saul went to the table and stood there.

The old man looked up, and his face, lit by a wick floating in fish-oil on the table, was creased and seamed, picked at by time as if it tried to reach the bone. Yet it was a clean face, not ravenous or savage. No, it was very cold and exact, almost like the face of a clock.

'Is this he?' the man asked of his companion.

'It is.'

'Saul,' said the old man, 'I see your father's looks in you. Your mother I knew nothing of. Will you sit down.'

Slowly, Saul did so. The old man had compelled him too, by some white authority, some power piled up behind the fallen face.

'I have been selfish,' said the old man. 'I have not begun to look for you until almost too late. Is it too late, Saul?'

'What do you want from me?' said Saul.

'That you will come with me and allow me to change your life. The heritage your father left you is penury and disgrace. I would like to rescue you from these things.'

'Why?'

'You're mine. My nephew.'

Saul sat facing them, sullen with enormous misgiving and a faint alarmed desire. Was any of it true? Or just some ruse to recapture or further enslave him?

'What proof do you have?' said Saul. He had not reasoned his words, and therefore when the old man took out a little picture in a silver frame, Saul looked at it blankly. His own face, much older, looked back at him. And yet not. This was a face of laughter and weakness. It had been happy.

'Who?'

'Your father and my brother. The family name is Angier, but it has been corrupted in this City to Anger.'

'Anger,' Saul said. He felt a bitter rift against his heart. *Anger* – his name it might well be.

'Why not,' said the old man patiently, a king to a valued simpleton, 'come with me. You have nothing to fear. Besides, you're wily and young and would easily get the better of us if we mean you harm. Come as my guest and see what I offer you. Then you may reject it, if you wish.'

'Why do you want this?' said Saul.

'I believe in judgement, and justice.'

High above the City, the house towered on its hill. That was its name, the Tower. Tall casements were framed in thick velvet, but it was not like the other velvet house, not at all. Food, though abundant, was plain. Dinner was served at seven in the evening. Servants as calm and quiet as mechanical things glided about, saw to everything.

Saul slept again in a bed of crisp, clean linen – or rather, he lay awake, and heard the Time Piece strike the hours far down in the valley of the river.

There was a heavy fog the second night he came there, and he and the old man, his uncle, sat in the dark dining room before the white candles and red plates with their veins of gold.

There was wine, but this too was abstemious, Saul found he did not really want it now. He felt tired and leaden, as if he had been running for years along the highway, and now he had flung himself down.

He did not mistrust the old man, who had not laid a finger on him and had brought no one else to do so. Saul had learned enough at last to distinguish between this building and this man, and other kinds.

Saul accepted that the old man wanted him since he was flesh and blood with him. Saul had even heard of such things, fairy stories of the workhouse; the rich relative who rescued and took away to a new life.

Saul was dressed now in sober good clothes. His hands were clean and manicured, his hair washed, his body full of meat and a little wine.

The old man said to him, 'Tonight I will show you all the house.' And the fog pressed at the windows of the conservatory behind him, whose door stood open, shutting out all the world. They might have been marooned on an island or a mountain top.

The fog lay too in faint mist through the house, as Saul had seen it lie in other rooms and on other stairways. The lamps had a pale yellow corona. There was a faint deathly smell, and by its token, Saul guessed his benefactor would not live long, and perhaps this was why he had been brought here.

The Tower was vast. Wide stairs carpeted in a crimson almost black, walls of inky wood, and ancient pictures of noble, priestly things, knights and cathedrals, and the coronation of kings, all done in mystic sombre colours, hung in shadow. On bureaux of oak, mahogany and ebony inlay, sat bowls of dull bronze, vases with draperies of malachite vine, pewter balls and globes of tarnished silver.

There were many, many rooms, some even for the use of guests, and these plainly had not been put into action for a decade or more – here the fog had massed about the undrawn drapes, the stripped beds covered only by a pall of velvet.

In the library were three thousand or more books, their spines gleaming like the backs of serpents.

Saul looked at them in disbelief. He could not read, what were they to him?

But his uncle said, 'I myself will give you lessons. You have much to learn. Are you afraid of learning?'

Saul did not know; he suspected that he was.

He said, 'If I'm slow—'

'Then we will go slowly.'

Last of all, Saul was shown the master bedroom, and even here no misgiving stirred in him. This old man had long been purified of sex, if not of gender.

A vaulted chamber with a canopied bed, midnight blue, and a great stone pillared fireplace where logs were burning against the turn of the season.

'This is mine and will be yours,' said Angier, who had become Anger.

Saul looked about. The shadows stood thick in corners, where small objects glinted like eyes. Another boy might have feared. But Saul had known fears of the world, and they had ousted the terrors of the mind.

'When you die,' he said, flatly. Even untutored, he was not crass. It was another testing.

The old man said, 'Yes, that's right. We have a year, you and I. Perhaps a little longer. It will be enough.'

Saul became a scholar in that house. It was not a dream, not after all unbelievable. He had an aptitude for learning and so, soon, a hunger. The old man taught him, and two others, one a youngish man, and one in heavy middle age. But all taught him well. He learned first to read, then mathematics, Latin and Greek, history, and something of the sciences and the world. From knowing only matchboxes and sodomy he came to have a wealth of knowledge in the cabinets of his brain, easy of access, an endless source of revelling pleasure.

This was where his happiness lay, to sit in the great library and to read all things.

It did not matter to him that seldom did they venture out. He took his exercise with a fencing master in a low beamed hall of the house. He walked the extensive garden, finding grottos and caves of ilex and yew, dark even in the snow of winter. Occasionally they might, the old man and he, drive out across the City.

Now he saw the river from a carriage, its metal length, the concrete embankment with its wall and ornaments of fish and dolphins, the tall obelisk that now he knew had been brought from Egypt, the sphinx of white stone, and the stranger statue of a dog-like beast done in blackest bronze.

At this the old man pointed.

'And who is he?'

Thinking, delving amid his knowledge, Saul answered, presently, 'A statue of the god Anubis.'

'Yes. And tell me what you know of him.'

'The Conductor of Souls, like Hermes of the Greeks. He led them to the hall of judgement, and weighed their hearts in the great balance, before the god of death.'

'Weighed them against a feather,' said the old man in a deep soft voice. 'And woe betide the man whose heart was the heavier.'

When they had returned to the house, the snow was falling again in feathery flakes.

The old man took Saul into his study, that led from the huge hot conservatory of palms and primeval ferns. Plants grew there as old as time, his uncle had told him, and in the study too were artifacts of stone that had been used on the plains of earth before men had a name for themselves, and bones of birds with teeth, and the tusk of a mammoth dug out of the ice.

The old man sat down at his desk and released a little drawer by a peculiar pressure of his fingers. He drew out an ivory box.

'Open it and see what is there.'

Saul obeyed him.

Inside the box was a ring couched in red damask. It was of thick gold and had a raised oval stone, black as jet, but dull, like a spent coal.

'What is carved into the cartouche?'

Saul looked and saw the beast god from the embankment, the dog-jackal of Egypt, Anubis, and lying in the same way, couchant, his head raised, his long forepaws stretched out.

He said so.

The old man said, 'There is a band of men, of whom I am one, who have taken this god of judgement to be our symbol. Put the ring on to the second finger of your left hand.'

Saul again obeyed, although now the hair prickled over his scalp. He had come into the presence of something for which no earthly degradation and no unfelt mental nervousness could have prepared him.

Smooth shadow streamed from the ring, he saw it like a light. It was flawless, terrible, sound.

On his finger it felt cold and hot. But it hung there. It was too big.

'One day,' said the old man, 'that ring will fit you, Saul.'

That night they came. The men his uncle had spoken of, and Saul was admitted to their ceremony.

There were nine of them, and his two tutors were of their number. But the others Saul did not know.

They went up into a room on the third floor of the house into which, before, Saul had never stepped.

Here ten black chairs were arranged about a long and polished black table. A fire burned on the hearth and candles everywhere, yet the light was rich with darkness.

There were no pictures, no other furniture.

The men sat down, and Saul stood by the door, which had been closed.

Then something peculiar, almost amusing, happened. Each man reached into a compartment under the rim of the table, and brought out – a head. A black, long-snouted head, set on a long black throat. And each man, without a word, fitted this jackal's head over his own.

Amusing, yes. But it was not. It was as if a sound began in the chamber, a low thrumming.

Saul caught his breath. It was not fear he felt, but that older and more perfect thing – terror.

Only obedience, perhaps gratitude, and a general dread to disturb, kept him from backing out of the door.

It was his uncle who spoke, his uncle masked as Anubis, and now the voice was muffled, hollow, *changed*.

He raised his left hand, and the ring was on it, and the fire touched the dark dull stone, and it flashed.

'We are here now firstly for our usual business. You have seen the boy now. He is mine. Is he acceptable to you?'

There was a murmur. It was assent.

The jackal who was Saul's uncle said, 'Come here, Saul. Pass behind each chair.'

Saul made himself move. As he reached the first chair, which was that of his portly elder tutor, the man put up his hand and touched Saul lightly on the left side. Saul did not flinch, though he shook. He went to the next chair, and was touched again. Each of them touched him, his uncle also, until he had completed the circuit.

'Saul,' said the jackal-uncle, 'you must swear now on this sword that you will reveal to no one in the world, even should they be dear to you, or your dearest enemy, what we do and what we are.'

Saul looked. The sword was there on the table. It had a hilt of black iron and a gleaming blade with one rusty edge.

He went to the sword and waited.

'Put your hand on the blade.'

Saul did so.

The men said, with one voice, weird and muffled, awful, 'Swear.'

Saul thought of *Hamlet*, which he had recently read. But he put his hand on the sword and said, 'I swear I'll tell no one. Ever.'

He thought, whom could he tell? Yet he knew the oath bound him like one of Lylch's chains. It was so heavy, he felt himself bowed and shrunken.

What must it be to put on that fearsome head that seemed made of iron? To look out from the corners of two eye-holes ringed by gold. To speak through that parted snout full of white alabaster teeth.

'Go out now, Saul. The rest will be shown you on another night.'

He stumbled to the door. Somehow he opened it. Outside his legs gave way and he leaned on the wall.

A faint murmur came from within the room, and he fled not to hear it.

That night he dreamed of a black jackal. It stalked across the stars and from its mouth came fire, and he was stumbling through the matchboxes to reach it when really he wished only to run away.

What had been done to him? Was this worse than any other thing?

The uncle of Saul Anger did not last a year. The snow stayed late into the spring, and on one of the nights of early April, when the City was white as a tomb, he died.

In the master bedroom the shadows had foregathered, though the fire blazed high in the pillared grate. The rosy lamps burned. Propped in the dark blue bed, the old man waited for death calmly, his pale striated hands crossed loosely on the sheet.

Towards midnight the carriages came across the thick white snow. They rumbled in beneath the windows of the Tower, the horses stamping and puffing out white breath.

The nine men of the secret society had come to see the old king go, to acknowledge the new king, his heir.

They climbed up into the bedroom, still in their outer coats, which had a massed white border.

Bareheaded, they stood about the room.

There was no talk beyond the first greeting, to the old man, to the boy.

The younger tutor, Kesper North, stood at Saul's elbow. He whispered, 'Don't be worried, Saul. No one expects weight of you, not yet.'

Saul bowed his head. He felt no pain at the old man's death. The old man had betrayed him like every other. And yet – he was bound. There stirred in him a thirst. For he knew by now, it had been revealed to him. He too—

The old man in the bed sighed. He slept.

They kept watch.

From below, now and then, the mechanical servants brought ruby decanters and crystal glasses, the salvers of sandwiches and toasts, the silver pot of coffee and the china pot of tea.

Far off, yet clear as a dagger through the icy night, the clock striking in the City. One o'clock, and two, and three.

Saul slept in his chair as the old man dozed in his bed.

What woke him was a thread of scarlet creeping over the room.

It was the stealthy snow-dawn from the eastern window, where the curtains showed a crack of light.

Saul looked at the effigy in the bed.

The old man had raised himself. He beckoned. He said, with exact clarity, 'I am ready.'

Death had come, or the Conductor of Souls, Anubis, the dark guide to the underworld.

Saul glanced, to see this new shadow, but nothing was there, for the dawn was like blood.

Then he saw the old man changing. On his frail body, the black mask began to evolve, not placed there, *drawn* there by supernatural means.

His head was that of the jackal now, with two black glowing eyes, a black tongue. Then the tongue was pulled in and the eyes closed. The mask lolled, and faded. And only a human corpse was in the bed, dead as a bone, a shell left by the sea. Empty, and indifferent to all that he had wrought.

CHAPTER FOUR

The Society

At a quarter to ten, Anger rose from his desk, and walked back through the conservatory and the dining room, up through the house.

When he came to the room on the third floor, he unlocked it. Only one servant was allowed in here, an old woman who had been young in the youth of his uncle. She it was who polished the table, and on cool nights laid the fire and lit it.

Anger paced about the room. There was always this restlessness, this need to possess the space before the others came.

Ten years had passed since the night of his uncle's death. Kesper North was grey now, and the fatter tutor had died – and been replaced, at the recommendation of three others, as the rules of the Society stipulated. They were now twelve men; extra chairs were set.

And those men, Anger had learned early on, their nature and their calling. Judges and lawyers together. Merchants who were valued in the City. A cleric even. And a lord. Here all were equal. It was their bond.

He heard the noise of a carriage in the street. But this was not one of the Society. Only on that night of death had they come in this way, and to the funeral. Now they walked the last mile or the last yards to the Tower, rung its doorbell, and mounted up its steps in a body.

He had never known one of them be late.

The Time Piece struck, and he heard the door sounding and opened, low down in the house.

They ascended now, and would soon be in the room with him.

Anger drew in his breath slowly. He crumpled the last cigarette into the fireplace as he detected their footsteps on his stairs. On his finger, the ring burned black.

By the year he was seventeen, Saul Anger had overseen the mysteries of the Society many times. Every three months it met, there in that room of the Tower. Before his uncle's death, he had known its aims, its methods, and its power.

Kesper North, who with four years had already grown grey, and far shorter than Saul, had been the whisperer, the one to instruct him in what he must do.

He had not, until he was fifteen, worn the jackal's head. The casque appalled him, and when he first donned it, he had almost fainted. But North was there at his right hand to whisper, whisper reassurance. The feeling passed. He grew used to its restricted vision, the echo of his own voice in his head when he spoke, the humming of the force of it, like the steam pipes under the house which worked upon the water and the temperature of the conservatory.

By seventeen he knew well how the business was laid out, each man speaking in turn. How this member had read this or that in the papers, or seen this or that, or been told of it by his agents. The two judges had perhaps got closer, and the three lawyers, to men who had appeared before them in the dock. The wicked ones who increased the misery of the City. Pimps who corrupted weak and stupid woman in her most loathsome guise. Thieves and cutthroats, masters of confidence trickery, burglars, murderers, the rubbish of the town.

And each man who spoke at that table had, every third month, one of these deviants in his sights.

Every third month, each of the nine and then the ten and then the eleven men, would select a creature of infamy, and for the sake of justice, kill him. Personally, at some risk. In disguise perhaps, or not, depending on the area and the situation.

The judges even had let men off from their grand altar, knowing the punishment of the law to be too lenient – a whipping, transportation to the sprawling colonies. Let men off and come at them, a day or a week later, in some alley of the black night. With knife or sword or pistol or club, they dispatched the offender. There must always be blood. It was the recompense.

At seventeen, Saul Anger had known what they would ask him. He was the king's heir, but once only, as his validation, he too must kill, in the manner of the Society of the Jackal.

Knowing they would ask it of him, he had prepared himself.

The long hours alone in the tall house, reading in the gold-flecked silence of the library, the mornings of fencing below, the minutes of standing at the high omnipotent windows, the sleeplessness that from the beginning had often dogged him, when he would lie and remember – these things had made up part of the sum of what, at seventeen, he was.

He had wanted, in the last of his horrible childhood, to kill men. The wish turned cold and marble in his heart. He was not afraid, at least he was not reluctant.

He had grown to a total belief in the Society. It upheld his reason for life, for, because of *this*, he had been rescued from the lake of despond.

'There are two of them,' he said, through the jackal's mask. And in the manner of the Society, they set up the judgement, fixing the hilt of the black sword into a socket, attaching to its upright blade, by a ring, a balance of gold with two shallow cups. In one cup, the perfect white feather, and into the other cup they threw two of the leaden hearts. With a clang and a clash, the balance swung down and hit the table, and the feather floated a moment above its higher dish.

'Only one is necessary,' said Kesper North.

'Not to me.'

He had already taken care to find out, and the small acute web of agents that served the Society had brought him all the word he had needed. It was fortuitous. Two at one blow.

The balance would stand now, on that table, until he came back to it, for this was first blood.

He had three months.

He did not need them.

It was summer, and the City busy at its riotous doings, the noisome coils of it full of maggots.

Mr Lylch, the overseer of the workhouse, had changed his mind since that day he told High Hat he was not inclined. Mr Lylch had become much interested, at least in the commerce of the velvet house, where Guinevere sat in his red dressing-gown, playing with a muff. Lylch had a share in the enterprise now, and so one night when he was summoned out, to journey with Guinevere in the carriage – some new and abashed client – he went.

They sat, this strange assorted pair, as the coach rattled through dark narrow streets to the proposed place of assignation. Lylch had been foolish enough to trust to Guinevere's sagacity and Guinevere foolish enough to trust that Lylch was sufficient bodyguard. The client besides, had required that they come alone.

'A gentleman, you say?' Lylch did wonder, as the vehicle went on. 'A funny spot to have the meeting, and no mistake.'

'Did you think he would meet us in the park?' asked Guinevere. 'He wants his little secret kept.'

They got down into a thoroughfare that was walled on both sides by pitch black tenements, not a light burning, and no noise but that of two cats fighting in a yard.

Then the coach slowed and stopped. A figure came to the door, and opened it and got in.

Lylch peered, but Guinevere desisted. Guinevere was used to those who arrived muffled, and with averted face.

This man had pulled his collar high and his hat low. In the dark he was a shadow, but he smelled of grooming and coins.

'Good evening, dear sir,' said Guinevere. 'Here we are, as you see, to assist you.'

The stranger spoke. He had a voice dark as the night, but musical and well-bred. Clearly he was worth a pound or two.

'My needs,' he said. 'Dare I explain them?'

'We are citizens of the world,' said Guinevere. 'We've seen and heard a great many requests. Nothing can shock us. Don't fear it, dear sir.'

'You want a boy?' said Lylch.

The stranger hesitated, as if composing himself – he was. He said softly, 'A young boy. About seven years of age. Slight and innocent. A virgin.'

'Oh my stars,' said Guinevere, 'a man of taste you are indeed. But I must warn you, such a little thing is quite hard to come by. Quite difficult.'

'It will cost guineas,' said Lylch.

'Money isn't in debate,' said the stranger. 'Whatever you ask. But can you supply me? I want him young and fresh. I want him tight as a girl.'

Guinevere laughed, velvety, as if a fat hand ran over a drape. 'Delicious. Of course, nothing but the best. And you shall have it. I have one now, a sweet angel only six and a half years old. Golden hair and melting eyes. Not touched. A skin like finest book-binding.'

'And you,' said the stranger to Lylch, 'what do you say?'

'I'll vouch for it. The blighter comes from my own establishment. I'm the fount of the honey, you might add. By the wisdom of the seven maidens, as the Good Book has it, yes. I pass on quite a few specials to my friend here.'

'But hasn't the boy a mother?' said the stranger.

'A mother? Some rackety whore died of the pox.'

'The child is clean as a lily, however,' said Guinevere.

The stranger breathed quickly. He said, 'But, you must understand, I'm urgent. I've had to wait. I may harm him.'

'Tsk,' said Guinevere. 'How honest you are, dear. Well, again you must be warned, any harm will cost extra. But don't fret. These little things are tougher than they appear. And he may like it. Many of my darlings adore to serve such gentlemen as yourself. Now, when shall it be?'

'Make it soon,' said Lylch, 'since you're so impatient.'

'Yes,' said the stranger. 'I think so too. It shall be now.'

Something gleamed then, in both his hands, which each man noted oddly were pale and very fine and without gloves. But what it was that gleamed they did not know. Did not even know when both the long Eastern knives were buried in each of their chests.

In astonishment, ridiculous, both men turned to the other for some explanation. But they had been struck in the heart and belly, and now the dreadful pain began. Blood spewed from the red mouth of Guinevere, even as he formed a question as to what had gone on.

Lylch died harder and took more time.

He fell in his writhings to the carriage floor, and Saul Anger stooped over him, and when the coachman shouted down what was amiss, Saul answered that one of the gentlemen had dropped his pipe and was looking for it.

If the coachman guessed otherwise, and doubtless he did, he made no move to interfere. They stood in that dark street beyond all lights, the horse like a rock, the coach itself black as any hearse.

And presently Lylch lay still on the floor and Guinevere sat upright in his jabot of blood. Saul Anger slipped from the cab as he had come, swift and silent, with his two knives stowed, and his handkerchief, sodden with gore, in a pouch.

He returned through the byways of Black Church, unaccosted, seldom glimpsed, and climbed up the cake-built hill to his mountain top.

In the room on the third floor he lit three candles, and going to the sword which upheld the balance, he wiped the blood of death along its rusted edge.

When they came again, the men of the Society, the leaden hearts would be out of the dish and the feather lifted high. In the journals they would read, a small piece only, of the deaths of the two Saul Anger had taken.

The cabby who had found them after half an hour had turfed them from the carriage on to the road, and so driven off. He made no witness.

Saul Anger himself did not sleep that night. Nor for some nights after. He prowled the high house, looking from its windows. He wanted more, and forced the blood-lust down deep inside himself.

He recalled the moment when his uncle had shown him the picture of a pyramid of Egypt, and how it had at once seemed to him like a matchbox of the Three Flames, standing up in the desert.

He sent for Kesper North, since the others were not yet due to come.

'You have done it,' said Kesper North.

'So I have. But there's more to be done.'

'Not by you. Now you're the king. Your uncle founded our Society. He killed only once. You need do nothing more.'

'But,' said Anger, 'I want—'

'You must be calm,' said North, as he had in their early days, when Saul rushed forward after learning. 'It isn't needful.'

'To me.'

'No. There's always risk. The leader must remain above risk. To hold us together.'

Later Saul Anger, alone, thought of what he had done to Lylch and Guinevere in the dark, and he turned cold as the leaden hearts flung in the balance. He found himself trembling as if with fear, but it was not that.

He considered leaving the Tower and walking away across the City. Taking ship perhaps to other lands. He thought of a wild freedom, and knew it was not to be his.

By the time they came again to the house, he was as calm as North had enjoined him to be. He did not want to go away, he did not want to murder men. He felt the power of the Society of the Jackal, and also its macabre ludicrousness. Something had gone from him but another thing had come to take its place. He could not have named either of them.

The twelve members of the Society entered the room mildly, greeted Anger, and sat down.

For a moment, before they donned their masks, they spoke lightly of the day and the City, one even alluding to the advertisement on the cloud for Tiny Tiger Tea, a popular brew of the masses. 'This isn't progress,' this man said, 'a barbaric custom, the sky plastered with slogans.'

'And,' said another, 'these carriages driven by steam, frightening the horses—'

'We go too far and too fast.'

They settled brooding at these words, and drew the masks from their compartments, and put them on.

Thirteen men now, with the heads of black Anubis, Conductor of Souls, Weigher in the Balance. Judgement.

They spoke one by one. This fellow had killed drunkards for their money. He would die. This one had swindled an old woman. He would die too.

Then there came the turn of the cleric. 'I am sick of these women,' he said. 'I've spoken before. I will be heard. These filthy conveyors of disease and wretchedness.'

Kesper North said, 'Women are fools and easily led. It's the men behind the whores who are to blame.'

'But I have heard of one – a notorious bitch of the streets, sick with syphilis, purveying it night by night. She laughs and says if she's to die, she'll take some of her gentlemen with her. *This* one I want.'

'No,' said Anger levelly. 'As North has said, you've spoken on this theme before, and we don't kill women. They are the lesser creation, good when well guided, wicked when encouraged to be so. Though harlots are the rubbish of the streets, without the men who make them so, they would find other employment.'

The rest of the table echoed this, but for the cleric, who said, 'My blood boils. I would eviscerate the lot of them and leave their filthy bodies for dogs to eat.'

'You have spoken your mind,' said Anger. 'Now let's hear your other choice. I don't think you so simple, sir, that you came here to us without one.'

The cleric writhed, and mumbled another name, the name of a man, a dealer in corpses.

This victim was acceptable.

So it went on then, about the table, until every man had spoken.

The balance was erected, and into it the leaden hearts were tossed, twelve of them. Later North would dismantle all and hide it away.

They sat in silence some while after business was concluded. Then one by one they took off their masks and stowed them, rose and went out. They left solitary, or by twos, not as they had come.

Not quite an hour had elapsed.

Kesper North faced Anger across the burnished table, where now lay only the blood-rusted sword.

'He's troublesome, Weams.' He referred to the cleric.

'Yes. His obsession with these low women inclines me to think he's indulged himself.'

North frowned. He did not know – none of them did – of Anger's past. Blunt talk such as this did not meet with North's approval.

'Surely not. But he's fanatical.'

'As are we all.'

North glanced into the fire. 'A flame to cleanse. You recollect your Virgil.'

'Fire can run out of hand.'

'You're here to prevent it.'

'The youngest of you all.'

'All the better. The cleanest and most strong.'

Anger laughed, shortly. No, North did not have an insight on his past. They smoked a pair of cigarettes and parted.

What had been needed was done. In three months' time, the fruit of it would be shown, the bloody handkerchiefs dipped in water to renew their potence.

Anger descended the house. He entered the conservatory of palms. The heat tonight was extraordinary. Perhaps the steam boiler had been stoked too high. He must speak to his man.

The advertisement had vanished from the cloud, and the cloud itself grown dim. The moon was sinking.

All at once a strange thing moved in the air. It was nothing mechanical, nor even natural. A shadow passed between the earth and the stars.

Anger beheld it without dismay. It could be nothing. Some smoke, or thing he had not been quick enough to see. Some trick of the eyes. A fancy.

CHAPTER FIVE

White Cat

Kitty Stockings re-entered Rotwalk Lane in the drizzly grey of earliest morning. She had got only one customer all that long night, and he had been rough with her, pulling her about and bruising her bosom. However, he was so excited that she had been able to press her thighs together and so prevent his proper entry, and he had released his seed in this way, not noticing. For this she was thankful.

Kitty had loved men in her younger days. Her sweet weak father, who had starved to death by giving all the scraps to her and her ailing mother. Some of her first clients who had been kind and jolly. But now she was more sceptical. A few were good sorts, but many not, and that beast had given her only a handful of coppers, and she had not dared protest.

As she neared the looming eyesore of the Rookery, Kitty noted something that surprised her.

It was, in the foul and fetid street, an image of peerless shining white, and it moved.

'Oh,' said Kitty, 'you poor thing. Where have you come from? Strayed from some big house, I should think, from the look of you. You won't like it here, you won't.'

And reaching down, she picked up the slim snowy cat, out of the mire, and held it in her tired arms.

Just then some nine or ten ruffians emerged from the Rookery door, and one, seeing what Kitty held, pointed it out to the others.

They were not above skinning such a novelty for the prize of its fur.

Kitty said, 'Just look, here's Grace's cat.'

'Gracie? She don't have no cat.'

'Oh yes,' said Kitty, 'for about three days.'

The men drew off. They would not hurt anything of Grace's. Grace was the talisman. They allowed Kitty to pass on into the house, and thinking of how the lie had better become a truth, she began to climb up the winding stairs.

This was no easy matter, for in places people slept on them, and the landings were thick with snores and a fug of stoves.

Reaching the attic at last, Kitty knocked on Grace's cubicle.

Grace called in her lovely voice that whoever it was should come in, welcoming all the world alike, and Kitty passed through.

The sun had strengthened, and light fell as if through a green forest, by the tattered but beautiful curtain, and dewed the mattress in beryls.

There Grace lay, white as snow – white as the cat – one arm over her head, and her hair like silk on the pillows.

There was a pretty smell in the room, unlike that of the whole house. Grace had always the ability to drive out poisons.

'Look what I found for you,' said Kitty.

'Oh, a cat.'

'Yes. And just your colour too. Better keep the poor thing or Ma Crow will put it in a stew.'

Grace stretched out both her arms, and Kitty put the cat down into them. Of course, it snuggled close at once, kneading Grace's hair and purring. It had not struggled.

'I wonder if we can get it some milk,' said Kitty.

'I expect it would like a herring,' said Grace.

At that moment, across the City, a young man was standing before a furious, rudely-woken doctor, sobbing. The doctor was shouting that there was nothing at all the matter with the young man, he was mad to suppose that he had a disease, and besides, should not have gone with women of the streets to catch one. This was the young man who had lain with Grace, at her address of accommodation, and had given her gold pieces.

Grace did not know this for a fact, but she might have done, for she smiled a secret smile.

The cat lay down with its face against hers. Its eyes were pale green like her own.

'You might well smile. But I've got some nasty news. Two of the girls were telling me. One of us was chased all along Black Church last night. She reckoned she only just escaped with her life.'

'Who chased her?' said Grace quietly.

'A great shadow was all she saw. She thought it was a big man, very tall, with a peculiar mask. She didn't see much. She knew he meant her harm. She said his eyes glowed *red*.'

'Perhaps it was bad gin,' said Grace.

'Perhaps it was another of those men who like to kill girls like us.' Grace said nothing. She stroked the cat. 'It's a cruel city, this,' said Kitty.

'So they all are.'

'How do you know?'

'Well, what do you think, Kitty?'

'I think I'd like to live on the moon, and eat strawberries and cream.'

They laughed, and gently moving the white cat, which curled instead to sleep on her pillow, Grace sat up.

In her old white nightgown, she looked mysterious as a priestess. Kitty marvelled at her, as she often did.

'I'm for my bed. I've been up all night, and only one brute who cheated me.'

'Have some breakfast with me before you go,' said Grace.

And she got up and pushed Kitty gently into the ancient chair. In a little cupboard there was bread and sausage, and this they ate with a cup of gin and water. Grace gave a piece of sausage to the cat, which it devoured daintily, nibbling her fingers.

'What'll you call it?'

'I don't know. Perhaps it will tell me.'

Kitty would not have been surprised if somehow Grace knew the language of cats.

'Shall I bring my music box?' asked Kitty.

'Oh yes. Let's have a tune.'

So Kitty went next door to her own tattered room, where damp limped through the wall, and took up her one proper possession, the music box her father had given her when she was only five. This too the roughs of the Rookery did not steal. They knew Grace liked it.

Sitting in the green curtain light, while the cat now washed itself, Kitty turned the handle of the box, which was of tin, and faded with patterns of pink flowers.

Unimpaired by years of pain and damp, out spirited a wonderful whirling tune, heightened by the click and whirr of levers.

Grace stood up and danced. Her erstwhile patron, who had taught her to read and write, had also shown her how to waltz, and now she did so, round and round, her balance flawless and unfaltering.

When the melody had run its course, it ceased with a clack – the only sign of age – and Grace stood still, glowing and marvellous, her hair electric, in a wave of silver.

'Oh, Kitty, how I'd like to dance in one of the gin-palaces. Shall we go?'

'Maybe. But we'd have to dress much better or they wouldn't let us in. Only the whores with class go there.'

'Yes, you're right. Well, one day. Make it play again!'

Kitty smiled and felt like a mother, although she was one year younger. She wound the handle round and round.

About midday, the white cat emerged from Grace's open window, and walked along the sills of the Rookery, jumping from disastrous ledge to ledge, and down and up the vertiginous heights.

It surveyed the slums, the winding streets that were in parts so narrow, only cats could walk two abreast. Also, from the roof, later, the distant avenues of infamous Black Church where, in antique times, dark priests had had a monastery, and worshipped the Devil.

The white cat seemed content with all this, and yet alert. It stared from point to point of the world of the City that it could see, and as the day advanced and began to go, it stared also into the radiant and unsullied sky.

Stars emerged, and then, as the evening began, a far-off cloud appeared that showed a girl and a kitten, and another cloud that showed a razor.

At these things the cat looked boldly.

Then, in the night, as the moon rose, the white cat sang. It sang in a high and sacred voice, until below in the house, the ugly, dirty, unmusical ones heard it, and started to shout.

Then the cat sang no more. It went down to Grace's window, and descended to her bed. Here it preened itself with a tongue so pale it was almost white, its lemon-green eyes half shut.

Grace was away. This did not matter. The grisly sounds of the house did not matter.

Sleep was good, and it was full of dreams old as the pyramids.

Grace and Kitty stood arm in arm, one in her red rags and one in her worn grey dress, at a spot half a mile below the better streets that rose from Black Church and the river. Here balanced a fantastic building, lit like a gigantic candelabrum.

REIGNING CATS AND DOGS

The gin-palace was made of glass, supported by pylons and girders of green iron. Its roof rose into a dome, and up there a hundred chandeliers seemed gathered like burning golden birds. Below, seen clearly through the crystal, gas lamps blazed on pedestals, shards of coloured glass swung, prisms blushed and burst, and below all these, a tirade of dancers cavorted.

An orchestra played there, a galloping polka filled the street outside with music, besides with the tinkle of glasses. A squadron of gins and brandies were being clinked and drunk, and on the upper tiers, the long flutes of pink champagne.

Kitty stared, like an outcast into Paradise.

'It'd be no good,' said Kitty.

'No,' said Grace. 'But one day.'

She was not sad, but wistful, like a child. This delicacy had not been corroded from Grace. She dreamed still.

Instead, Kitty and Grace polked on the pavement, madly, with bacchante gracefulness, round and round.

Until a moustached policeman, his hirsuteness slightly disarranged and caught in a moustache bandage, came hastily to move them on.

There was no place outside Paradise for happiness.

CHAPTER SIX

Jade Cat

In the red-lit kitchen of the Rookery, fifty persons stared, as a drama went on.

The newcomer was a small crooked man with a battered black top hat, whose clothes, despite the smallness of his body, were yet too tight for him. He carried a cane with a piece of ancient, valueless green glass at its top, and this he now waved under the nose of one of the bully-boys of the tenement.

'Where's my cut, where's my cut, I say?'

'I've given it you. Get off and leave me in peace,' said the bully, Jack Black, red and jolly with gin in the firelight, tickled still and too omnipotent to resort to violence.

But the crooked little man ranted on.

'No you ain't. You give me coppers. It was worth more than that. I know – I found it.'

'Bit of old plate was all,' said Jack Black dismissively. 'Bullock didn't give me nothing for it. And that what I've give you is your share. So take it and get off.'

'Get off he says,' cried the little man, raising his screwed up, sallow face, which was the largest part of his body, and like a dirty peeled potato. 'Get off. And cheated. I'll tell you, my fine lad,' said the little man, 'I got men and dogs outside. Yes I have. Big men and fierce dogs as'd take your leg off with a bite.'

'No you ain't,' said the bully. 'I know what you've got. Now off you go or do I make you?' And he rose to his burly height, his shaven head bristling like a porcupine.

The little man shrank back.

'You're a cheat, that's what you are,' said he, and turning he scuttled to the kitchen door, jeered now by the assembly. Outside the black night loomed, vaguely lit by a skein of stars up in a remote sky.

By the gutter stood his reserve force, one big man with a wooden leg, and one medium sized disreputable dog, with hair like a balding brush.

The kitchen door was shut.

'Couldn't get nothing out of him,' said Ralph Mooley, leaning on his cane, regarding the big man and the dog.

'There now,' said the big man. He watched as the dog urinated up against the side of the house.

'That's it, Buskit,' said Mooley to the dog. 'Filthy warren. Den of vipers.'

'Where now then?' said the wooden-legged man, essaying a hopping step.

'We'll visit the Biscuit,' said Mooley, 'and see what's doing. Then maybe down the strand, to see what we can pick up.'

'Picked clean, that mud,' said the other.

But they made on, along Rotwalk Lane. Each had a curious gait: Mooley's rather like a crab, as if he attempted to go sideways, while the big man, an old sailor by the name of Albert Ross, hopped stolidly. The dog too went on in an odd way, rambling and bobbing. It was altogether an unsightly specimen, ginger in colour had there been light to see, and with sticky fur of many different lengths. It had a nose like a box and with a great many spiky whiskers. Its scruffy tail was carried jauntily, however, for Buskit was, against all reason, an optimist.

They descended from the lane into the horrid streets that slithered to the river, and after about twenty minutes, which they passed mostly in silence, the dog occasionally watering various upstanding articles, they reached a timbered public house that lurked against the quay.

The Barrel and Biscuit catered for the riff-raff of the streets and off the boats that put in there, an evil motley crew, to which Ralph Mooley and Albert Ross were quite well known.

They squeezed into a booth in the dark light, and supped their beer, and Mooley now and then hailed men who slunk about the shadows.

The dog scratched under the table.

'Nothing up,' said Mooley, 'nothing doing.'

A resigned depression covered him. He sighed, and gave Buskit a kick. Buskit shook himself and took another scratch.

'I'd heard,' said Mooley, 'there was a supernatural thing frightening the whores in Black Church. Now *there's* a chance. When girls run they drop things. Bangles and coins.'

'There was a spectre once, on a ship. The old clipper it was. Three nights it chased the watch below. It was a doom, for a month later she run aground, and half the hands was lost.'

Ralph Mooley paid no attention to this. Albert Ross was a fund of lies, which sometimes would enthral the drunken or the stupid, and earn free drinks.

They finished the beer and rose, and Buskit sidled after them, his thin orange legs picking between the great boots of the customers.

Outside once more, they walked along the quay, got down the rotting slippery steps, and stood on the river shore.

A huddle of shipping creaked at its moorings, and here and there a dull lamp shone. Further on, the strand was almost deserted and black, with just the river shining beyond, eerie and lapping, in low sluggish gulps.

'Fishers are out tonight,' said Mooley. There was a steady trade in corpses on the river, boats that plied up and down to fish up the murdered and the suicide for hair or watch-chains. Near the tide-line a boat had been pulled in and a small group was there, bending over something that faintly glowed.

Mooley and Albert Ross and Buskit approached, sufficiently known not to cause alarm.

A pasty face turned, and greeted them.

'We've got a good one here. Look at her. Only a night she's been in, I'd say.'

Mooley and Albert Ross looked down, and saw, spread on a rug, a dead girl like a mermaid, pearly greenish skin and a long wet tangle of hair.

'One for the students,' said another man.

'No. The artist'll take her. She's a beauty.'

'But he likes to paint red hair. She ain't a redhead.'

'We'll dye her hair, make her nice.'

Across the wet black ribbon of the river, another phantom ship passed, rowed silent as a corpse herself, out hunting.

'There's Creakle's boat. What's he got?'

'Nothing from the look.'

They spread the girl out a little more, like a fine and delicate carpet. In her hair was caught a deceased eel, which one man pocketed for his supper.

Buskit looked on, and gave a little whine.

'Shut up, you bastard,' said Mooley. 'What you got to grizzle at?'

They walked off, Mooley and Albert Ross, the dog pattering behind them.

Presently they went by a sewer hole, from which, at certain times of day and night, a fetid sparkling fountain poured.

Past this point the shore was wide, a paving of thick mud, pocked with large depressions. An old boat lay and rotted on its side, and for a long way the land caved in towards distant warehouses, black and broken-windowed.

Cloud had come above them now, and up there was the image of a razor. And next to it, a tub of bubbles. Advertisements for shaving and for soap at which the two men looked without interest.

They began instead to search the mud, Mooley with his cane, and Albert Ross with the ball of his wooden leg. Buskit sniffed warily after rats.

Their haul had been, over the years, patchwork. Horses' teeth, and bones, chains, coal, rope, and sometimes coins. The tide had now and again washed in china and dolls and watches and earrings, but these were special finds. Others had unearthed golden guineas, pens, and ladies' corsets. The shore was a mire from which anything, it sometimes seemed, might be dug.

Aside from scavenging, Mooley had often earned his bread as a lookout for robbers. Albert Ross relied on begging, and his tales of shipwrecks which had never happened. He had a letter in his pocket, falsely signed by a make-believe vicar and two squires, which attested to his survival from the downing of the ship *White Pigeon*. Like all the rest, this being a lie, he did not often resort to presenting it.

Mooley found a penny, swore at it, wiped it with his scarf, and put it in his pocket. Albert Ross turned the mud over, phlegmatic and silent. He never expected anything and seldom got it.

The dog ran to the edge of the black river, and stood staring off, lost in some doggy dream.

'If it weren't for the rats,' said Mooley, 'I'd not keep that dog. But you got to protect yourself.'

Buskit howled thinly.

'Be quiet, you brute,' shouted Mooley.

Buskit turned, and came cantering towards them. He rushed to within three feet and sank suddenly in a slough of mud, up to his belly.

Here he struggled, yelping.

'Bloody fool of a dog,' complained Mooley, and going over, he put his boot into the mud below Buskit and heaved him up. Great clods and sloshes came with him, and Buskit rolled over, biting at the muck. Something fell from him with a thud.

'What's that? Some stone—'

Albert Ross leaned close. 'No, it ain't. Don't know what it is.'

They went, hopping and sidling, the dog trailing them, down to the water, and Mooley washed the mud away.

'What is it?'

'A doll, is it?'

They stared, by the faint light of the stars, and the luminescence of the advertising clouds.

Certainly, it was the figure of a cat, sitting bolt upright. Its face was feline and enigmatic, carven with eyes and whiskers. Its four paws were delineated like the heads of flowers. It was of a dim greenish material that gleamed now the mud was gone, and in one pointed ear was a ring of encrusted metal.

'Is it worth something?'

'I should say it might be.'

Mooley gnawed his lip, showing the find this way and that. 'Here, Albatross, will it do for Bullock?'

'Bullock's the best bet,' said Albert Ross.

Buskit scratched, sitting in the mud.

By starlight, Albert Ross rowed downriver, and Ralph Mooley and Buskit sat like effigies in the black boat.

The oily water curled round them, and on the banks the buildings stood stark and ghostly, seldom with a light.

They had passed through the docks where the great ships waited at stone quays, and where there had been lamps and sometimes noise, and once they were challenged, but they slipped by. Out here the marshes ran into the river, thick with reeds, and duck sometimes splashed or called in weird voices.

The church was sited across the river from Dogs Island, near the bridge, a white oblong with a pointed tower. St Darks was its popular name, it had no other. It had been begun a century before and then abandoned, only a shell, with two pylons marched into the water where, by night, two torches burned like red bushes.

They rowed in quietly to the pale steps, and hesitated, sitting in the boat. Behind the high uncoloured panes of St Darks' glass, a faint glow was visible. Bullock the dealer was at home to callers.

'Shall we go up?' said Mooley. 'Is it wise?'

'Better had,' said Albert Ross.

They tied the boat to an iron ring in the right-hand pylon, and got out awkwardly on the steps, the dog as clumsy as the men.

Then they hovered in the torchlight, which reflected below as if the river also burned.

A duck hooted, and rose from the reeds like a flying gargoyle of dark green.

'Best go up.'

They went up the steps, and so to the tall black door. This Mooley pushed, and it opened a little way.

Beyond, the church was all one hollow chamber, pillared, with a roof only partly carved in octagonal designs, partly left blank. A silver star glittered in one eight-sided shape. A single star, no other.

In the pulpit was visible a huge man. He was well over six feet tall, some twenty stone in weight. A mane of dark hair poured round his large and brazen face. His nose was strangely flattened. He was like a gargantuan, bloated angel, a tiger-angel, unkindly, and knowing.

'Knew we were coming,' said Mooley to Albert Ross.

The being in the pulpit spoke.

'Of course I knew. What have you got for me?'

Bullock was a fence of prodigious reputation. His spies haunted the byways of the river. He was fair but exact, and his retribution on those few who had tried to undo him, famous.

Ralph Mooley slunk sideways towards the pulpit, Albert Ross at his back, and Buskit last of all, a cowed Buskit, who did not choose to lift his leg against the pillars.

Reaching the pulpit, Mooley pulled out his find, wrapped in a soiled handkerchief, and offered it up.

Bullock came out. He was now even more massive, on two columns of legs booted in red leather. His belly was big as a world and swathed in a waistcoat of grey embroidered silk.

He leaned down and took the object Mooley extended, shook off the handkerchief. The green cat shone.

'What's this?' said Bullock in a terrible, soft voice.

'We found it,' said Mooley. 'Rightly, the dog found it.'

'Where?'

'In the mud up along the strand of Black Church.'

Bullock gave a quiet roar and the church echoed like a barrel of a cannon.

'Do you expect me to believe that? You lying turd. Take it back to the one you stole it from.'

'I never—' protested Mooley.

'I won't touch it,' said Bullock, 'and if you've any sense left, nor will you. Do you think I'm blind? Can't see, eh?'

'No, no,' bleated Mooley.

'Found it in the mud – this comes from the sand. The hot sand of Egypt. Go and give it back and ask his pardon.'

'It's true what Mooley says,' put in Albert Ross solidly. 'We found it.'

'You too, eh?' said Bullock. 'Save your wind. I won't touch it. You see that?' He indicated where, behind him on a platform, a telescope pushed up through the roof of the church. 'Do you think I can look that far and not see what's under my nose? Get out.'

Mooley took the green cat back from Bullock's enormous paw. The cat was hot now, as if it had been seethed in fire.

'Pasht,' said Bullock, as if to himself, in a mumble. 'Sky goddess. Patroness of the stars and the cups.'

'This here?' asked Mooley.

'Get out,' said Bullock.

They retreated from the church, and Bullock stood there, by the altar rail, in the unsanctified hollow, staring after them from huge angel frog's eyes, until they were gone.

Out on the steps they leaned together, at a loss.

'Won't handle it,' said Mooley.

'No, he wouldn't.'

'Must be bad. Better hide it.'

'Yes, better do that.'

Buskit whined, and Mooley kicked him absently. They went down in low spirits, and got into their boat, for the long row back upstream.

CHAPTER SEVEN

The Apparition

The girl had been sent out for beer. This happened every night, but now there was a reason why she left the house so blithely, toting the white jug. Her hair shone under her cap, and her aproned waist was cinched particularly tight.

At the corner of the avenue, she began to look out for him, her young man. He had said he would meet her hereabouts, but casually, in case they were seen. For she was not allowed a sweetheart; the household where she worked was very strict.

The summer twilight was coming down, softening and blurring the edges of everything. A lamplighter moved in the distance, waking up the lamps of the broader streets. The public house that supplied the beer was only a road away, and the girl started to fear disappointment. He had not come.

She crossed the street, and idled a moment under the doorways. A black shadow drifted around the corner.

For half a second she thought it was a man, and that it might be him. But then she saw it was not like a man. It was not like anything.

The girl stopped quite still, holding her jug, the deep blue sky above her pierced with the first needlepoint of stars.

She saw a thing that was firstly like a black hump. Next it opened out, and she saw a frightening enough image, which was a black dog, long-snouted, with a lean body and long legs. This kept as still as she and stared at her, and gradually she realized its eyes were red as fire.

The fine hair rose on her body and her legs turned heavy and cold. She did not dare to run.

Then the dog – stood up. That is, it stretched upwards. It reared into the sky like a black fan that had spread, like a devilish umbrella, although it was still a dog shape. And now it was tall as the house-fronts and it craned over her, black and impenetrable, with its red eyes on her, and a faint shimmer around its muzzle.

A shrill weak scream escaped the girl. But she could not move. Only the jug dropped from her hands, and smashed. The noise was far away.

And now the dog, the huge dog that filled the sky, came forward and passed – right *through* her. She felt it like a wave of ice, freezing her blood. Her breath thickened and turned to water in her lungs. Her heart stopped beating and she fell dead as a stone on the road.

Since the sewers stank, the man who had entered them had wrapped a handkerchief about his nose and mouth. He carried too a lantern against their darkness. From his waist was slung his pan, which he would hold under the flushing conduits. Water and excrement would gush through, and any valuables remain. He had garnered some things in his time – a gold chain, some silver coins, even once a pearl.

As he trod the filthy passages, that in places let off a yellowish glow, knee deep in the foul water, his sharp eyes searched for anything that glittered.

Above, the City roared and chattered. It sounded like Hell in a dream.

He paused and directed his light. Something blazed under the tide of murky liquid. He bent to see—

And as he was doing this, a great cold entered the sewer, and then a great dry heat. Surprised, he hesitated, raised his lantern and looked about.

Rats clustered on the ledges, their moist black bodies clinging together like jam. Now they crouched low and had become very still, their eyes gleaming like dead coins he would never want.

A black pillar stood up from the water. It was strong but oddly fashioned. Of iron it must be, but it had not rusted.

On a reflex, for he was careful, the sewer man glanced about. Not one pillar, but four. Two very straight and two with this curious curve to them.

Where the water met them it flashed strangely, as though little fires were going off in it.

Then the pillars moved. They moved forward, and directly through the wall of the passage, through its stone and slime and stink, and were gone.

The man stood trembling. His hand which held the lantern shook as though he had the palsy. He stared at it. The hand had withered like an old brown flower. It was useless to him. It was not his.

He gave a low cry, and the rats came spilling off the ledges and swimming away, and there one floated, dead and belly up, and he saw it was white in the moment before the lantern died.

Up on the embankment the obelisk rose into the clear night air, black basalt, and on either side the creatures lay, their paws stretched out, the white marble sphinx with the face and hair and breasts of a woman, and the body of a lion. The black bronze Anubis that shone as if wet. Jackal-dog, the Judger and Weigher, motionless, an interesting landmark on the river's bank.

The policeman stood looking at these things, unnerved as he always was by this spot. A ghostly suicide was seen here, and he had seen it, a woman in a cloak and loose hair, who climbed on to the wall, poised, and let herself go over into the long chains of the river.

Now he would always pause, the policeman, to see if it would come again.

But the night was soft. It smelled of soot and grime and the steam and oil emissions of the traffic, of horseflesh and dung, of summer stone, and, in vague candy wafts, of the flowers of market-gardens on the City's edge. Of the river too, sewage and fish, and some other smell – age perhaps.

No harm, surely, in this night.

The policeman went up and stood under the obelisk, and looked downriver to Minster Bridge.

Now that was odd. Some effect of the hazy lower air or the alternate clarity of the sky— The bridge was too near. It hung across the river, black and arched, but its pylons were to be seen only at either hand. It had a head formed like the head of a dog.

The policeman stared on. His heart palpitated and caused him to cough, and in the City things rattled and trotted, bells sounded from some church, everything continued. But here. Here from this place he saw a black dog bigger than the domed cathedral, crossing over the river. And where its feet disturbed the water, pale fires rotated.

It went on to the farther bank, and there it dwarfed the houses. Lighted carriages were passing on the road, and the monster stepped over them. They did not see. Nowhere did any see what he saw.

It vanished in the shadow of the City, one with it.

The policeman knew he had witnessed some awful thing, over which he had no power, of which he might tell no one.

Against his own body, sobs burst like gunfire, and he leant on the parapet weeping, not knowing what would become of him.

The girls of Black Church had been wary for some nights. They went about by twos and threes. Daisy had seen a devil and Rosie had seen it too. A black shape that pursued in silence. God knew there were customers with bizarre tastes, but this was not in the book.

The two redheads, not pretty enough any artist would want them for romantic pictures, walked through the back lanes of the area, searching out the lawless men who strayed there, burglars with a haul, roughs who had taken a purse. These men might be good for money and besides a drink and a laugh.

They found one at the turning into Priests Court.

He wore a tattered tan coat with big pockets stuffed with loot, and catching up to them he planted a smacking kiss on the rouged cheeks of both.

'All alone, girls? That's a shame.'

He said he would take on the two of them, and they were glad enough, for even in a pair they had been nervous.

Above, ancient buildings lifted, with a faint candle flicker in only one window. There was a reek of washing and bones. But down the road the tavern was, the green and yellow windows and the bright bottles.

He was friendly, the robber, he would conduct them there.

But it was not to be.

A dim sound came. It was like slender bells tinkled on a wand. It moved like the wind across the court, and with it a wave of heat.

'What's that?' asked the smaller redhead.

'Old Nick himself,' said the robber. 'Don't be frightened. You've got me with you now.'

And then blackness was there in the court with them. A blackness not like the night, but of the night, of the night's bowel.

It entered and they saw sway up over them the head of something, and two ruby lights, and teeth – so many white teeth.

It took him first. He was lifted with a shriek, and all the bounty fell out of his pockets. They saw it snap off his head, and then he fell – but there was no blood.

Both girls were screaming. One tried to run and the other to hide.

Death had both of them. It sheered through them, mincing their necks, tearing off their breasts. They too fell one by one, down in the courtyard with the man, on the jumble of sovereigns and gold rings.

No one had looked forth from any place. If screams were heard in those alleys, it was better to be ignorant. Closed doors, shut windows.

Besides now, nothing was there, only the three bodies in a line.

No blood at all lay on the cobbles. No blood on the white skin. The robber's head was on. And yet, it was an altered head. Like a walnut, seamed and pitted, the mouth fallen in on black teeth, the thin hair crossing the wrinkled pate. His fingers were still young. On his breast the pocket watch had melted, its hands stuck fast.

And the two dead girls, how could they be otherwise. One a hag of a hundred years, her torn dress showing her withered dugs. And the other – it would cause worse terror – the other had gone a different way. A woman's body, but the head of a child, too small, its features untouched, the mouth a rosebud, the soft hair shining in the glint of the solitary candle high above.

CHAPTER EIGHT

A Visit, and After

Anger was dreaming.

He had not slept for two or three nights, and now, seated in his study, sleep overcame him as sometimes it had overcome the old man, his uncle, Angier.

Anger's face was cold in sleep, a knight upon a tomb. His mouth firmly closed, his hair silken. His hands lay on the chair arms. A graven image, even unconscious.

But inside his skull, another matter.

In the dream it was his father who approached him, his father with Lylch's face and Guinevere's dressing-gown. And Saul lay tossing in a fever, so hot that he seemed to be on fire. And this made his Lylch-Guinevere-father very angry.

'Be still, can't you. Be still.'

But Saul could not be still. And so the father went out, and helpless, Saul watched where he went. It was to a blacksmith's forge, and a black hole that fleered with flame. 'Make me a brand,' said the father. And the blacksmith, a faceless giant, hammered it out on the anvil.

The father took it. He flung down a silver coin, the way Saul had seen so often, so many men with silver coins.

And then the father was in the doorway of the room where Saul lay, and the brand was white-hot, like a sun.

'Lie still, you little beast, or you'll have this.'

But he could not lie still, and the father came to him and pressed the brand home on his naked flesh across the heart.

Saul cried so loudly in agony that stars fell into the room. But the brand said only his name. The brand that marked him read *Anger*.

He woke.

His man was positioned, couth and unflurried, in the doorway.

'A gentleman has come to see you, sir. One of the gentlemen.'

Anger knew what he meant. A member of the Society. It must be Kesper North. Anger felt relieved. He did not, in the aftermath of the dream, just for a minute, want to be alone. And North never stayed long. A game of chess, or half a game. A book recommended or borrowed. The vestige of their former relationship, when Anger had been a boy.

He got up, and went out through the conservatory and the dining room, into a small parlour. Here the furnishings were of the same rich darkness; two lamps had been lit on the mantel – Angier had never inclined to fit the house with gas.

At the centre of the room, twisting his hands, stood, not North, but Spartacus Weams, the cleric.

Anger felt now a wash of distaste. This man appalled as much as the women Weams loathed.

'Yes,' said Anger shortly, 'how may I help you?'

'Oh, Anger,' said Weams, 'give me time.'

'Sit down then. Will you take a brandy?'

'A brandy? Yes. That will be of use.'

Anger went to the carved sideboard, and poured out the brandy kept for infrequent guests.

Weams took the glass and drained it. He sat back in the scarlet chair and touched his eyelids with his fingers.

'I need to speak to you, Anger.'

'Then I'm all attention, of course.'

'It isn't easy for me. I'm so burdened. Picture a man beneath a stone, the classical fate for a sinner in Hell. This is me.'

'Why?'

'You're too direct. Oh, you must give me time.'

Anger said, impatient but level, 'You've sought me.'

'The leader and the figurehead of our Society. Our pure and honourable Society. Oh, Anger. Something's happening. Haven't you felt it?'

'What is happening, exactly?'

'Something – terrible. Something that claws at the roots of reason.'

'What, then?'

'I don't know. I *feel* it. Do you read the newspapers?'

'As you know, I must, now and then.'

'Then have you seen – reports—'

'Of what?'

'Of *something*. How can I say?'

Anger said, almost sweetly, 'But you must.'

'I'm afraid – to speak it aloud – we have – *unleashed* something.'

'Death,' said Anger. 'Justice.'

'No – not in the way it's been for us. Our ventures. Not that. This is – something *moves* through the City.'

Anger said, 'Weams, this is gibberish.'

'My guilt,' said Weams, 'my guilt makes a fool of me. I need to confess to you. But – I can't.'

'Then what can I do?'

Weams motioned towards the brandy. 'Will you oblige me?'

Anger did so, pouring out a double, a triple measure. He wished only to be rid of this man.

'You must understand,' said Weams, 'that I am – plagued by – inclinations.'

'You've bought women,' said Anger. 'Well.'

Spartacus Weams laughed. He laughed horribly and stupidly and drained the glass again.

'You're blind,' he said to Anger, standing up. 'Like a priest king, blindfold. Is it your fault? I think so. You were a child when he gave you to us. I remember you. So cool and sure. What guilts do *you* carry, Anger?'

Saul Anger felt a shield rise up in him like steel or a glacier.

'That's not what you came here to discuss.'

'I can't talk to you,' said Spartacus Weams, 'you're a rock. You're iron.'

Anger said nothing.

'Well then,' said Weams, 'I'm damned. Be damned to you as well, Anger. *Your* fault.'

'Go now,' Anger said.

'Oh, I will. I will. Go to what? We shall see.'

The cleric passed from the room and went down the stairs of the house like a roll of heated air.

When he was gone, Anger lit a cigarette at a candle. What Weams had said had made no sense. And yet, it had left a shadow on him, like the burning brand of the hideous dream. What was his judgement worth? He was a figurehead, no more. The Anubis they had named their Society for. A god in a mask.

* * *

The way down to Hell was, naturally, easy. Through the dim-lit streets and so into the dark streets, and so to a street that had no lights at all.

Spartacus Weams left the carriage, not fearful of the spot or the hour, only of himself. He went to a low door and knocked. The door was opened a crack. 'Ah,' said a voice, 'it's you. You've been absent a long time. We expected you nightly.'

'I would have kept away,' said Spartacus Weams.

'There, and that would be a shame. How disappointing for us. And such a trial for you.'

Weams passed through, and into an odorous corridor, and up a stair. At the top was a room, lighted or perhaps shadowed by the dullest and most smoky lamps. Under the threadbare carpet boards creaked and mice rustled.

A young man rose from a sofa. He came towards Weams smiling. 'Will I do, tonight—' Weams stared at him. He was about twenty or twenty-three, Anger's very age, and not unlike Anger, after a sort, pale and very dark, with dark cool eyes. But he was not icy like Anger, not adamantine. No, he was friendly and wanting to please.

'Yes,' said Weams, and they ascended the stairs to another upper room, that had in it a couch, a wash-stand, and two dismal candles that the mice had chewed.

It was not the velvet house, nor did it deal in little boys, yet it was of that type. It was a house of Sodom, and Weams feared it now, because here he had known his only true pleasures, pleasures so awful they made him scream. Pleasures so transient they must be often repeated.

Had he been able to make his confession, he would not have come, would not have been able or perhaps even allowed to come here, and that he would have been glad of. Even as his flesh writhed, Weams would have rejoiced. For every teaching of his life and of his calling had warned him that this, which he did here, was a vice worse that any other. A crime against God.

The young man, the whore, had stripped to his waist, his pale hard body like alabaster in the fitful light. He drew Weams in lightly and held him like a trembling child.

Weams was already molten with desire. He began to beg for use, and the young man teased him, inflaming him further, saying Weams would have to ask him very politely, persuade him. And Weams heard his own voice offering the young man poetry, almost Biblical phrases, while the room swelled and diminished with the surge of his blood.

At last the young man, capable and accustomed, bent him forward against the footboard of the bed. With swift strokes Weams was laid bare, parted, tickled so that he whimpered, packed full of delight.

Ridden, Weams gripped the wood and tried to hold off, but the torrent took him. He grunted, hearing his voice again with a shame and dismay that did not matter. The great wave came and he shouted, his belly dissolving, biting his tongue in the fit.

The male whore withdrew from Weams at once, glancing at his member to see if it were soiled. *He* had had no pleasure in the act. His strength was in his lack of it. The look he turned on the back of his customer would have made Weams cringe, if he had seen it, but he did not, leaning on the bed's foot, gasping.

Instead the whore saw something, something else. It was obscene. From Weams' buttocks there dropped out something black, and the young man swore softly, thinking his lay had fouled himself from excitement.

Yet the black thing was clean and almost clear. It rested on the bare boards, and now it shifted. It *grew*.

The young man made a noise and stepped back.

There was a huge thing rising up on the floor. It was coal black, and now it had a pointed head. Two eyes roasted red.

A gigantic dog confronted the prostitute. In terror he backed now to the wall and gave a frantic cry.

Weams turned.

He saw the black jackal, big as a hunting hound, its sleek sides shining in the almost dark. And then it launched itself. It took the young man by the throat. A flare of white teeth like awls. It had him. It shook him.

The young man's shriek was stifled. There had often been such noises in this room.

The dog-jackal shook, terrible, as if with a rat, the body lifted from the floor.

Weams could see the glazed eyes of the victim, the open mouth. Then he was flung down.

The huge dog faded. It was a shadow. Then it was not.

Weams could not move, but finally he forced himself. He went to see. He kneeled down.

The man who had pleasured him lay in a heap against the wall. Oh, something unspeakable—

Weams retched and turned his head.

Anubis the Jackal, exacter of punishment. It had not torn out the throat. It had worked some miracle of deletion.

The body ended at the neck. Here the head, so beautiful and cool and young, had disintegrated – had *decayed*. Like rotten vegetable matter, and in this, the sallow rim of the skull. One perfect eye, yet open, pitiable, loathsome.

Spartacus Weams pulled up his clothes. He saw to himself, then crept across the room and fumbled for the door. After him, in the corridor, he closed it, and went down the house.

No one intercepted him. He reached the outer door, and opened this, and there the carriage waited in the black dead street.

Weams ran to the carriage and jumped in. At once it started, bearing him away.

What had it been? Was it some sick dream? No, it had been real. It had been retribution. Not upon him, the sinner, but on the innocent wretch who had served him for a coin.

Weams' apartment was by night an autumnal brown, with Persian carpets on the walls. A great black Bible from the seventeenth century rested on a stand, with a bookmark of crimson and gold-leaf.

Weams uncovered the page, and looked. He saw the word *Repent* and nothing else.

He went to the bureau, and pulling out a sheaf of paper, scattered it before him. Leaves fell to the ground. He paid no heed.

He wrote: *Anger, I have met death in the pit of sin.*

Weams stopped. He dipped the pen into the ink.

We have unleashed a terror. It is our pride. It is our wickedness. We are not worthy, not one of us, to obey such a master. I least of all. And now he has come to chastise us

Weams dropped the pen. He picked up the shaving case he had brought from his bedroom, and opened it.

The silver razor was in his hand. He felt nothing and everything. A jumble of thoughts and needs, none good, none tangible.

With a sure hand, he cut his throat, across and across.

And as he coughed and choked on blood, he thought at last. *What have I done?* But it was too late.

He fell across the desk and blood splashed on the letter, not concealing the words.

REIGNING CATS AND DOGS

To Saul Anger, as the Time Piece struck the hour of five in the morning, this letter was conveyed. Weams' man had summoned not only the police, but a grave man of the Society. It was to be hushed up.

'He died of a sudden seizure, sir,' said Weams' servant to Saul Anger. 'There was blood. I regret some has splashed the letter.'

Anger read what Weams had penned. Unfinished and hysterical, it had the power of all missives fashioned before death.

Weams had been mad. Always unhinged, now this.

The night had turned cold, and they had lit a fire. Anger crumpled the letter and cast it in. There it burned and was no more.

Anger seemed to see cities blazing on the coals. Red eyes looked through. With a sigh he turned back to his sleepless bed, and lay down there, silently, to wait out the long still night.

CHAPTER NINE

The Runaway Carriage

Full of relief, Kitty Stockings entered Grace's room as though she brought flowers. It was a fine morning, and two of the Rookery boys had stolen some milk from the cart that passed through one of the better streets. A cup of this Kitty bore into the room.

'Look what they got.'

'You have some,' said Grace.

They shared the milk, and from the pillow the white cat came and stared with spring-leaf eyes, until it too had had a portion on a little powder tray.

'I've got some good news,' said Kitty. 'I hope you'll be pleased, Gracie. We don't need to work the streets.'

Grace waited.

Kitty said, 'Yesterday evening, when I was by the Hollow Tree public house, this man come up to me. And he said I could make some money having my photograph taken, in exotic poses, for gentlemen's private viewing. He said,' she added sadly, 'I'd like the photographs, they'd make me look younger. And he told me if I had a young friend, to bring her too.'

'Yes, why not,' said Grace. She smiled. But then she never said no.

Kitty said, 'I think he was quite genuine. He gave me a shilling, for nothing, and the address, which is in quite a good part of Black Church, where the drapers are. And it's not safe, those other streets. The newspapers are bursting with some horrible murders done four nights ago – a pair of poor tarts and a man in Priests Court—' Kitty could not read, but there was the scribe of the Rookery, who made his pennies writing false testimonials, and he would sometimes read out loud from a third-hand paper. 'It's a very strange thing,' said Kitty. 'The bodies had no mark – but they'd gone wrong.'

'What do you mean?' Grace asked. Her look was very attentive.

'Two were young, but their faces, and parts of the women, were old and shrunken – and one – had the head – *of a child*. I tell you, our kitchen was agog. Ma Crow said it was a pack of lies. But there it was in black and white, and they wouldn't print what wasn't true.'

'But how could it be?' asked Grace. She stroked the cat absently.

Kitty replied, shuddering, 'They said it was someone experimenting with science. Like they do all the time now. These new-fangled machines—'

'Such as cameras,' said Grace.

Kitty laughed. 'No, that'll do us some good. It's these bicycles that fly and railway trains and steam carriages. Where will it all stop?'

Grace said, 'Was there anything else the paper said?'

'Yes. There were sightings of the *thing*. The apparition. Sometimes it's a man with a mask like a dog's head, and sometimes a giant hound – but black as night. Some think it's a masked man with a great dog to guard him. He takes his victims aside and the dog won't let them move. Then he works his science on them, and they die. But obviously, he hates women. And our kind of women mostly.'

'There was a report,' said Grace, slowly, 'of a servant girl who dropped dead in the street.'

'And a policeman went mad on the embankment by the obelisk,' said Kitty. 'He sat there by the sphinx, and urchins were throwing dirt at him.'

Grace played with the cat, trailing a sash for it to paw and bite.

'She has teeth, look.'

Kitty said, 'They're calling the atrocities the Black Church Terror. We'll go up to that man's room in the afternoon, and be back before dark.'

Grace gave over the sash to the cat, and sat, her chin on her white hand. She was thinking, carefully and stilly, of everything that Kitty had said, and her mind had turned back as if pulled by a cord, to that night when they had heard together the weird wild cry cut through the dark. Terror had been there from that moment. All this while it had attended on Grace, a slim black shade that stood just behind her left shoulder. And yet – she did not fear it. Psychic, she sensed a vast evil, something fiery and yet cold, hot yet drained of light. But, a woman, she knew a curious anticipation also, that made her blood electric. Something was in store for her. Not death but life.

Again the carriages were gathering, not in the bloodless snow now, but in the bright summer afternoon, for the funeral of a member of the Society.

A sudden seizure, choking, a haemorrhage. Anger had learned from a second source, one of those responsible for this very pretence, that Weams had slashed his throat. Augmenting this ominously, there had been another murder on that night, in a street where Weams had carried out charitable work. These murders too were to be suppressed. The public had grown agitated, led astray by the too-vivid reports of the journals. Already there had been a small riot over the river, where apprentices had smashed the windows of a workshop that produced typewriters. Modern things were out of favour. A mad scientist who practised on slum-dwellers and whores was a dangerous symbol. Caricatures had appeared, an absurdly long lean figure in a black greatcoat, his face hidden by the mask of a dog, with, in the fist, a hound on leash, its lips dripping foam, and in the other hand a vial marked *Poison*.

Rivals to such things were the unpublished photographs the police had taken of the mysterious bodies, and the cadavers themselves, preserved already in formaldehyde for study.

Weams' death had been a simpler one, the age-old means.

The place of burial was St Davids-by-the-Meadow, the white church of the pointed tower and two pylons, that stood above the sweep of lower Black Church like a good thought.

Here in the wide green graveyard, overhung by cypress and yew and early roses, the fine ebony coffin was let down into its black slot, that promise of things to come, and if they were not now, yet they would be.

Each man who stood above the grave, and all the Society was there, the two servants of Weams, and not one other, was conscious enough in those moments of his own mortality.

To Anger, so young, no taint in him that was physical, the pit looked promising, indeed. He thought of sleep at last, of utter noiselessness and serenity. The grave did not frighten, rather it allured, and he imagined how facile it would be, to fall down into it and be at peace.

But then, straightening up as the priest closed his book, Anger forgot these thoughts, and stood looking about him at the men of the Society of the Jackal, at their sombre faces unclad by the mask of Anubis.

Clearly, from this fount, the rumour of the dog-man had sprung. The man who murdered the riff-raff of the City. Odd it should have taken so long for such a connection to grow. Although, of course, now the Society was inadvertently blamed for deaths it would not design to effect, those of street-walkers and sodomites, servant girls, such strays.

They spoke a minute, the twelve men, there in the leafy paths, between the tall grey stones which one day would be all that remained of any of them.

'He was insane. We would have paid the price. He would have run berserk. Betrayed us.'

'Better that he rests and leaves the work to us.'

'I've heard he had strange fancies. He'd been reading the papers no doubt. His mind . . .'

There was no wake. They did not go to drink wine or to eat mutton over the corpse of Weams.

Behind them, as they walked away, the gravedigger, a gaunt, bent man, shovelled the earth on to the coffin lid.

Anger reached his carriage and got in. He drew the black hat off his head and held it in his hands, as if he removed the mask of the jackal.

The day was so sunny, and the interview so hopeful, Kitty had put on her yellow muslin dress and Grace her pale cotton.

They walked up through the lower streets, and coming into the better ways, paused to peer in at the windows of dealers in junk and fantastic curiosity shops, where azure parrots swung in cages and skulls rested on ancient books.

At a barrow they bought a saveloy and shared it, licking their fingers.

The sky was blue, without a cloud, and even the faint persistent haze of the dirty City did not much impair it. Birds flew over on white wings.

But the thoroughfares were buzzing with talk of the murders, and everyone who knew their calling, from the costermongers to old crones with brooms, shouted out some warning, coarse and mocking, or deadly serious, causing Kitty to shiver and take Grace's arm.

They walked into the quarter where the drapers worked, and after some eighth of a mile of sweat-shops, whose poor slaves were sometimes to be seen out on the pavements smoking or merely slumped in exhaustion, they came among the tiny shops where cloth was sewn. Here and there in a window was an example of work, and now a green dress caught their eyes.

'Oh, look at that for you,' said Kitty.

'When I go to the ball,' said Grace.

'They'd let you in the old palace and no mistake,' said Kitty, 'with a gown like that.'

It was of silk, the shade of leaves or clear summer river water, of water-lilies and Venusian dusk. It glimmered, deep-bosomed and little of waist, with twenty flounces to its hem.

'And jade earrings to go with it,' said Grace.

'Or in the pawn shop on Drop Street there's a pair of green glass.'

'And what will you wear?' asked Grace.

Kitty said, 'I shan't go. It isn't for me.'

And Kitty knew a lonely darkness, there on the warm street. She had always guessed her way went down. Through gates of pitch she would be going, not of crystal, to the clink of chains or knives, not champagne flutes.

Anger's carriage travelled quickly, although it was funereal and gloomy, the horses black: the chariot of Hades.

Along the broad streets it coursed, and other traffic made way for it.

Then came a turning, and a rapid check, the driver calling and cursing.

Something had blocked the road.

Anger did not lean out to see. He did not care.

The black horses sidled, jinking. The carriage rolled.

In the middle of the street before them, another carriage had been halted. *It* had no horses, or it had two horses fashioned of black iron. The carriage rested at the back of these, and even now it gave off fumes of steam and oil. A modern conveyance, a steam vehicle.

The driver had got out and was remonstrating with a little crowd that had turned quite nasty and was berating him.

'Satan's coach it is!' cried a big woman of the lower streets.

She was seconded by three burly men.

An egg was suddenly thrown. It landed, broke, and poached on one of the hot iron horses at the front.

With no more preliminary the driver was pushed to the ground. Men swarmed over him, bounding into the carriage. Crowbars and hammers were instantly at work on the mechanism.

A roar began to come from the carriage's rear end. Other spectators drew off. Oil spread on to the road.

Then came an abrupt gout of scalding steam, which filled up the area like a fog. A clang, a clatter, and next an explosion, with fire, and part of the carriage ripped off and skidding down the roadway. Men and women scattered screeching.

Anger's black horses reared and burst forward in fright.

The driver shouted, standing up now and fighting with his team, but they were too strong for him. The equipage tore down the street, past the pandemonium of the exploded coach, towards the lower ways of Black Church.

The onslaught threw Anger sidelong. He was not stunned, more galvanized. He sat up and held to the side of the carriage. It was immediately apparent what had occurred.

He knew a dire elation. He thought of the grave into which he had stared.

The carriage was running very fast, and all at once, Anger felt the concussion and change as the driver was shaken off the box. The man lay dead or injured in the street, and the horses, terrified, furious, tore on, like the steeds of Pluto truly.

Nothing would stop them now until they had smashed the carriage to splinters.

Anger saw the craning buildings fly past, and pieces of the sky, and frightened faces pulled away.

Out of control. Lost. He gave himself up.

To Kitty, the black carriage, as it erupted into the street, was like nemesis. It appalled her and she shrank back with a cry.

It was all black, all burning-seeming, with the lather of the horses, their red mouths, the sparks that shot from their hoofs and the wheels. The sun flashed off the carriage windows like lightning.

Surely it would run them down, career over them, uncaring or perhaps intended, leaving them mashed like paper roses.

But Grace did something quite mad, quite lunatic. Worse than the carriage. She stepped into its path. There on the road she was, white as a bird and with the sun flaming like silver on her hair, and she held up her hands.

And Kitty waited in abject fear and a horror beyond expression, to see the horses pile over Grace, and her blood rushed up into the sky.

But this did not happen.

The horses shied and veered, ran together, and halted, and the carriage ran into their backs and vibrated as if it would fall apart, but it did not. Everything was intact. Everything was perfect. The horses unhurt, with Grace stroking their midnight noses, and the carriage whole on its four smoking wheels, rattling.

Kitty said a prayer to God, in whom she did not believe.

Grace, leaving the two horses with lowered heads and heaving sides, walked around to the carriage door. It had opened at the impact of cessation.

Inside a man sat quite still. Not a hair of his head seemed disturbed. He was like the god of the underworld, as the vehicle suggested, Pluto or Hades, that she had read of somewhere when she had been taught to read.

Grace looked at him. His face was as familiar to her as day and night, but she had never before seen him.

She looked into his black eyes.

'What do you want?' he said.

'Are you unhurt?' she said.

'Yes. Thank you. The carriage stopped.'

'So it did. Can I help you?'

'I need nothing.'

He got up and came out of the enclosure, and stood beside her on the road.

Grace gazed up at him, memorizing everything, the line of his brows, the shape of his bones, the way his hands moved and fell back, elegant, indifferent.

He stayed by her only a moment. Then he had walked around to the horses. He observed them as if they were mechanical things which had gone wrong.

Outside the little shops, young women in grey aprons had gathered to see the event.

Kitty darted forward. She approached Anger diffidently but without reverence. She said, 'Excuse me, sir, but that girl there, it was she stopped the horses.'

'Did she?' Anger glanced at Grace. 'That was very brave. You knew how to do it.'

'They were frightened,' said Grace simply.

Anger came back to her.

'Allow me to thank you properly.' He had produced a silver coin and held it out.

Grace took it silently.

Kitty, panting still with fear, grinned. This was what she had wanted.

'And now,' Anger said, 'I need a man to take charge of the carriage. And one to run back and find my driver.'

A fellow stepped forward. He was decently dressed and tipped his hat.

'I can drive you, sir. I used to handle my dad's coach. It'll be nothing to me. My boy there will run back.'

'A guinea if you can get up the hill,' said Anger. 'The tall house.'

He was light now, almost frivolous.

He nodded to Grace and stepped back into the carriage, unshaken, unmoved, as if nothing at all had happened.

But everything in the world had happened. Everything.

Grace and Kitty stood together, and outside the drapers' shops, the young girls lingered whispering. They had thought the man in the black carriage very handsome.

'A fine gentleman,' said Kitty, as the carriage was taken calmly off up the road. 'And he behaved well. That's what I like to see. One that knows how to carry on.'

'Did he?' asked Grace.

'Of course, you silly. Didn't he give you that silver?'

Grace looked. The coin was not more brilliant than her hair. Less brilliant than the green stars of her eyes.

Suddenly she blushed a faint dawn-like red.

Kitty laughed. 'Why, you fancied him. And who can blame you. He was lovely.'

'No,' said Grace, 'not lovely. Bitter as hemlock. But yes, yes. I – fancied him.'

'As if you never fancied another,' chided Kitty, exuberant with shock.

It was true. For all her gifts of kindness and love, this one had never stirred. Snow she looked and was. Till now. Something of his fire had touched her. His cold, cold fire colder than her snow.

'We'll be late,' said Kitty. 'Come on.'

'Where?'

'You know where. You are in a state. Well, you can dream of him while the man photographs you. See how that will do.'

CHAPTER TEN

On Reflection

Within the mirror, what did the young woman see? The surface was speckled, tarnished, the glass so old it had a greenish tinge. And so her face seemed to float in water like a lily. A pale face, with wide-set eyes, the long pale hair let down. Grace looked, trying to fathom her own self. Until now she had never tried. She attempted to make out what he had beheld when he glanced at her. But certainly he had not seen her, only a figure that was there and then was gone.

The silver coin lay on the table. She had not given it away. It had been his. How often had he touched it?

Grace moved a little. Yes, she was beautiful as sometimes she had been told. She had known this. It had not much concerned her. Now it did. She was a lamp, and he must glimpse her light all across the dark City. But she doubted that he would.

A man had come to the cubicle door, and cleared his throat. Evening was in the window.

'Are you on for a go, Gracie?'

She had never refused them, there had been no need. Yet now, for the very first, a primal aversion took hold of her. She put it away.

'Come in.'

The man of the Rookery, as he lay down with her, experienced some new thing in her responses. He did not know what it was, she seemed tender and willing as ever. But when he had exhausted himself, and stretched out for a moment by her side, he said, 'Oh, I'd like to make an honest woman of you, Gracie. If I had the money, I'd set you up. A little house, a nice little garden. If I could.'

Grace smiled her immemorial smile.

On the window-sill, the snow-white cat sat watching them.

* * *

The Seven Brides were in Black Church. They had not been seen there for a year.

They had got among the throng of the great market off Drop Street. And winding through, they were noted in spasms.

The market was lit for the night, tall saffron gas flares streaming into the air, and lower down the red drizzle of tallow dips. The barrows and stalls showed off their goods, worn coats and patched shirts, pots and jugs that had a chip in them. On boards stood grey pies and piles of sprats, from barrels came a slurp of beer. A man played a fiddle, and as the Brides went by, callously and unsuperstitiously, he struck up the Wedding March, alerting the crowd.

'Look there, there they go!'

Seven women in their middle years, but with the countenances of raddled young girls, eyes expanded like blue saucers. Each in the rags of a wedding gown, and all the same, creamy satin that had gone yellow, festoons of lace, the fashion of twenty years before. Wedding veils like cobwebs on the cobwebs of their greying hair. And all knotted, all caught together, the hair, the sashes, the rills of lace and undone loops of dressmakers' pearls, holding them meshed in one floating, moveable spider's web of mummified marriage.

'Step back. Don't let them touch you.'

They were unlucky, poor doomed things. They had roamed the City a long while, now and then vanishing for months. Next seen in the south of the metropolis, next the north, somehow, sometimes simultaneously. They did not seem to rest, yet there were anecdotes of policemen who had found them, all clotted together like white insects under a bridge, in some black yard, and how the Brides sprang up wailing and ran away, each a mirror image of the others.

They were in constant flight. They seemed to feel neither summer heat, nor winter cold that powdered their veils with frost, nor rain that soaked them. There was a smell to them like stale dolls' clothes.

Now they passed through the market, their awful flimsy feelers brushing in peril close to the sallow lamps. They made a soft moaning sound, or was it only the wind of their passage?

The story told of them was universal. Seven sisters, they had been betrothed to seven brothers, comely, wealthy young men, employed in the army. But before the wedding day, there had been a male celebration. The seven young men went, each of them, with a celebrated whore, and found presently he had, each one, caught from her a terrible disease. On the morning of the wedding, seven corpses in full uniform, shot neatly through the brain, their own handiwork. The seven sisters waiting at the altar in a white lacy line, the news brought, the screaming. They had run mad. Those sent after them had constrained them to no avail. They would cunningly escape, put on their wedding dresses, and set off again in perpetual flight about the City. At last they were left to their fate.

From what did they fly? The bad news they had already received? Did they eat or drink? Did they truly sleep, or only lie nightlong behind the black rope of the river, moaning and rustling in their cocoon of grief?

'A sad tale,' said Albert Ross, as he ate a sprat. Buskit pawed his leg, and another sprat went down Buskit's gullet with an orange gulp.

'Hags,' said Mooley.

They turned their attention to the business of the night.

Ralph Mooley, as he had told Albert Ross, had been thinking, cogitating. It had come to him that if they could not pass on the green cat they had dug from the river mud, there was another way it might make them money.

Now they hopped and sidled into Drop Street, and came to the shop of Balthazar the Jew. It was a large-fronted emporium with, above it, its three yellow balls hung like curious fruit. A lamp illuminated the dusty glass, behind which lay all manner of abandoned objects, compasses and mallets, brooches and fans, a baby's ribboned bonnet, a chair, a set of knives and forks. A forlorn window.

Ralph Mooley inspected it. He held his bag close.

He would not be sorry to get rid of the cat. It had a peculiar way of looking at you. It had shone there in the dark of his hovel, until he put a cloth over it. Some pagan thing. Had Bullock been afraid of it or only of its presumed theft?

They pushed open the door, which gave a mournful tinkle.

Things loomed, old paintings and pieces of furniture that had been brought from sundered houses on the backs of carts.

From behind a moth-eaten curtain, the Jew moved out to his bare counter. Balthazar had a thin amber visage and drooping, moat-black eyes. The sadness of a ceaseless visitation of destitutes had settled on him, to augment the brooding sadness of his race. He was bowed by it, and leaned his fine creased hands upon the counter in an open motion, inviting, passive. *Do what you must*, said the hands of Balthazar. *I am here.*

'A fine night,' said Mooley. 'Not a drop of rain.'

'The City is thirsty,' answered Balthazar, in a beautiful baritone.

Buskit craned to see over the counter, and Balthazar in turn peered down at him.

'Back, you bugger,' said Mooley, toeing Buskit away.

'An intelligent dog,' said Balthazar, 'he watches everything.'

'Bloody useless booby,' returned Mooley.

Buskit backed further off and breathed sprat on a roll of carpet.

Mooley put the bag on the counter.

'I have here,' he said, 'an heirloom. I won't say it's valuable, but I won't say it ain't. See what you make of it.'

And he unwrapped the cat and sat it on the counter between Balthazar's hands.

Balthazar stood up. He straightened. He hung there gazing for some moments. At last he said, 'Have you stolen this?'

'No,' cried Mooley, 'it's honest come by. But I'm down on my luck. What'll it fetch?'

Balthazar did not answer. He said, 'Pasht, the Egyptian goddess of joy. From a later period, when jade had come into use.'

'Jade is it?' asked Mooley. 'Well, I never knew. Nor my ma, what passed it down to me. Been in the family for a hundred years. She'd turn in her grave if she knew I meant to pawn it.'

Albert Ross coughed.

The Jew said, 'I will give you two pounds.' His eyes did not widen or narrow. His face was like a smooth plate.

'Four,' said Mooley.

'Two,' said Balthazar. 'I am risking my livelihood. Such a thing as this.'

Mooley sulked. 'It's worth five pounds or more.'

'You will never redeem it,' said Balthazar. 'You want to be rid of it. Now I must take it. Look how it burns green.'

They looked.

Albert Ross said, 'There are great fish what shine like that, in the tropic seas. And one day the bosun catches one, and when it was opened, it was full of emeralds. But the ship run aground and they was lost. Thirty men lost their lives, but the captain wept for the emeralds. Bad fortune they was.'

Balthazar, Mooley and Buskit ignored him.

Mooley said, 'Well, I'll take it and be damned to you, Jew, you robber.'

Balthazar said nothing. He was accustomed to insults and hatred. Waifs threw stones at him, and all of his children had died, most in infancy. Such was life. Indeed, there was always some call for a goddess of joy. It came into his mind as he counted the two pounds in Mooley's grubby little hand, the great festivals of the goddess, drinking and making love, and the little spotted cats which had roamed her green-walled temple. But Balthazar believed only in one just and stern God, who brooked no other.

He took the statuette of Pasht and put her away in the small room behind the shop. There she glowed like a green moon, and he heard a faint high singing. But Balthazar doused his own imaginings and made a brew of tea, which he drank black, and full of sugar, in the natural silence of his shop of sadnesses.

It was Kitty too who was counting money in her untidy cubicle, in the attic of the Rookery. Normally she hid her coin in a stocking, and kept it beneath the mattress, having nowhere else. No one had stolen it – she was Grace's friend.

Now there was a gold coin, the fee for the taking of photographs, which Grace had pressed on Kitty. The man had been saucy but not laid a hand on either of them. They had been given flimsy girdles to wear, collars of gilt and glass stones, beads and cloth lotuses for their hair, which he had wanted taken down. They were to be temple maidens, bare breasted, and the poses he required were stiff rather than naughty, their hands outstretched, their heads held high. Each plate had taken a minute of absolute stillness, during which Kitty felt her hair curling, the tip of her nose itched, and she longed to blink.

What would become of these photographs she did not know. The man had been very pleased with Grace, and quite pleased with Kitty. Probably they would never see the results, although he had asked them to call again, in a month's time.

After the episode of the carriage, Kitty had been in a daft giggly condition, but Grace was magnetically still.

She's fallen in love, no doubt of it, reflected Kitty, with a slight tremor of unease. For it was unwise to have such feelings for a gentleman – and he had been a real one. Kitty knew, she had loved in her youth, loved and lost so often.

She had not expected it of Grace. Grace had somehow fallen, become human. No longer a white goddess. Only – a girl.

Kitty stowed her wealth. It made her feel warm and secure. But this was only an illusion and she knew it, like the gleam of gin. There was no safety, just as love could not prosper. Even Grace was mortal. And Kitty – she was brittle as scorched paper.

CHAPTER ELEVEN

Jackal's Hide

'Eating is always such a pleasure,' said the neighbour of Kesper North at the table. 'And there aren't so many. A frisky woman, perhaps, that might measure up. Or the theatre when the songs are lively. But food, now that you can rely on.'

Kesper North looked at this man, Tadlow, with distaste. Tadlow was fat, wobbly as a jelly, and encased in gaudy chocolate and puce clothing, with excrescences of mauve. His large round face balanced on three thick chins that moved beneath like the layers of a concertina. Tadlow's mouth was small, but it stretched as into it he shovelled huge helpings of roast chicken, gooseberry relish, and potato.

Kesper North would not have chosen him as neighbour, but when he had sat down, the table had been full, there was no other place. Now the board had cleared, but it would be the ultimate rudeness to move.

North's club was a shabby but respectable establishment set high above the river. One long table, draped in an impeccable cloth, dealt with all. And round the table ran the iron railway lines of service, which even now were bearing forward a fat pink turbot on a dish of lemons. A Tadlow from the sea.

'Look, there's your fish,' cried Tadlow to the other remaining diner. This man smiled thinly and allowed the turbot to come to rest beside him.

Tadlow said to North, 'You're such a meagre chap. You pick at that chicken. Don't you have an appetite?'

'It digests better,' said Kesper North, 'when taken slowly.'

'Oh, trouble with your guts. I never have that. A pint or two of wine takes care of it. A little wine for the stomach's sake, eh, North? And then a stroll. And then a good sound sleep. Now for sleep I recommend a goblet of whisky. Not a finger's depth. A proper stoop. It clears the mouth and calms the mind.'

Kesper North considered that Tadlow, a fellow tutor, had none. He pictured the menace lying on a great feather bed mounded with pillows, snoring like a volcano.

Tadlow touched a dial, and the silver dish of gooseberry relish ran round the iron rails and came to his place. He helped himself to his fourth vast dollop.

Kesper North laid down his knife. He was disgusted by gluttony as by all excess. He rose now without apology, crossed the dining room, and went out on to the broad balcony, which afforded the members of the club a view across the avenue and down the hill to the river.

The summer evening was at its last, the light condensing with a golden soupiness, as in some antique painting of Italy.

Kesper North drew in the dusty smoky air, and caught the perfume of chestnuts in the parks, the aroma of horses and violets.

Over the spire of St Davids, the sun was going down, and there the air was blushing. Poor Weams. The sunset would colour his tomb.

Kesper North withdrew a cigarette and struck a match. And heard a heavy footfall and the pushing open of the balcony doors.

'What an evening,' said Tadlow, his voice full of suppressed belches. 'A beauty I think it will be. Now here's a night for walking abroad. Perhaps a theatre. What do you say, North?'

'I have books to study,' said North.

'Silly man. What's it worth? The young puppies don't listen to a word that's said. Confound them, I say.' Tadlow, the tutor, stretched, and popped into his mouth an infernal cigar. 'Confound them. Keep the papas sweet is all you need. Ah, young Horace does admirably well, a genius in the making. Let them fudge their Homer. Let them waffle through their sums. Life's for good things, North. And the young fools can always be taught later by someone more strict than gentle Tadlow. See how they like *that*.'

'You are a villain,' said North suddenly.

He was angry that Tadlow had come, that Tadlow professed to enjoy the sunset, that Tadlow existed.

'I? A villain? I'm an angel, North.'

They stood, the two men, gazing out to where the sun was now a flaming globe behind the spire of St Davids.

North thought of the Society. Such things, to a Tadlow, would be fairy tales, legends he would not bother to teach.

Tadlow burped softly, and observed the sunset begin with a connoisseur's eye. He was mellow, with wine and food, and had besides an apple pie and Stilton to look forward to, with the addition of the club's inferior but quite palatable port. Tadlow did not mind that he was fat. He minded about nothing. He took things as they came and were. Pleasures were few but *pleasing*. He inclined to indulge himself. He was not unhappy.

The light of the sky melded to carmine. It was majestic, epic, the silhouette of the City upraised against this glorious screen. While far below the river shone like – port.

'Now, what a view, I say,' said Tadlow, and turned to Kesper North, to wring some tribute from him.

But how odd. Some phantasm of the light . . . North's head had massed into a blodge of shadow. Tadlow squinted. Yes, how bizarre, now North looked as though he had the head of a dog. Black as jet, the ears upstanding, the muzzle pointed and long. One searing profile eye stood out, redder than the atmosphere, bright with a fleck of the dying sun.

'I say, dear fellow,' said Tadlow.

And the dog head, the *jackal* head, moved round to face him. So he saw it all. The blazing eyes. The points of teeth.

Tadlow was unable to move quickly. He had never had to. He blundered back against the balcony rail. He had no idea what went on. He uttered a tiny choking noise.

Then the jackal stepped free of Kesper North. It was on its hind limbs, and it walked like a man. Its skin glimmered, black silken hide, with, down its breast, the six flat nipples of its canine species. Its head tilted and the jaws spread. The tongue was black. Tadlow was astonished by that tongue. Then the whole casque of the head split wide and darkness fell across the sunfall.

Kesper North crouched against the farther end of the balcony. He could do nothing but oversee. And hear, that too.

Tadlow, the man he hated, gave off a succession of loud squeaks, and then he was absorbed, his head taken into that enormous jaw. The head consumed.

For a moment the black jackal crushed and gorged on Tadlow, and then Tadlow was let fall, like a scarecrow, boneless, on the floor of the balcony.

The jackal dropped to its four feet. It stood, motionless, and melted into the bloody sky.

North could not move. He seemed turned to stone. Then feeling came like needles and flames. He straightened and balanced there, stupefied.

There had been no outcry, only Tadlow's foolish little squeaks. The thing itself had given off no sound. And no one had come to see.

'My God, my God,' said North.

He covered his face in his hands, and looked again, and saw again Tadlow, lying fat and crushed against the rail. But there was blood only in the sky. None had splashed the balcony.

Kesper North went forward, not wishing to. He leaned above the body of the fat man.

Something had happened to the mauve cravat. It had unravelled, it had become – the fibres of a plant. So much North could fathom. And for the face above, the face which the beast had mouthed—

'No,' said North.

He stooped closer. The light misled. The light described. This was evident: the face of a fat and hairless baby. A baby's skin that had no mark. And too small for the collar and the cravat of fibres. Far too small.

North stepped over the body of his dead enemy. He pulled on the doors of the balcony and went back, closing them, into the dining room. There he nodded to the last diner at the table. North paused, as though transfixed.

The railway line was humming as a silver dish of cream ran over it.

North burst into laughter. Then begged the pardon of the last diner, and got out of the room.

In the hall below he took his coat and hat and fled through the simple door and into the street. In the red afterglow, the carriages jostled, and late walkers strayed along the pavement.

Had he gone mad? Should he go back again and look, and be sure? But he knew that Tadlow lay on the balcony with the head of a two-month-old infant. And soon others would find Tadlow. Soon the roof would fall.

North hailed a carriage.

The cabby thought him drunk, but there, a gentleman did take too much. That was no concern of his.

It was very hot in the conservatory.

North looked round, not properly seeing anything. The great palms towered into the domed roof, where stained glass stood now, in darkness, in black ovals and dull golden scrolls. A curious place. Old Angier had been fond of it. The heat agreed with him. He would sift the white sand through his fingers, feed morsels of meat to the red-lipped preying plants, pluck spotted leaves. Anger did none of this. He had finished dinner not long before North's arrival, and had sat at the table drinking wine.

Only as they moved into the conservatory, had Anger said to him, 'You're agitated. What's the matter?'

'We're men of the modern world,' said North. 'How will you believe me?' He was pale, a pallor the heat increased, yet he had spent much of his force in self-control. He was used to mastering himself, and did so now.

'Weams came to me with an outcry, not so long ago. I was unable to help him.'

'I don't seek help,' said North. 'But you must listen.'

'Is it the same thing, I wonder?'

'What thing?'

'These reports of the black dog,' said Anger, nearly idly.

North said, 'You know me to be impartial and quite sane.'

'Yes, I do.'

'But tonight I wondered. Either I've lost my wits, or something happened that has no right in the thinking world.'

North had been Anger's tutor. Anger had grown to manhood attending to him. And some of Anger's abstemious coldness had been drawn from Kesper North and his self-control. No, Anger did not doubt him. He said, 'Tell what it is. You know I value your judgement. You're not insane.'

'Wait until I've spoken. Tonight I killed a man.'

'You've often killed men. As the Society dictates.'

'This wasn't a felon. He'd done nothing – but annoy me. Irritated me. And then.' Anger waited. North said, 'Something came out of me. It was pure darkness. And it took on a form. It was the shape of the jackal god. Of Anubis, our symbol. I don't speak metaphorically. This is the truth. I saw it. I saw its *skin* gleaming, and its eyes. It took him and tore him, and when it left him – he had the head of a baby. He was dead.'

'Yes,' said Anger. 'It's hard to believe.'

'But you do believe.'

'If you say that it occurred, it must have done.' Anger's face was unreadable. He opened the box of cigarettes and offered them to Kesper North, who shook his head.

'I want nothing. No consolement. Till I've finished.'

The conservatory whispered about them. Broad leaves lifting and falling, blossom breaking out in the sweat of heat, spilling in white and carnelian drifts. Water dripped, beads descending stem to stem, running away along the channels in the floor. Red creatures the size of the tip of a pin slowly devoured a drooping plant.

'Power is generated,' said Kesper North, 'from nothing, by the action of one thing on another, like steam. And somehow our actions have made this thing. This beast.'

'Why?' said Anger. 'How?'

'I don't know. I wish to God I knew. What did Weams say to you?'

'That we had unleashed a demon.'

'So we have. I saw it.'

Anger smoked his cigarette. He glanced at the windows which showed the descent of the City into Black Church, and so to the river. 'Why did it choose you, North, for its manifestation?'

'It might be any of us. Or none. The newspaper stories have been suppressed. They caused too much alarm. But from what I've heard, it comes and goes. It's a phantom, yet it kills. It kills by *time*.'

'You think that I've caused this,' Anger said.

North hesitated. He said, 'Yes. Inevitably you. As a child causes malevolent spirits to appear in a house. You are the inactive member. Where does your strength go? Your passion? Into this? We kill, but you're the figurehead. We're a pack of dogs, and you are the leader. The king dog.'

'But I know nothing about it,' said Anger.

'All the more reason to think you are the cause,' said North.

'And yet you saw it, not I.'

'A man sees everything,' said Kesper North, 'except himself.'

Anger laughed, very softly. 'What can I say to that?'

Somewhere in the conservatory a branch groaned at the weight of its sap. An insect crouched in the soil, laying her eggs like silver mercury. Green flies fed on the sugar of the leaves, and flew away into the web of a spider that hung like death, motionless and waiting, from the side of an urn. She let them tangle themselves, and then she glided down on her rope of silk. The room was full of tiny unheard screams.

'The Society must be called together,' said Kesper North. 'It prides itself on justice, on removing dross. But this – apparition – kills indiscriminately. The innocent, the stupid. Poor silly whores, young girls. Anyone perhaps that we would dislike or disdain. Like that fool tonight. If you'd seen—' Kesper North put his hand up to his face. Despite himself, he was not in perfect command.

Anger said, 'I should like to.'

'*Like*—'

'It's not that I doubt you, North. But I'm accustomed to judging for myself. You taught me that.'

'Go out into the City, and see, then.'

'Yes. I'll have to, won't I. Or do you say it won't come when I'm near?'

'Who knows? It's part of you.'

Anger raised his brows, ironically. 'Conveniently, it seems.'

Kesper North said flatly, 'Another man, Anger, would have some vice, however small. He would want women, or a wife at least. He would indulge himself in something, however mundane. Do you know that I cripple myself buying books? I can't resist them. But with you, everything is in moderation. And yet you *seethe*, Anger. You're a black sun. I saw it in you as a boy, a great might contained, locked up inside you. One day it would get loose. And now, it has.'

'You've never favoured me with this analysis before.'

'It's the time for it. *You* are the fount of this.'

The spider fed in the web. On the wall a sapphire beetle crept, with claws outspread. Death too had her enemies. Moulds and microcosms hovered in the burning moisture of the air, funguses and viral atomies. The two men stood debating their issues of fate and the supernatural in a scalding sea of movement and surcease.

Outside the street sloped down into the dark.

'I'll call the Society together,' Anger said. 'Will that content you?'

'Partly. It may be too late.'

'And I,' Anger said, 'I'll seek for it.'

'Where?' said Kesper North. 'It's inside you now.'

'In the City. In Black Church.'

Over the roof something white loomed on wide angled wings. It was a gull from the river, and in its grip, an eel.

Kesper North thought of things classical, eagles bearing wolves and snakes. Omens.

'I must go now,' he said.

'Take my carriage.'

'No thank you. I'll do better walking.'

'Then good night.'

When North had gone, Anger moved about the paths of the conservatory. The beetle had the spider, ripping away the web. A bug devoured the eggs in the tray of soil. A leaf detached itself and dropped on to the path.

Anger saw none of this. His mind had closed itself to everything, including the soul of what Kesper North had said to him. He would go out into the City, but to search only for a spectre. It did not and could not exist. And yet there was a quickening in him. There had been that night when he had killed his own two devils, there in the carriage in the dark. He had never forgotten that night, although it had lain dormant and still as glaucous water.

What would the streets of the City present to him? What was the reality behind the nightmare beast which men seemed to see? Look, there on the glass pane of the window, a shape . . . His own shadow.

A bat flew by, hunting from the old tower of some church. Moths fluttered at the glass, attracted by the lamplight. The root of a fern split open and maggots coiled like a string of seed pearls.

Then again, had North gone mad?

Along the street, the party came, three men and two women and three children. This was a decent avenue, lighted by lamps, and by a cloud above which read, in luminous pink letters, *Boyne's Pickle*.

They were laughing and merry. One man carried a basket with bottles of wine, and a woman a basket of new-laid eggs. The children had been frothily dressed. They were off to a celebration.

Death who had no enemies came at them around the corner in a gust of black wind.

The heat smote them and skirts skirled and a hat was blown off.

Then the children screamed.

The adults stared. They knew what it was, although they had not credited it.

They saw its gigantic figure that was bigger than a carthorse, the up-curved blades of ears and slender muzzle. Red eyes that dulled the lamps. Above, the pink cloud went out.

The men put the women behind them. The women clung to their children.

But then the black wind of the jackal swept over. They felt the rasp of its skin. They were flung and picked up and shaken and dropped down, like leaves. For a moment all was shrieking and shouting, and then all was silence.

From the houses round, the lights went up as blinds were drawn and curtains pulled back. There was nothing in the street but a heap of bodies.

Men came out presently to see.

Never would they forget.

The woman with the dead child, and she was a crone, and the child was a crone too, grey-haired, withered. The man with the tiny hairless head. The others all joined, a muddle of whole limbs, small and brawny, one fair with a bracelet of garnets. And the rest gone so far it had decayed like rotten vegetables, and the terrible smell rose from it, corruption, like an open grave.

Nearby, some broken bottles from which had burst out, purple and glossy, grapes, and the dark leaves of vines. And hatched on the road from broken shells, some things that scratched and cackled and ran away quickly into the interstices of the night.

CHAPTER TWELVE

Love

Against the sooty wall and two pale bodies, the men danced the dance old as the world.

Kitty was released first. She let down her skirt and the man chucked her under the chin. The man with Grace took longer, achieving his climax with a hoarse noise.

Above the wall, the twilight.

'Run home now, girls,' they said, the customers, 'and don't let the black dog catch you.'

They parted gaily, as if all was well. Kitty counted over the money. She wanted to hurry now.

They went down the alley and out into the lamplit street. Some doors up, a public house shone like a gold coin and a piano played with a riotous thump. But they went by, outcasts in the coming of night.

Kitty stole glances at Grace. Grace was not the same.

'Let's go to the pie-shop,' said Kitty.

'Of course.'

'No, only if you want. You need cheering up.'

Grace smiled. She was sad now. Never before had Kitty seen her so.

'It's a rotten life,' said Kitty.

'But we should live on the moon,' said Grace. Her voice sounded far far away, as if she were already there.

They passed a gin-shop, but there were rowdy women outside, their sleeves rolled up. One fed a bottle of spirit to a baby as white as rice-pudding.

'Poor thing,' said Kitty, 'she didn't ought to.'

'No,' said Grace, in her far away voice.

Kitty thought, *She's thinking about him. About her gentleman with the black eyes.*

When they got over the sewer and into Rotwalk Lane, and up the Rookery stairs, they had no supper and no drink, and went into Grace's room, and sat down there.

The cat was away, up on the roofs. The sky showed in the open window, an eerie sulky darkish blue.

'I should like to see the stars,' said Kitty. 'They say you can see them all from the park on Dogs Island.'

Grace sat like a beautiful statue. Had she heard? Kitty knew she was no use to Grace. She went out and down to the kitchen, where Ma Crow gave her a herring in a crust of bread.

Kitty began to think, in long deep progressions.

Presently she went back up again to her bolt hole, and here she took out her music box. She stroked the pink flowers, and the memory came of her gentle father. Kitty wiped her eyes. That was so long ago, it seemed like a century. 'I look like it, too.'

She put the box on her knee and turned the handle, and the flighty music came, like a spell.

It was no good. It was not a fancy. Grace was in love. How strange, for Grace had seemed impervious, like a white bloom that never faded. Now she craned after the sun, and somehow it was not absurd. If she could find him again, how could he ignore someone as wonderful as Grace? And then, if only for a little while, Grace could be happy. For if Kitty had never seen Grace sad before, had she ever seen her joyful? Grace lilted through life. She deserved much more. It could not last. But it would be worth it. To touch the moon and then to fall.

Kitty got up and went to Grace's cubicle, knocked, and was admitted.

Grace sat in the old chair by the window, looking out across the wretched roofs, and into the lucid sky. After all, there was a star, a very bright one.

'Do you see?' said Grace.

'Just goes to show,' said Kitty. She stood and folded her hands. 'Gracie,' said Kitty, 'if you went to the gin-palace to dance, you might meet him there. Gentlemen go there.'

'He never would,' said Grace.

'He might.'

'No. He's darker than the night. He wouldn't go to that place.'

Kitty said softly, 'But you can work magic, Gracie. You know you can. Do you remember when I had the toothache and you took it away? Do you remember the baby with the fever and you made it better? Yes, you can work magic. You can *make* him come there.'

Grace turned and looked at her.

In the deepening of darkness, Grace's whiteness seemed to drift. The petal of her face altered. Her green eyes widened.

'Could I?'

'Of course you could. If you want him.'

'It was as if,' said Grace, 'I'd seen him every moment of my life. And yet everything was changed.'

Kitty said, 'Then you must.'

'But,' said Grace, 'they'd never let me in.'

'Yes they will,' said Kitty staunchly. 'I'll get you that green dress. And those green earrings.'

'How can you?'

'You'll see.'

'No,' said Grace, 'Kitty—'

'Oh, so it's always you who must do everything for me, and I can't ever do a thing for you? You can't stop me, Gracie. I've made up my mind.'

Morning came, hot and dry, and stenches rose from the back streets, and dogs fought in Rotwalk Lane.

Kitty Stockings picked by them in her cerise shawl, her red bird tilted on her hat.

She went through the avenues to Drop Street and straight to the shop of Balthazar the Jew.

'What'll you give me for this?' said Kitty, putting the music box on to the bare counter.

Balthazar leant forward his amber plate of face. He touched the handle of the box, and music ran up into the shop. It sprayed over the doleful rugs and lost pictures, and startled mice in the rooms beyond.

'A very nice toy,' said Balthazar.

Kitty named a sum.

Balthazar looked at her. His second daughter, who had lived longer but who was dead, had been pretty in this dark and slender way. Balthazar was not sentimental but the world was very cruel. It did no harm, now and then, to redress the balance.

He brought the money and laid it before Kitty, who flushed with excitement. She said, 'And that lovely green item. I'll see that.'

Balthazar too started.

'But,' he said, 'how can you know?'

'Know? Of course I do. What are you asking for them?'

Balthazar was confused a moment, but driven by a compulsion, he went behind the curtain and lifted down the green jade cat from its shelf. This too he brought and positioned before Kitty.

Her eyes grew wide.

'What's this?'

'Didn't you ask me for it?'

'I meant the pair of glass earrings.'

'Ah,' said Balthazar.

The cat stood on the counter, surrounded by an aureole of light. Kitty reached out one finger to touch, then drew it back.

'What is it?' she said.

'She. Pasht. A goddess of Egypt. The Queen of Cats.'

'Pretty puss,' said Kitty. 'Grace would like that.'

Balthazar moved the cat carefully to one side. He brought instead the green earrings.

'The cat in any case,' he said, 'is in my keeping for a while.'

Kitty paid for the earrings. She slipped them into her little red crocheted bag.

When she had gone, Balthazar drew the cat once more into the back room, and replaced it on the shelf. Shadow sank away from that spot. The cat was full of light, as if she stored the moon. He lifted the music box, and put it beside Pasht. A single note came from the box, and flitted away into the air like a moth.

The dress was not so easy. A stout woman loomed with louring brows. They could not hire the dress, oh, no. Two sluts such as these would bring the dress back in ruins. So much was evident, and so much she did not say, but she implied. Then all the coins were produced. The money from the music box and the savings that had been secreted in the stocking. The tune changed a little.

Finally the young girls in their grey aprons were adapting the green silk to Grace's white body, taking in the waist, fluffing out the flounces. The young girls were enthralled by beauty, to have it standing there and to be attending on it. They drew from drawers and boxes white undergarments and cascades of lace threaded by green ribbon, kept for richer clients in a hurry. Everything was managed, and the last bright coin went on a pair of slippers like silver, that had been sorcerously conveyed from somewhere, and which fitted.

Returning with their parcels, Kitty and Grace were hailed by men, and laughingly turned them away. And such was the mood of the day, these men only laughed back at them and let them go.

In the street by the Rookery, a gang of youths mocked them, fine ladies who had been shopping, but nothing more.

Above, in the green-curtained chamber of the attic, they stared at each other in wonder.

'It can all be sold again,' said Grace.

'Perhaps he'll take care of you. You won't need to sell them.'

'Perhaps I shan't see him.'

'Hush,' said Kitty.

They got jugs of hot water from the kitchen, and by now the rumour was going round. Grace was off to see a gentleman. A relay of snotty-nosed small children, black with grime, came to the attic with further basins of hot water, one after the other.

As Grace laved herself, the beautiful scent of her flesh increased, and filled the room. Kitty had washed Grace's hair with lavender soap. The cat wove round their ankles, purring, and the day deepened in the window.

Kitty dressed Grace with the utmost care. Then stepped back in silence.

Grace gazed into her mirror.

'You're a picture,' said Kitty. She felt replete. She had sold her own future for some yards of silk, two slippers, two earrings like angelica that were now hung from the white earlobes of Grace. But then, who knew what lay in store? Fate might snatch Kitty before she had a use for her savings. Better to live in the moment.

Grace turned about. The dress sighed like a wave upon a shore.

Her hair she had plaited and wound up upon her head in a crown. And her hair was like the moon on water. Her white neck soared, her waist was like the green stem of a plant. Her shoulders bloomed with soft light. Her face was too beautiful for that room. It belonged in the sky. The green stars of her eyes rested on Kitty.

'A real picture,' said Kitty, and bit her tongue that she could not bring out something better. But this miracle was beyond her, and the room and the street and the City. Into heaven Grace should be carried. But then, she did not want to go there.

'Who shall I pray to,' said Grace, 'for my wish?'

'Pray to that green cat I told you of,' said Kitty skittishly. 'You should have seen it. Pasht, he called it, the Jew. He's a good man.'

Grace bent and picked up the white cat and held her high. 'Give me my heart's desire.'

The cat miaowed. In the darkening room, girl and cat together shone like a lamp.

On the stairs, the Rookery stood to watch. They whispered. Not one touched Grace, afraid to soil her gown.

Below, Jack Black presented himself, his shaven head bare and his red neck puffed out.

'Street's filthy. I'll carry you over the muck, Gracie. Get a carriage at the turning. The old bastard owes me a favour.'

This was done, and Kitty followed, and about twenty children from the Rookery. The cabby obliged Jack Black without a murmur.

Away it went into the sunfall then, the fairy coach with the young woman in it, in her slippers of silver and her earrings of glass.

CHAPTER THIRTEEN

Night Work

The youthful policeman kept still as a waxwork, as the razor glided over his chin. It was, the barber had promised, a very close shave. In his heart, the young man was sorry – he had been growing a moustache.

'Cheer up,' had said the officer. 'Just think. Have you ever seen a lady with a moustache?'

'Yes, sir.'

'Be quiet.'

The barber straightened now, and wiped off the last of the soap. He stepped back and the officer came and touched the young policeman's cheek. 'That's very good.'

Then the woman was there, powdering white and rose. She dabbed blue on his eyelids, and the policeman winked at its sting. The wig was next, musty and blonde, and then the little hat.

He stood up awkwardly.

'Very pretty,' said the officer.

The policeman blushed under his make-up. Round his legs the skirt of the dress frothed and curled. There were enough layers to hide the truncheon.

Morgrave's Girls they had already been called. Morgrave, the clever colonel who had come to oversee the investigation of the Black Church murders. It was supposedly his idea, young, strong men, done up to look like whores, ambling through the rougher areas of the City.

It would take more than an unhinged scientist to get the better of him, the policeman thought, ushered into the van. The horses set off at a trot, and inside fifteen minutes he and his partner were let out again, at the edge of a warren of crawling benighted streets, only wide enough for their dresses to pass by.

'Remember your whistles. There are constables patrolling with pistols. Don't be too hasty.'

They walked out in the barrage of skirts, and stood on the corner of a lane, as the van went off.

'And how do you like it, Billy?' asked the young policeman's partner, a burly fellow called Moans.

'It's a penance,' said Billy. 'If my girl could see me.'

'I don't know,' said Moans. 'Well, I don't.'

He moved with a waddle and a swish, liking, to his surprise, the ripple of petticoats over his calves, the greasiness of the red salve on his lips.

Billy was more slow. He stumbled in his skirts, putting down his feet like a rhinoceros.

From an alley a drunk came rolling.

'Evening to you, girls,' he cried, and circling on Moans, added, 'You're a fine big lass. You remind me of my mother.'

Moans beamed and patted the drunk on the arm. 'Want to come to my room, deary?'

The drunk considered. 'How much?'

Moans tittered. Billy stepped forward and shoved the drunk away. In a deep masculine voice Billy snarled, 'Clear off, you varmint. We're on police business.'

The drunk gave a frightened squeal and went staggering away.

Moans said, 'That's no way to catch our murderer.'

'He wasn't. Only some sot.'

'How do you know? Perhaps some cunning disguise.'

'Watch yourself,' said Billy.

Moans swung his hips and smacked his lips.

They moved down the street. The lamps were isolated and burned a flickering yellow, casting strange shadows. In a doorway a man leaned, thin and black as a twist of night.

'Good evening, deary,' called Moans.

The man cursed him, and they went on.

After the lighted street there began a maze of back alleys and dismal yards, above which towered the black frontages of tenements. Here they were only once accosted, by a washerwoman with her load, who called them filthy harlots and spat at their feet. Moans giggled excitedly, and Billy shuddered.

They were in the paved lane behind the Wayfarers' Tavern, hearing the sozzled cries of the inmates and the clunk of vessels of beer, when a hot wind came up and passed them. Both men checked, and turned about. The jolly sounds of the public house went on.

'Funny weather,' said Billy. 'We could do with some rain.'

They stopped and the faint glare of the tavern buttered over them, and all about the brick and stone of the City stretched away, closed and airless, where the flame of the wind had gone.

Then there came a howl.

It was not from the public house, but out of the labyrinth beyond. A human noise dehumanized, like that of a beast in pain. And then, once more.

'By God,' said Billy, 'something's up.'

'That way,' said Moans, lifting his skirts.

They ran heavily, by the lighted house, and down into the black. The night heaved with their motion. Around one corner, around two. No more howlings. Only a great still heat, as if something burned there unseen.

They ran into an alley closed by a high wall. No one was present.

'Yes,' said Billy, 'look.'

They went forward. On the cobbles lay a heap of clothes. Nothing appeared to be in them.

Moans got a matchbox out of his bodice and struck a light.

A man's breeches and boots, his coat and waistcoat, shirt, and a striped handkerchief for the neck. Flared on the ground was a sheaf of bank-notes. And a glass bottle that ended oddly in a spill of sand.

'What's that?' said Billy, peering forward.

'Dead rabbit, is it?' asked Moans.

Billy turned and spewed violently against the wall of the alley.

Moans leaned nearer and saw what Billy had seen. Moans had beheld such a thing before, in a black parlour of the slums, laid out on newspaper. It was a human foetus, perhaps in the seventh month, exactly formed, its huge head half-transparent, its small webbed hands equipped with every finger.

Moans pushed his whistle between his lips and blew. The whistle sounded shrill and foolish in the raw darkness. Who would come?

But at once feet stampeded, and he heard the solid shouts of men.

It was Billy who, through blurred eyes, glanced up and saw the effigy in the sky. With searing hate he pointed.

'This is a dead-end. But there he goes.'

Moans too looked into the sky, as the two uniformed policemen erupted into the alley.

'Up there – bring the bastard down!'

A constable raised his shotgun. He took aim at the lone, low-flying flycycle, pale on the black sky, its floating bat-wing like a sneer.

The explosion was very loud. A flash lit up the alley and the monstrous thing upon the ground. Then came an answering detonation above. The shot had hit the flycyclist's gas-bag. They heard him shrieking.

'Good, let him *fry*.'

The flycycle, a star, was engulfed in fire. It tumbled through the night writhing, giving off fireworks of sparks and long streamers of red burning gas.

They watched in amazement and terror, the four men. But all about now the night was loud with whistles and the sound of feet. From the public house they were gushing out, the women flushed with gin, frightened and electric, the men clamouring to see, waving their mugs.

The star of the flycycle went down into the river. They made out, even over the high walls, the glow of its meeting with cool water. And then the dark came again.

'By Christ,' said Moans, 'if we got him—'

Charles Morgrave left his carriage, and walked towards the alley in Black Church where the men of the force waited. The idiots from the tavern and the hovels round had been cleared away. Already a photographer had come to take a picture of the thing upon the cobbles.

Morgrave was tall and narrow, dark skinned from his sojourns in foreign climes. In Egypt he had helped unearth the foundations of a temple, and vast statues with the heads of birds. But now he was here, his narrow light eyes busy on the City and these men, who were imbeciles.

They had fished the wreckage of the flycycle from the river. Some rich adventurer en route to some pleasure or other, now ashes.

Morgrave reached the alley. He saw lined up the two young men in preposterous women's garb, one big and ludicrous, the other younger, who might perhaps pass as a boyish girl. They looked at him dumbly, saluting and afraid.

The imbecile with the shotgun waited nearby.

Morgrave spoke.

'Well?'

'The alley was a dead-end, sir. And then I saw the flying vehicle. It was the only way he could have done it and escaped.'

'You fool,' said Morgrave. 'Where is the landing place? From where could he take off? Have you never heard of a man who could climb a wall?'

Billy hung his wigged and hatted head. Moans said, 'But that object, sir—'

'Perhaps,' said Morgrave, 'he had the foetus with him. If he is a scientific man. He left it there with some clothes. To – play with us.'

They stared. Morgrave glanced at the policeman who had fired.

'You bloody imbecile. Consider yourself finished.'

He stepped past the shivering men, and went to stand over the mess on the ground. He looked at it impartially. He had seen worse.

Morgrave knew that someone or some persons were killing the dross of the City. This had been so for some while. He welcomed it, the cleansing of chaff. Only the method was puzzling; unless it was some clever trick. Morgrave would like to catch the man, or men, talk to them. He would protect them. His philosophy was in accordance with theirs. The rabble proliferated. Better contain it.

He turned to the photographer.

'Have you done?'

'Yes, sir.'

'That's good.'

Morgrave strode from the alley. He looked about.

The slanted brick lines of this site, like rubble, appealed to him. He liked low life, and would have liked low women if they had been safe. But half the drabs of the metropolis were diseased.

However, up the hill were better chances. The whores who paraded there were worth a look.

He said to an assistant, 'Take care of this. I'll go up the hill. Wherever he went, it was away from here.'

Morgrave entered the gin-palace almost indifferently. It had no glamour for him, decidedly no magic.

Nevertheless, he looked about, and saw the dancing floor, where couples pranced, the balconies hung with dark green plants and red velvet rope, the bank of the orchestra. The long bar was backed by shining mirrors, where every jewel-like bottle and vessel reflected. Lights spun in the glass walls and from the necklaces of the fiery chandeliers.

He took a goblet of champagne, and rested his eyes on the long walk where the women went up and down.

That one there, in the black and blue, the curve of her bosom so milky, and the gold comb in her hair. Or that one, rather plump, in satin the colour of a sound white wine.

Morgrave smiled and sipped. He liked to drink but never to excess. He was the same with women.

His eyes travelled about the glittering room, the cages of bright birds, and stained glass baubles that hung down.

There in the air, on a balcony, he saw a dress like an emerald. He had never seen hair so blonde. Her skin was like fine china, but would be so soft.

Men would be going now to a fashionable house, speaking to the servants, entering a tall room full of furniture and stability. Imparting to a weeping fainting woman the death of her husband in a tragic flying accident.

And as this happened, Morgrave watched across the crowds and the dancers, the white girl standing on her balcony. Was she waiting for someone? Certainly she was.

Perhaps he would not arrive.

CHAPTER FOURTEEN

Grace and Anger

He walked along the path above the coiling river. He had no anxiety concerning assault. The moves of defence he had been taught by fencing masters would also serve when unarmed. Besides, nothing was farther from his mind, and his aloofness acted as an amulet. Only once had some figure approached out of the reaches of the night, and this one, seeing him properly beneath a solitary lamp, had stepped back quickly.

Formerly he had roamed this land of shadows, destitute, at the bottom of all things, careless.

But now he was vigilant. He did not look for men. Yet, men were all he saw. Mortal things. What had he expected?

An old shed leaned below the path. A lantern was alight there, and voices argued. A young man stood on the slope, his hands outstretched. 'She's too far gone. No use to me.'

'But a redhead they told us. Look, we had her up only yesterday.'

'She stinks. She's rotten. How you disgust me.'

Anger paused in the curve of a broken wall to listen. Something was here, corrupt and disquieting. In such a situation, what might not come?

'I'm an artist,' said the young man below. 'What do you take me for?'

There were growls and oaths, and all at once the young man took to his heels and ran away.

From inside the shed a man muttered, 'What shall we do with her then? She's worthless.'

'Cut off her hair for the wig-makers and then throw her back. Let the fish have her.'

Anger walked on, and as he passed the slit of window, he saw a white form stretched out on a bench, a girl lying on her back, and a man was cutting off her long red hair. She had been drowned in the river, plainly, for her skin was like cheese.

As he progressed, Anger came up with the artist who had run away. He was static on the path, and stared at Anger wildly.

'Spare me a cigarette, sir.'

'If you want,' said Saul Anger, and handed him a couple from the container in his coat.

'Do you have a match?'

'None.'

'Useless,' said the artist, as he had of the corpse. But he put a cigarette into his mouth. 'I was a happy child,' he said.

'Were you?'

'Not a care on earth. What brings us down?' Anger did not reply, but as he tried to go on, the artist snatched at his arm. 'Come to the inn with me.'

'No.' Anger gave him a coin.

The artist said humbly, 'I never begged before.'

Anger left him standing on the path, and took another that led up from the river into the hollow streets.

All about was an intense silence, disrupted in spots by islands of noise. In one hovel a man beat his wife, in another a woman sung a despairing lullaby over some forlorn crib. A gin-shop shone with a feeble greenish light, and here there was a different singing. A man had fallen in the gutter among the filth, and lay there.

I have come back, Saul Anger thought. But he knew what had brought him here. He did not believe in it, yet he must search for it. A beast, a phantom.

By its own accord the night seemed to guide him upward now, up from the lower streets and into better ones, with the occasional lighted window, and then he was among the lamps, and idlers were on corners, and two women passed, their arms linked, and looked sidelong with cool eyes to see if he were willing.

Glitter and light. It was like broken glass. All around her a thousand rainbows, and none of them real.

Grace stood in the middle of the air, and below her, below the balcony on to which she had strayed, the orchestra made its music. She longed to dance. To be at one with it. And indeed men had come to her, but softly she had turned them away. She wanted only one.

This was new. She had never repulsed any others, she had never made a space for herself. Yet now she did. A lagoon in the sea of movement, into which *he* would advance.

But there was no glimpse of him. None. A hundred men, some handsome, some dark, moved to the heady rhythms of a dance. The heavy golden light hung down like wreaths.

Grace stood alone, and half the ballroom was inspired to look at her, she was so beautiful, so fresh and sheer and sparkling in her dress of leaves and her hair of moonlight.

But she was like a child shipwrecked on an alien shore. None spoke her language, none knew her, and none could assist.

The dancers whirled. The chandeliers flamed and revolved slowly.

Into this world she had come, and here she was, the best, but yet, nothing more. Half of herself. Unpartnered. She waited in a crystal.

For the first time in her life, Grace burned. She was on fire, brighter than the lights of the lamps. When had she ever really wanted anything? She had *been*, that was all, she had existed. But now, like a rose that rises out of the earth, she stretched herself.

Her yearning was imperious. She demanded something of the night. At last, the answer to her questioning sweetness.

The doors beneath opened and closed, and men stepped through, and women too. All was shimmering and coloured.

The orchestra struck up a dance like a clashing of knives and through the upper air of the palace dazzled a rain of red, green and purple, as the prisms turned on their cords.

The gin-palace towered before him. It was itself like a gigantic lighted gas lamp, ornamental, translucent, filled by flame and movement.

Anger stared. Here he was, miles from the slough of darkness, confronted by this gaudy dolls' house, monument to vulgarity, icon of pseudo-brilliance.

He turned his shoulder to walk by.

At this moment seven women blew down the street in a fog of sundered lace. Seven hags with paper faces, their arms outstretched. He had heard tell of them, but never seen. The Brides.

Anger stood back to let them pass, for their world was empty of anything. They seemed to see no one. Perhaps the City, for them, was like a black grotto, a succession of caves and precipices, unpeopled.

They came near and he thought of moths. The fluttering ochre garments that had been white, the ropes of lightweight pearls. Their eyes were like holes into stony pools. They murmured.

Anger felt horror. He watched them whisper by. It was possible to descend this low – God knew what one was, but what might one be?

Suddenly the solid yellow lamp of the playful, sinful, stupid palace attracted him. He turned and looked at it again.

An old-fashioned gavotte sounded through the glass, and above it the tinkle of goblets and the rush of voices.

The Seven Brides had gone by. The night had them.

He did not want to enter this place, and yet his hand was on the door. He was well-dressed, although not in evening clothes, they would not stay him. A rich man after his pleasures, drink and girls.

They had been girls once, the seven outside. They would grow ancient in their bridal gowns, and perish one by one.

He had opened the door and the huge noise came bursting out at him. He did not want it. This was not his mission. He thought, however, of a glass of wine. And for the first time in ten or eleven years, this glass appealed to him. He wanted it. To raise the glass and take the wine. To feel it in his mouth and throat.

A million scents were on the air, a million variants of flowers and alcohol and hot young flesh, of illuminations and waxes and the infiltrated dark.

But there was no darkness here. Outside, the darkness was, pressing its face against the glass. Let the dark be damned.

The area is massive, like a lighted star in space. It reminds him of something he does not recognize, which is the celebration of Christmas, a tree with vitreous balls and burning candles. He has never seen such a thing. In his youth it did not exist, for him. The old man, his uncle, had never indulged it, and nor did he. Perhaps in a novel then, some description. An intimation of happiness goes through Saul Anger, but not enough to be known.

And she, across that multitude of people, does not even see him, though all her senses are strung up to see only him, so much so that every dark-haired man who has emerged into the light she has taken to be him, for one whole second.

The orchestra plays a polka, and the crowd dances. On the avenue to one side of the room, among the monstrous potted ferns, beside the balustrade, beautiful whores walk proudly in fine dresses, feathers in their hair.

Something motivates Grace. She leaves the balcony and goes down the stairs to the floor. Here she stands, and people look at her. A man comes and tries to take her wrist, and Grace says quietly, 'No,' and the man is somehow pushed away, as if an iron arm had come between them.

She watches the dancers. She raises her eyes to the platform where men and women drink gin clear as water and brandy like a brown river, and the champagne corks pop, and there are fountains of light.

Where is he? Ah, he will not come. All was for nothing.

Anger lifts his glass of wine, the colour of the glowing air, and drinks. He drinks it straight down as if very thirsty.

At once the room takes on an extra dimension. It becomes funny, habitable, not unpleasing.

He walks from the upper tier to the edge of the floor.

Is it possible he will ask one of these women to dance with him? The fencing masters had insisted that he learn also to dance. He knows the steps, used before only for balance. But the polka is a fool's exercise, lumbering and clownish.

All the women here are prostitutes, of course. Not one unsullied. The inferior sex, led astray, debased. Yet, even so, he sees as if for the very first in all his life, the white curve of their throats, the satin breasts that nestle in silk, the eyes of that one, the hair of that one. Would it be appealing to take them in his arms, to feel the pressure of a lithe frame against his?

He does not think of it, but he has never had a woman, never lain down with one. Never even kissed a woman's lips. He is not a virgin, a host of men saw to that. Yet he is ignorant of everything. It comes to him that he might learn. And for a moment, this idea does not enrage him. He considers it, and drinks the second glass of wine.

Grace sees Anger in the way that lightning strikes the earth. One instant the world is only spinning coloured tinsel, and then it centres into one thing. He is there, standing dark and still among the mass of so many, each of whom, an individual life, is suddenly nothing. People pass before him, the dancers go by. They are transparent. Grace sees through them all, and there he is, unmistakable. She absorbs his black hair and the blackness of his eyes, his dark clothing, the topaz glass in his hand.

Incandescence spreads from her, crosses all the distance between, and reaches him.

Anger sees Grace abruptly caught in the press of people like a green jewel. He is mesmerized one moment only by the colour of her dress, which seems the only green gown in the palace. There she herself becomes apparent to him.

Has he seen her before? He does not remember, thinks it is only her flawlessness that makes her seem familiar. She too must be a harlot, or she would not be here. But she has no taint of this. The best of the others, walking to and fro, has some tawdry gloss upon her. But this one is unlike that. She seems to have risen from some lake or perhaps out of the sea. He thinks of water and plants that grow from water, and one with a lily's face.

His impulse is immediately to shun her, to take, if necessary, the arm of another.

But something is drawing him, like a silver chain, around the floor towards her.

Dancers spring by, Anger is jostled, he pays no attention. Somewhere he puts down the empty glass.

Then the green and white girl is a few feet away, and she looks up at him. Her hair is a blonde only written of, it could not have occurred, yet here it is. Two green water drops spangle from her ears, reflecting on the white of her neck. Her eyes are those of a cat, so large, and with every light of the room held in them.

Why does she look at him like this? He thinks he must have noticed her illustration in a book, she is the likeness of a picture he has seen.

He does not speak to her at once, because no greeting is adequate, all seem insane. And she, she does not speak, does not seem to breathe. And for a minute he half believes she is some illusion, and she is thinking the same thing, as she gazes up at him, that she has imagined that he has come here, but it is not true.

And then he draws in air to speak to her, and she draws in air to listen to him.

But exactly then, the polka ends, and the voice of someone else resounds through the hall.

'Ladies and gentlemen, your regard. We have here, for your amazement and delight, the magical piano which plays itself, of which you will have heard.'

A rustle of excitement goes through the crowd. Beside the tension of the two who stare at each other, it is nothing, yet it intrudes, distracts them. They turn, bemused.

Up on to the podium of the orchestra a black piano is being wheeled. Its lid is raised and like a gilded fan its inner workings are laid bare. Attached to it is a serpents' nest of tubes that end in a squat engine, chaperoned by two portly men in evening dress.

REIGNING CATS AND DOGS

All is positioned and the crowd applauds. The two fat men bend over the engine, which judders, and lets off a puff of steam.

'The steam-driven wonder,' cries the man from the podium. 'You shall hear it now play that old favourite, "Flowers and Tears".'

He steps back. The engine is cranked and one long lever pulled down.

The black piano gives off a little ripple of notes, and then begins to play. It plays the waltz 'Flowers and Tears'. And the viewing crowd see how the ivory notes and the black go in and out, without a hand laid on them. The piano plays by itself, over the wheeze of steam.

And great clouds of steam are coming out now. It gets into the lamps and causes them to blink. Into the elaborate coiffures of women and limpens them. The floor is slippery, and there is a fine dew.

But no matter, the miracle of science is playing. 'Flowers and Tears'.

The crowd begins to sing in chorus. Their throats propel the sound up into the vault of the glass dome.

The piano tinkles to a halt, and the fat men are red and wheezing too, but the steam has stopped.

There is much clapping and cheering. And, required at once, the orchestra picks up its abandoned instruments, and now a greater waltz is flooding forth.

Anger turns and takes Grace into his arms and they move out upon the floor, which is covered by dew.

They are dancing together, he and she. Their bodies touch and part, touch and part. His hand is on her waist, in the other hand he holds her hand. Her face is tilted up to his.

He wonders what he is doing. But it does not matter. Like the surrealist piano, it is only a dream. He feels the tender pressure of her body. Though others dance on the floor he does not see.

She does not see. They are alone in a golden globe. They move as one. She is so full of joy she almost laughs, but the pain of joy constrains her. It is too much, too much.

The waltz must never end. It seems that it will not. New instruments are added to the orchestra, instruments not yet invented.

The walls of the gin-palace liquefy and the floor flies up into the sky.

They are dancing there now, far above the City, the towers and spires below, the river, lost in a honey mist. The stars are so close, one might put a finger to them. Comets sail softly by with scintillant trains.

There is nothing to say. Their bodies say it.

She is so near now. They have grown together. He feels the pressure of her ribcage and her breasts against him and under his arm her waist moves like a snake.

He is devoured slowly by desire. At first it is nothing, he can ignore it. But then it fills him. In the dream-state of the waltz, he knows it will be simple and easy. They will dance and then they will be elsewhere, and he will possess her. His readiness does not dismay him, he is inebriated by it, as by her. His veins are full of fires.

She is aware, even through the flounces of the dress, of his eagerness. As she melts into his body she acquiesces. Never has she ever in her life known sexual desire. But it is such a natural thing now it occurs. Like flame or rain.

The stars swim round their heads now and their faces are drawn together. Already her scented breath is on his cheek, his clean breath faintly tinted by wine on hers.

They are the only people in the world. The first lovers who have ever met, as all lovers are. They have invented love together, as the gods invented fire.

She must speak to him now. He must speak to her. The yearning rouses in them like the sexual melody they feel. And yet they do not need voices. They need only lips and tongues.

Closer and closer they combine, and the waltz turns them like planets through heaven.

And the waltz ends.

They are there, in the gaudy glassy hall, surrounded by others who sweat and laugh, and the floor is slippery with spent steam.

He holds her still, her form pressed into his.

Where can they go now? What must they do?

The wish of both of them is to dissolve or consume. To master and be mastered. To be alone in the depth of the forests of the darkness, with stars to cover them and to seize.

But they are here. Here is the City, the rapacious and wicked City, with its lolling doors and quaking lamps. Here there are poisons and lies. And she is a whore, and he a gentleman, and she is innocent and he is ruined.

And then, from the outer void, the Time Piece strikes.

It strikes twelve for midnight. The bridge between the day and the night.

Saul Anger steps away and lets the woman go.

A comber of disgust breaks over him.

And she, inside her form of alabaster and jade, she shrinks. She feels his scorn and self-hatred. His eyes are cold. He would thrust her far from him if he could. And so she too steps back.

They are now separate. They are now alone, not with each other, but each with themselves.

Grace can say no word. It will do no good. And he, he is choked with fury. It seems to him he has been duped. He has been made a fool of. Dancing with a slut in a cheap green gown.

Anger makes after all a sound. In it are all the curses and the denials he is too polite to utter.

Grace lowers her eyes. If she sees an abyss at her feet, she does not falter. She lets him go.

He goes. He leaves her. He strides away across the floor, between the laughing couples who have nothing but ordinary lust and leisure to enjoy.

Grace moves, from courtesy to all these others, whom she had forgotten, to the rim of the dancing floor. And now they are striking up another raucous polka.

He pressed across the floor and reached the spot where the young woman stood now, surrounded by men.

Morgrave had watched, but he had seen her dance only with one, and this one had gone away. Now they were all at her, like some choice leaving of a gull cast down on the ground.

He parted them quietly with his jasper-headed cane. And, sensing what he was, wealth and power, complete indifference, these men gave way.

And there she waited.

Yes, she was extremely beautiful, very choice. He doubted she had had many men. Eighteen years of age, no more. But so pale, and her eyes heavy-lidded. Someone had mistreated her.

Well, he could put that right.

'Good evening. Will you take a glass of champagne with me?'

She looked at him as if from far away. And then he saw her come back into her own eyes. He took this for her recognition of his strength. He did not realize it was her resignation.

'Thank you.'

'What's your name?'

'Grace.'

'How suitable,' he said. 'You're the prettiest here. Shall we go somewhere private, after our drink?'

'Of course,' she said.

They drank a bottle, and a soft colour rose into her cheeks, but she did not seem animated. A severe blow then. Perhaps the man who had danced with her had been her first, and put her off.

Charles Morgrave had no doubts he could improve her. After him, she would know whom she should value.

When she led him to an accommodation address – a four-poster with worn coverlet, a cracked gilt mirror – he was a little disappointed. 'I shall have to make you happy,' he said, as he viewed her white body with its silver fleece, the rose-bud nipples, the little waist.

He took her as he always took a whore, without crudeness and without ornament. He did not expect her to thrill to this, and despised the ones who pretended, or, God forbid, the ones who liked such treatment.

Grace was only willing and gentle. He said, 'I'll give you a little house for a week. How will that be? And some things girls like. It can't be for long. I'm a busy man. You won't anticipate too much?'

'Oh no,' she said. She smiled. How strange, her smiling aged her. She was mysterious as a sibyl. He took her again.

CHAPTER FIFTEEN

Hatred

Every colour was exaggerated. Windows loomed crimson, with bars before them, like the guards of braziers. Lamps green as the leaves of limes fluttered in a rising fitful wind. And in the shadows white faces and claws, things that beseeched – but he had no time for those.

He was sickened. Sick of himself. He had been dancing with a whore, a witch, and she had made a spell on him. He had been ensorcelled.

The night was hot and pressed low on the City, the black sky cloudless and here and there adorned by the knife-point of some bright star. A new moon had come and gone, like a wandering child.

A flycycle passed overhead, and Anger looked up at it in contempt. The world was mad.

The piano had played by itself. He was the same. His body had reacted mechanically to the scent of skin and hair, the movement of a little waist. Cast her out, this demoness. He did not want the flesh. His mind had triumphed all these years. Yes, he was strong.

He stopped, and saw he had come up on the embankment, and beyond, the barricade of stone with its leering fishes; the river lay down, smelling of the sea and thick with night.

Anger moved to the parapet and stood there, his hand on the stone.

Below a barge chugged by, its wake spangled by the combustion of its funnel.

Why was he here? To seek the impossible. The other thing was over now. He might forget it.

In that second, a gentle hand alighted on his sleeve.

He turned, and there she was. Woman in another form. A pale thin girl with curling auburn hair. Her face was rabid, but her voice mild.

'Can I help you, sir?'

'Help me? How?'

'If you were lonely, and looking for company.'

She was another harlot, soliciting his compliance.

Anger said, 'Get away from me, you trull.'

The girl turned without demur, like a leaf veered by an autumn breeze. She drifted away along the pavement, and he watched her go. The lamps lit her as she went by, her red leaf hair and narrow back. And between, the shadow took her in.

He felt a measure of compassion then. He might have given her a coin. The price of lust, which perhaps would have enabled her to desist tonight. But there was always tomorrow. She was lost.

He leaned back on the stone, looking towards the tumble of the City. A white church rose from the darkness with a pointed tower. He was gazing at this, when the night passed in between.

It came as naturally as the gusts of the wind, it came like smoke. He saw it, Anger, and did not believe in it, though they had told him. And then it stood on the street, substantial as the darkness, tall as a house, and two windows were in it, crimson windows, without bars, and slowly they slid to him. And he saw it was real, it lived and had being. The Jackal. Anubis – but not the god, some ghost of a god that they – and God knew how – had summoned.

He saw its legs, straight and curved like a dog's legs, going up, and the curve of the tail, and the arch of the belly, and the long head, and the ears of it, like the images he had been shown, like the image on the ring.

Anger said softly, 'Why are you here?'

And it waited. It waited and it looked at him. This was not the right question.

Anger said, 'Are you mine?'

The jackal raised its snout. Starlight outlined its blackness.

It was *real*. But the street was empty, but for the prostitute, who had walked on and did not see.

Saul Anger said, 'If you're mine, do what I say. Go back. Go back into Hell.'

Then the jackal put down its head. It opened its jaws and he saw the lines of teeth that were like the teeth in the masks that thirteen men had worn.

'In God's name,' he said.

But the jackal, though it was not the god, was yet *a* god. Its crimson eyes sunk like slumbering candles in the moment before they cease. And then flared up like torches.

It stepped on along the street, along the bank above the river, stalked by him, not touching him. And he saw it go past the lamps, but they did not light it. No. One by one they went out.

There it was ahead of him, and the lamps flashing into extinction.

He followed. And as he did so, it seemed a thread of its darkness came from him, came *out* of him, like the casting of a shadow. But it was the shadow of the demon, cast back over him.

He thought, *This is madness, some illusion—*

But the night burned, and above the stars were like a silver fever. It might be anywhere, this place, any great river of the world, under any flaming sky of night.

Presently, the embankment curved . . . like the leg of a dog.

Ahead of him, beyond the shape of the jackal, Anger beheld a strange play.

It was the woman who had solicited him, the girl with red hair, and before her stood the artist, the tattered wild young man Anger had met with earlier in the night. They had been brought together.

They poised confronting each other. The beast was one with the night, they did not apparently notice it. It could not be real. It was of no importance.

Anger heard her speak the words: 'Can I help you?' She was coquettish now, sure of a few coppers.

The artist said, 'Your hair's red. How long is your hair?'

'When I undo it? Down to my knees.'

The jackal moved. It was like a black engine, but silent.

Anger noted this, still disbelieving. It would go by them, the pair above the river, and they would not see it. Why should they? It was the spirit of his soul only.

The black columns of the legs stemmed forward. One went right through the girl.

She flung out her arms. Anger saw, the withered hand protruding from her sleeve. Her face was half like a skull. Her red hair rained out from her hat – she had not lied. it was very long – and it was a grey waterfall. She fell over backwards without a sound.

But the artist screamed. He turned to run.

The jackal did not seem to go more quickly, and yet it caught him. It lifted him up, shaking him, worrying like a dog with a rat. The screaming stopped.

Anger watched. The demon shook at the spine and the artist was a rag doll, high in the air, and next lying abruptly on the pavement.

The beast picked over the body. It stood now against the parapet. It seemed again to be waiting.

Anger went slowly to look. He paused above the girl. Half her face was so *old*, like crumpled cloth, the lips and chin still smooth and young. Her withered hand was lying loosely there in the sleeve. Red in her grey hair. Farther on, the man . . . Anger halted.

The jackal rose against the sky and the stars blazed round its head. Perhaps satisfied, it crossed the street, and again the lamps failed one by one.

The church was there, the church with the spire and the two pylons outside its door. It had seemed a long way off, yet there it was. The jackal approached. Grotesque, it lifted one black hind leg, and urinated against the left-hand pylon. A stream of something like black fire poured from it. A stench of ancient things, hot as a furnace, filled the night.

Saul Anger regained himself, leaning on the parapet, his head in his arms. The awful ancient stink had faded.

Death lay on the ground, and underneath, the river ran, its black muscles pulling the reflected lights like chains.

The beast was gone. Gone where and to what? And from where had it come? The spaces between the stars—

It was the method of the Society which moved him. He must go himself at once away from the corpses of those the jackal had killed, before any glimpsed him.

He walked quickly, firmly, along the pavement, and the impression came, vertiginous and terrible, of the whole City flowing backward, backdrops as if in a theatre, wheeled away, leaving only the darkness in the wings.

And into the darkness he came.

Back among those infernal streets that he had traversed earlier in the night. He was drawn there, as he had been drawn into the lighted globe of glass, as he had been drawn to the whore in green. Yet this was different. He submerged himself. He had seen the jackal. The night was full of it. He had burrowed in under the night, to hide.

Of this he was dimly aware. A curious craving was in him for the bright place where he had danced, but he reasoned this was the need of strong drink.

REIGNING CATS AND DOGS

Now he drank the sweet evil gin of the slums in a little dirty goblet, leaning on a counter in the dark light of cotton wicks floated in oil. All about was other flotsam of the dark, but they left him alone. It was not the first time they had seen, these hungry drinkers, a gentleman leaning here, drinking as they drank. They looked at him with quiet and almost comradely hatred.

Anger stared inward at his own brain. It too was full of rage and hate. Not a diluted easy hate like theirs, but sharp-edged as a broken bottle.

The black was packed hard against the inside of his head, a tunnel that led on and on and never reached the light. His hellish past, his arid elder youth, amid the clever books and fencing swords. The old man who gave him that new life of coolness. The balance, with its feather, than which a heart must not weigh more heavily.

Anger did not dissect what he saw, but he felt it over, each bitter or warped or cold thing that was there within him. And each thing weighed very heavily. His brain was black lead. And so his heart must be too.

It had come from him, the jackal. It had done what he approved of. It scoured the streets of their dross, and of the innocent yet worthless. It made room for great things – but what things these were, who could know.

Anger gritted his teeth and drank the gin and called for more. He stood now high up, and looked about the City as if he had perched on the pinnacle of the cathedral. Merciless, he looked. Let them all die. What use was life?

And as all this went on, he sensed it, the dog-god of the darkness, stepping through the avenues of the City, and the dead fell away from it like scythed grass.

About two in the morning, Anger left the shack of gin and went out on the alley.

At once, others followed him. They gathered at his back and one said, 'Well, my lord.'

Anger half turned his head.

The man who had spoken said, 'Now I should recommend my Molly. She's a nice girl. She'd please you.'

'Yes, she's a jolly girl,' another said.

Anger turned now to walk away, but he was unsteady a moment, and out of the throbbing night, their hands shot and caught his arms, as if concerned.

'Don't go. What, a gentleman not having his pleasure? You'd like something else then? I know a lad.'

'Take your hands off. Go to Hell.'

'He ain't civil,' said one. 'And we was being polite.'

'Teach him his manners,' said another.

One struck him across the back, and although Anger had guessed the violence to be coming, he was not ready. He staggered forward, and came hard against the filthy wall.

A boot kicked at his legs, but somehow he had gauged this one more quickly. He got to one side and rounded on them. There were three, in a half ring, keeping him to the wall. The biggest man aimed a meaty blow with his fist, on which a yellow ring caught the vague stagnant light of the gin-shop. Anger blocked the blow. He struck the man full in the face between the upper lip and nose, and the fellow reeled back barking in pain.

Then the other two set on Anger.

'Be sure he ain't armed,' said the smaller one, as he punched and kicked. The middle man said, lunging into Anger's ribs, 'He ain't. I'd have seen it.'

Anger lay in the muck of the alley floor, staring up at them from a haze of drink. He had barely felt the beating, nor felt it now as the smaller rat-like one kicked him again in the side. They could not harm him.

'Be careful,' Anger said, and laughed.

'Careful of what? Who's to see?'

'Something – may come,' said Anger.

The big man leaned back and slammed down to deliver a fist to Anger's jaw.

But Anger was still conscious, though powerless as a child, while they tore off his coat and emptied the pockets, ripped the silk from his neck, tried his hands for rings and let them go with a curse.

'He can lie there,' said the big man. 'He can look at the stars.'

Anger swallowed the blood which was trickling down his throat.

The little one spat on him, and they went away with the money and cigarettes and the fine coat and neckerchief.

Look at the stars. None were visible. A faint cloud floated high above, without a sign upon it. There was the sound of bells, or were they only in his head?

After a while, Anger tried to sit up. He succeeded in propping himself against the wall. This was all he could do.

He had been a fool, and got a fool's reward. But nothing mattered. For he had seen the jackal of hatred stalking the City. Soon the City would be bones and the wind would whistle through its streets.

Perhaps he slept. He was roused by a figure bending over him, and there was the odour of noisome clothes and unwashed body that meant a human thing, here.

'There,' said the new one, 'he's been mistreated. Took his coat. Take your money, did they?'

Anger said nothing. He saw the man, flat and luminescent, like one of the advertisements that were played up on the clouds.

'But you've cash at home, I dare say,' said the man. 'I'll take you somewhere. You've had a nasty beating. But we'll put it right.'

The man began to haul him up, and miles off protesting spikes of pain went through Anger's frame. He did not resist.

They were walking now, the man partly carrying him, talking all the while in a soft, ugly voice.

'The best in the City, I promise. You won't know you was hurt.'

Streets angled down, and crazy twisted dwellings went by, so crooked that only posts kept them upright. No lights burned, but there was a murmur of night life, things that rustled and coughed and growled.

Then, after a senseless time of this blundering advance, Anger glimpsed the masts of ships above the roofs, black combs full of witches' hair against the paler sky.

They rolled down a cobbled slope and the river slipped against the stones. Smurred half-blind lamps shone like fabulous beetles up in the air.

'Not far now,' said Anger's guide.

'Where?' Anger managed to say.

'The lovely place to what I'm taking you.'

Anger smiled and his cut lip smarted. The jackal would come and devour this lovely place, wherever it was, among the shambles of old ships.

Now they careered, the footing was slippery with oil, and there an elderly man sat on a coiled rope, and looked at them with dead incurious eyes. And here a brazier burned like a red coal, and there was far off singing, hideous as the song of the damned in the pit.

And then another dark area, and slewing up and out, and a lurching hulk upon the pane of the river, with an opening like a scarlet wound.

'Up the ladder we go,' said Anger's guide in Hell, and somehow up the ladder they went, and in at the scarlet valve.

There was smoke, as if from a great fire, but sweet, sweet and bitter all at one time.

A grinning monkey-being slid to meet them, with its arms welcoming.

'He's been in a fight,' said the guide, 'robbed too, but there's coins in his lower pockets, they missed 'em. And then, what'll he pay you after, once he's got used to the delights?'

Anger was let go, and the monkey put its hand, gentle, on his face, then shied away as he swore at it.

'Here, here,' said the monkey. 'Try, try.'

And it held out to him a long-stemmed pipe, and in the bowl of it something glowed like a gem.

Opium, it was opium. Saul Anger looked and saw it, and smelled the smell of it, and beyond, the shelves were stacked up inside the eldritch boat, stacked up with dreamers. Opium, the flower that brought joy and peace.

Anger moved to push the pipe away, and his fingers closed on it.

'Come, sir, come, sir,' said the monkey, which wore a faded gown of azure brocade stitched with gilt. 'Will find a bed.'

Anger drew on the pipe. The perfumed smoke soaked into his lungs. He coughed, and then his throat was soothed as if by purest water.

What did it matter. The jackal would devour it all. The ship, the river, the shadow, the smoke.

Anger rested on the hard cushioned shelf the monkey had led him to. Above and below, others lay in silence. They had no identity. He had none. Let the night have him.

CHAPTER SIXTEEN

Buskit at the Biscuit

Ralph Mooley peered across the hovel at an untidy heap of ginger fur.

'Dog sleeps all day. Useless article.'

Albert Ross, engrossed in pouring hot water from the kettle into a cracked pot, grunted.

'Useless, I say,' said Mooley. He picked up an object and threw it at Buskit.

Buskit woke with a yip, stared about him, scratched, and wagged his chewed-looking tail. The optimist was not put out.

Albert Ross brought the tea-pot to the table, which was a part of an upturned boat. Years before they had seen it beached in the mud above the river, and no one would go near it, not for the wood or the nails. It was unlucky, the story went. Nevertheless, they had brought a bit of it home. On it now stood the tea-pot and two chipped cups, a tin of sugar mostly lumps, and hard as a brick, that must be mined for use, a bent spoon, some unpleasant cheese, three newspapers months old, a knife handle lacking a knife, a whale's tooth, an empty brown bottle, a dish containing three pennies, and a lighted oil-lantern that fumed.

The room was dressed in no less festive vein. Everywhere stood shapeless things that might have been stacks of papers, logs of wood, bits of other ships, or merely hills of debris and dirt. All were covered by rags and the soot of the fire, for the chimney was never swept, and constantly coughed down black dust – it did so now; Buskit sneezed and wagged his tail. In places sat things that Mooley had scavenged and which had been unsaleable – watches without faces, vessels lacking most of themselves like early moons. In one corner was a collection of bottles that presently might go for a handful of coppers. On a hook in one wall hung a net that had been the property of Albert Ross, and nearby a small anchor carved of wood, from another hook.

Above, reached by a dangerous stair, was a supporting room, containing a stretch of old canvas sail with a quilt upon it, and here the two slept with Buskit and his fleas for company. In the corner up there rested only one other thing, the second shoe that Albert Ross no longer needed, and, by night, his wooden leg lay down beside it.

'Buskit,' said Albert Ross, 'rats.'

Buskit looked round. He had caught a rat or two, but generally avoided the unsafe task. The bold rats were too fast for him, although his mere presence deterred the more cowardly. Now he tried to evince an eager willingness to leap and snap and rend, his boxy face contorted and winking with unease.

'He's a good dog,' said Albert Ross, and poured the tea into the chipped cups. One by one he and Mooley excavated the sugar and each brought up a big grey chunk which was added to the brew. Buskit relaxed.

'I been thinking,' said Mooley. 'That money the Jew give us won't go far. A turdulence on him.'

Albert Ross cut a piece of the nasty cheese and ate it slowly. He said, 'There's bad words said of the Jews, but I remember one could tell the weather. He'd know days before if a storm was coming, or if there'd be no wind. Then he was in a fight ashore, and they broke his nose. And after that he couldn't tell nothing.'

Mooley ignored this. He said, 'I been thinking, that dog's a ratter. We could sell the dog.'

Albert Ross frowned. 'Ah, no,' he said. 'Old Buskit? No.'

'Yes. Useless wretch. And his fleas itches me. Better off gone.'

Albert Ross shook his head. 'No one'd take him.'

'At the Biscuit. It's dark there. Spin 'em a yarn how fierce he is. They'd take him to scrap and make bets on.'

'Poor old Buskit,' said Albert Ross.

And the optimist, not understanding, wagged his tail.

The Barrel and Biscuit was doing much business, the throng pressed up inside its tilted walls, a fug of smoke in the dim yellow air.

Ralph Mooley balanced leaning on his cane with the green glass top, a mug of beer in his hand. He indicated the creature at his feet. 'Prime ratter. Never seen one so daring.'

The drinkers at the Biscuit came and inspected Buskit with long leering eyes. 'Looks like a bit of old carpet.'

'Ah, but beauty's only skin deep. No, he ain't handsome, I agree. But have a glance at his teeth. He'll take a rat and cut it in two with a bite.'

Albert Ross stood by, saying little. Occasionally an anecdote of a ship's dog would rise to his lips. The dog that rescued the crew of the clipper, dragging them through the waves. The spectral hound that haunted the ship and howled as they drew away from land. But no one paid heed.

Buskit lay quiet. The attention made him uncertain but he did no more than blink. Once or twice men bent to gaze at him and laughed. Then Buskit smiled, not showing the famous ratter's teeth, but twisting up his cheeks so his tattered ears stood out sideways.

'Try him,' Mooley invited. 'You'll be amazed.'

The evening passed, and was irksome. At length Mooley and Albert Ross sat down in a vacated booth, and the dog went under the table, spared the knowledge that he was a disappointment.

'The swine's ankle it is,' said Mooley. 'If I had a pistol, I'd shoot the bloody thing.'

'He's a good dog,' said Albert Ross. 'He's as warm as a coal on winter nights.'

'He's a drain on our resources. Eats our meat and drinks our tea. Not worth skinning. The swine's ankle.'

Creakle's boat had put in below the tavern, and Creakle entered with his men, merry with pickings from the river. It was a fine night for everyone but Mooley.

They sat brooding, Mooley on his beer, on his ill-luck, the nights he had worked as look-out for various gangs, who had cheated him, on Bullock, who had done him the unkind turn of not receiving the green cat from the river. But Albert Ross dreamed of the sea, the one voyage that he had made, uneventful but for one single thing. This thing he had told to no one, indeed had not told Ralph Mooley, through all the years of their cohabitation. Albert Ross considered it now, and a milky calm stole over him, and against his wooden leg, through which he had feeling as if it were yet his own flesh and bone, he felt the rough flank of the dog leaning on him.

A big man pushed in on the table, smelling of fish and murk.

'Hear your beast's for sale.'

Mooley came alert. He looked up and saw the man called Mason, and Mason's two daughters, equally big healthy girls, with their sleeves rolled up on muscular arms, and having each a mop of luxuriant and filthy tawny hair, topped by a man's flat cap.

These daughters were noted for their names, for long ago Mason, who could read, had found bits of a dictionary, the words clear but all the meanings muddied and illegible. Taken was Mason however, with the looks and sounds. So now they were beside him, Calamine and Hyena. There had been a Eureka, too, but an infant malady had claimed her, she was lost.

Mooley toed Buskit out before the Masons, and Calamine exclaimed, 'Coo, what a sight.'

'He ain't handsome,' reiterated Mooley staunchly, 'but he's a warrior, that dog.'

Buskit looked warily about him. For the first he sensed danger.

Hyena loomed forward, seized Buskit's jaw and opened it.

'He's got his fangs.'

'Take a man's arm off,' said Mooley, thought better of it, and added, 'well, he can snap the head off a rat. Seen him do it often enough.'

'Ratter is he?' said Mason. Plainly he was in two minds.

Calamine Mason said, 'He's got no spirit, da.'

Mooley kicked Buskit. Buskit shook himself.

'Look at that,' said Mooley. 'Obedient.'

'I'll tell you what,' said Mason, 'we'll take him with us, give him a trial. Here's a shilling. More if he's any good.'

Mooley was insulted. He rose and puffed out his chest. Mason took no notice, clapped the shilling down on the table, and proceeded, with a piece of cord pulled from his pocket, to secure Buskit by the neck. Buskit whined.

'Da'll see you right,' said Hyena. She slapped Mooley playfully, and this knocked him back into his seat.

Mooley watched with angry doubtful eyes as the reluctant Buskit was hoisted from the room.

Outside the Biscuit the familiar smell of the strand assailed Buskit's nose, the mud and slime redolent of eels and tar, the sky above the river.

He glanced about, the dog, as best he could for the noose of cord on his neck. He had tried to look back, to see why Ralph Mooley and Albert Ross had let him go with these new aliens, in their rough skirts, trousers and boots.

Mason walked foremost, with Buskit. Behind came the two daughters, and one of Mason's men who was courting Hyena.

'Go to the sewer opening, da,' said Calamine. 'Plenty of rats there.'

She glared jealously at her sister, about whose waist the attending lout had put his arm.

They straddled down the shore, in a veil of darkness, only an intermittent gleam from secret buildings far away, and the stars above bright but ungiving.

Before too long, the sewer opening yawned in the bank. A trickle of water came from it, but inside it was a vault, shiny and shadowed at once, the mouth of a monster.

They lined up before this. Mason prodded the dog.

'Smell 'em, can you? Nice juicy rats.'

Buskit for sure could smell the rats. He bristled and swallowed.

'I'll let you go,' said Mason coaxingly. 'But you must catch me a good big one.'

Buskit felt the noose undone from his throat, a relief offset by the knowledge that something was wanted of him, and he suspected that he knew what.

'Go on, you brute,' said Mason's man, leaving Hyena to deliver a shove with his boot.

Buskit bobbed forward, and stopped, some feet nearer to the sewer entry, his hackles up and his tail down.

'Mangey cur,' said Calamine. 'He ain't good for nothing.'

Mason whipped Buskit smartly across the hindquarters with the cord.

Again Buskit sprang forward.

Now he was very close to the entry. With animal vision he could see into the cave. He beheld what they could not.

A hundred flecks of ruby eyes, staring out at him. A million wicked tiny teeth.

Another aroma came then, in a wave, like a wind. It was the scent-marking urine of a dog. But a dog made of night and fire. Confused and terrified, worse than the fear of the rats, Buskit put up his head and cried aloud.

Mason growled, 'Go on, you bugger.'

'It's no use, da,' said Hyena. 'He's only good for cats' meat.'

But her beau strode forward, and picking up Buskit in a bundle, took him to the entry and threw him headlong in.

Buskit screamed. Next instant he had landed in a stinking pool. Around and above him the ruby eyes glittered. And he saw that the rats too were petrified, frozen into stone. It was not because of him of course. They also had caught the aroma of death and power sprayed out upon the City. Transfixed, they kept their counsel, their thoughtless brains like drops of ice.

He might run among them after all, and kill with ease. They had no will, no cunning, not for these moments.

Buskit backed away. Though he was frightened of them when they were alert, he would not massacre them in their inertia. Their blood would reek of panic. Their terror would poison him.

Buskit moved about and re-emerged from the sewer. He stood there and gazed at Mason and Mason's daughters and Hyena's courtier. They could not smell the night. If they had been wise, they would have turned to stone like the rats.

But Hyena laughed and Calamine jeered. The man cursed, and Mason gave a grunt. So much noise, when the only wisdom was to be very still.

Buskit observed them in worry and dismay.

And then the shadow passed, it went away, like a cloud off a moon. And he heard the rats begin to chitter and crackle like paper on their ledges.

'What'll you do with him, da?' asked Calamine, making up her mind to pull her sister's hair when they were at home, for now the courtier was kissing her.

'*I* don't want him,' said Mason. 'He's no advantage to *me*.'

'Mooley don't want him back,' said the courtier.

Mason aimed a kick at Buskit. It was a very heavy and potentially quite crippling kick, and Buskit skedaddled to avoid it.

'Get off, you bloody runt!' roared Hyena's wooer. And taking up a stone from the mud, he pitched it at Buskit's patchwork hide.

The stone struck the dog and dashed him sideways. Buskit yelped. He ran off a little distance, and stood there, viewing them from bewildered eyes that still hoped for pardon.

But they were all armed now, all casting stones and mud at him, laughing uproariously as they did so.

And so he lolloped off along the strand, to get away from these enemies, wondering as he did so, where Ralph Mooley had got to, yet not expectant of any sanguine answer.

Near one in the morning, Buskit found his way back along the shore of the river, and came up to the Biscuit, where he pawed nervously at the door. But no one approached to let him in, and though now and then men tumbled out, they booted him off or fell over him and cursed him afresh.

There was no familiar odour there of those he knew. He was aware the two who had brought him had gone away.

Buskit had no notion of the route home to the hovel in the street of hovels where Ralph Mooley and Albert Ross brewed their tea and ate their cheese.

Buskit had few ideas.

Optimistically he had wagged his tail as the drunkards fell upon him. Now his tail drooped like the pennon of a lost war.

He crept away along the shore again, and sat down against a bank of rank sere grass. The night was wide and filled by risks. Within its boundaries something prowled, too awful to be thought on – this Buskit instinctively grasped. But worse than that was the fact that he had been mislaid. For it did not seem to him that Mooley had sent him away, rather that he had been taken – which Mooley had somehow not seen, and now here he was alone in the emptiness, and only Mooley could find him.

But Mooley did not come. Not a footstep, not a word. Only the slush of the river and the creaking of ancient boats. The Time Piece sang the hour and was silent. A shooting star rayed overhead, and Buskit watched it. He lay down and heard the callous rumble of the City through his bones.

CHAPTER SEVENTEEN

The Courtesan

Across the table, he looked at her.

The trouble with her was, she was so beautiful, and he had grown tired of it. It not longer moved him. But then, he had never wanted, Morgrave, any woman for long.

The little villa lay out among the market-gardens, and even by night there lingered the scent of roses and other flowers. It was quiet here, the occasional wagon passing on the road, and nothing more demanding than a milk cart. The villa was furnished pleasantly, and there was a girl to cook and clean. He called about ten or eleven, for a late supper. He had come there every evening for nine days.

The candles burned in their pewter sconces. The gas was turned low. The table-cloth was white lace. A tasteful scene, and most attractive of all, the alabaster girl with her coronet of silken silvery hair. The gown of peridot satin he had given her had brought out the colour of her eyes. She should be painted. Someone who loved her should see to it, before she lost her looks. But then, she was only a common prostitute, and Morgrave would not pass her on. She must go back to her dreadful fount. He had made up no lies, he had been honest about this. She knew what to expect.

But she behaved well always. Never impertinent or fawning. She seemed to anticipate nothing. And he recalled her look, so deep with some tragedy, when he had met her, a fathom of green water sunk to her heart. She had not foregone that look. She was sad. But she made no drama of it. She had not imposed on him.

Yet... She was too deep, too lovely. She was like a river, and he had no time for excursions. He did not wish to know about her, her life, her aspirations, her wants. He had been generous and sensible and she had seemed to rely not even on that. It was as if she had come with him – from kindness. But naturally, he knew better.

'This fowl is a little tough,' he said.

Grace inclined her head. She did not apologize. She was not the lady of the house, only his guest. It was the cooking girl's business.

Morgrave poured the golden wine into her glass and into his.

'A tiresome day,' he said. 'These stories of a phantom dog that haunts Black Church. Worthy of some crackpot writer.' Grace said nothing. Something moved Charles Morgrave to add, 'Did you hear of it?'

'Yes,' she said.

'Then there are tales of an insane scientist. Certainly there have been deaths. Curious deaths. But everything has an explanation. Meanwhile, another riot. A printing press torn apart and a paper warehouse set on fire. A stupid action in this dry weather. Why is paper scientific, I wonder?'

'When people are afraid,' she said, 'they do such things.'

'Yes, obviously.' He was impatient. She had spoken to him as if she revealed a basic truth of which he was unaware. 'The ignorant rabble, scared by a shadow. Whoever he is, he kills among the lower orders.'

Grace averted her eyes. She seemed to do this out of tact. She too was one of the lower orders, and had been exposed to the chance of murder.

Morgrave discarded this. He inspected the Stilton and the decanter of port. Both were impeccable – but then, he saw to the wine.

'You must take some port, Grace. You're too pale.'

'I'm always very pale.'

'It will do you good.' He filled a small glass for her. The drink was like blood. 'I'm very much afraid our little holiday is coming to an end.'

'Yes?' she said.

'I may be called away. I can't be certain when I can visit you again. You should have your freedom. But we've been fine friends, haven't we, Grace? I've treated you fairly.'

'You've been very generous.'

'I'm glad you think so. And, of course, a few farewell tokens of my esteem. Things I trust you'll like.'

'You're very kind,' she said.

She was properly grateful. She had not made a fuss. A perfect mistress. A shame he could not keep her. But then, he did not want to. She was not for him. Rather fascinating, however, her nun-like chaste quality. She might have been a virgin – he had nearly taken her for one. And he had begun to let sentences slip, he had almost told her that the killer of Black Church murdered only rubbish and why not. He did not intend to be indiscreet but somehow her serenity drew words from him, as if he must cast bread on her calm water.

Then again, how beautiful she was. A waste. She would be destroyed. She would sell off his presents and live a year maybe in haphazard affluence, or until her pimp discovered the trick and robbed her. And after this, the downhill road into the mire.

God knew, the murderer might have her indeed. What ruin would he make of her white body?

An icy hand fell on the intellect of Morgrave, but only for a second. She was nothing to him. He had had her, it was done.

As for Black Church, it was a nuisance, for there were still no clues. Only disasters, such as the slaying of that flycyclist. The papers had been suppressed. Rumour alone carried the news, and that was of ghosts and devils.

Probably the episodes would simply cease. He had seen such things in other countries. Horrific killings that began without warning and ended without trace, coming and going like pustules.

She was turning the red glass of port in her fingers, a red flower. One could look at her for ever. He declined. Nevertheless, his eyes lingered on the curve of her throat and bosom. Tonight he would make much of her. Their last union.

'Champagne,' he said, 'for later.'

Grace smiled her sweet smile. Yes, by God, she was being nice to him. She did not care about champagne or sex or being left to fend for herself. He had meant nothing.

He was irritated, but again only for a moment. She was a fool.

Yet Grace did care, for suddenly she had felt that very thing he had euphemistically offered her, her *freedom*. She had refused no one, had not refused this one. And for nine days and nine nights she had been here in this pretty house with its garden of arbours and honeysuckle. She had lived like a lady, somewhat, waited on, needing only to serve one man. But it had been a jail. It had been an interval. The price she had had to pay for the minutes of that dance, the exquisite waltz pressed to the body of her lover.

Aware of balances, she was aware of that one, the throwing in of herself against the feather of lust. Morgrave had claimed her as his spoils, and, abandoned, she had *been* only that.

Now he would release her. The blankness of rejection became again possibility.

As for Morgrave, she had been unable to give to him anything. He took, but that was not the same. Was the fault in her? To the coarsest and roughest and least courteous, she had generally been able to pass some mote of herself, some healing amorphous thing, so that they left her, imbued, perhaps altered. But to Morgrave no gift had seemed feasible. He was closed against her utterly. And sensing him in the night, when he slept, soundless and careful even then, she knew that physically he was quite whole, and yet there was within him something like a cancer. He had so walled it up and set it round with iron and mastiffs, the wandering uninsistent influence of her power could not get near. Or so it seemed.

She pitied him, but he was beyond her, as the man she had fallen in love with, locked and bolted though he also was in a tower of darkness, seemed not to be.

She pitied Morgrave, but she was so glad now that he would let her go. He had been her atonement, the stone in the balance for the gem of delight that had been the dance.

Morgrave drank the port, and poured a second glass. He said, 'How lovely you are, Grace. Classical perfection. It was my fortune to know you.'

At this, a slight breeze ebbed through the room. It folded the candle flames and put them upright again. The light was richer and there came the perfume of roses, wallflowers, honeysuckle.

While from outside the chamber, a sound rose, mysterious and eerie, like silver pipes slightly out of tune.

'Good God,' said Morgrave, 'a cats' chorus. A great many of them. Some female puss is holding court in your garden.'

Grace rose to her feet, lifted by some impulse of the sound, the savage music. She turned and went to the window and drew back the curtain.

The garden ran below, thick with trees and plants. The night was moonless, only the stars were out, and one particular star, standing bright above the rest.

But down in the garden, a casket of emeralds had been thrown. So many green, green eyes shone up at her, the stars of cats, who sang.

Morgrave was at her shoulder, his hand dry and bitter on her bare arm.

'By God. How many are there? Two score of the brutes. Did you call them by magic, Grace?'

'Perhaps,' she said.

She raised her white arms, and the song of the cats increased, going up in instrumental tiers.

REIGNING CATS AND DOGS

Across the way, another curtain was drawn back, and light spilled out upon the path.

Grace glimpsed the shape of cats, like pear-shaped pots sleeked over with fur.

And then Morgrave's hand slipped down on to her breast and the music faltered, tapered, and ended.

She saw them dart like snakes through bushes and under the clumps of flowers, around the stalks of trees, away into the night. Darkness into darkness. And the flames of their eyes went out.

'See Sirius there,' said Morgrave, holding her close. 'That bright star. Dog days. The Dog Star. In Egypt equated with the goddess Isis. But all goddesses are one.'

He turned her back and the curtain fell. She knew he wished to have her there, against the window, but he said, 'To bed, Grace.'

And so they went to bed.

In the night, he told her a story. He did not mean to.

He had possessed her almost violently, pinning her arms, struggling upon her body. She saw his face above her, the face she had seen so many times, a mask worn by a hundred men. And yet, in several cases, it was the true face, thrust forth by orgasm, all the masks torn away.

He subsided, and they drank the cold champagne. He put a little silver pendant round her throat, a tourmaline like the drop of a tear.

After half an hour, he took her again, less vigorously, moving more sluggishly. This was his second phase, greed not need. And after that he lay back to sleep.

Grace lay apart from him, her head on the pillows edged with lace and scented by violets.

She thought that tomorrow she would go away. She would go back to Rotwalk Lane, and there she would see Kitty, and Grace was glad. And then Grace thought of the white cat.

The cat stole with her into sleep. It walked before her to the entrance of a shop above which hung three brass balls, the shop of Balthazar the Jew. And there inside a green cat was, called Pasht.

On the counter lay a golden key. Grace picked it up.

She woke with her hands clasped around it, but nothing was there, and by her side her proprietor slept in his cocoon of cautious sleep.

He had said to her, had she called the cats by magic. In this jest his scepticism had manifested. But Kitty too had said that Grace could work magic, and it was possible, for she had drawn him to her, the man with black hair.

Half asleep herself, Grace leaned over Charles Morgrave, sensing like dead embers his own calcined dreams.

What did he know that she must know? Why must she know anything? Why, to regain her love. That was why.

He had shown her the Dog Star, Sirius. He had spoken, obliquely, of the phantom dog that roamed Black Church.

Grace put her lips to his ear. Softly she said, 'Tell me about the dog.'

Morgrave made a noise. He pushed back his head on the pillow. He said, 'There is no dog. It's a fact, the corpses are strange. It's some artifice.'

'But there is a dog,' she said.

He rolled away from her, and she thought deeper sleep had claimed him. Then he sat up and slid his legs over the side of the bed. He stood up. She saw his eyes were still shut, his head still lifted. Morgrave assumed a stance, as though speaking to an assembly. 'They do see a black dog. Even over the river it's been seen, though it does its work in Black Church. Whatever that work is. You'd expect a dog to bite and tear. But those aren't the marks. No, only abnormalities. What to make of those?'

Grace lapsed back. To herself she murmured, 'And there are the cats.'

Morgrave chuckled. 'Dogs and cats. Traditional enemies. Well, what else. Take Egypt. They worshipped the cat. Pasht. I remember some story in their picture writing, the greasy Arab told me. Some disturbance in the city due to dogs or jackals. They carried a statue of Pasht downriver to the temple of Anubis. She pacified him. But they're full of that twaddle, the old texts. Cats and dogs.' He turned his head, eyes still closed, towards the window. 'Are they out there, your cats?'

Grace said nothing. Morgrave stole back to the bed. He pawed at her lightly. 'Please,' he said. 'Please let me. I must—' He made a growling in his throat, savage and urgent. Leaning to her he pulled her round, over on to her belly. He mounted her from behind, snarling now, holding her down, mouthing her neck. She had had clients who were rough, and was not afraid. Besides, he was bestial only in the way of a beast. The noises in his throat went on. She realized it was a crucial purr, translated through the medium of the human throat.

As he spasmed he bit and clawed her, then withdrew instantly and sprang away. He crouched in a corner of the room. Behind him, something rushed

– it might have been a lashing tail. He had become a cat.

Grace touched her shoulder. He had not drawn blood. It was the gesture of his arm that had made the rushing movement.

In the garden a ghostly song went up, once, twice, and melted into nothing. By the time she had reached the window, there was also nothing to be seen but the arbours and earthenware pots.

She could smell wallflowers and roses, and at her neck the tourmaline moved. Through all the hall of night there was no sound but for the breathing of the City. And Sirius, the star, was removed in cloud. Where in the world was she?

Grace bent over Morgrave. 'Come back to bed.'

He went with her, docile, climbed in, lay down heavily. He looked relaxed and pleased. He said, 'A man hanged himself in the clock, the Time Piece. Found dangling from a rope. They were concerned for the mechanism.'

Grace said, 'Why did he hang himself?'

But Morgrave swam on to his side, and for the first time, she heard him snore. The snore filled the night, the room, isolating it, shutting the dark, the world, outside.

And slowly, beyond the walls of the garden, as Grace watched, an advertisement appeared on the cloud. It was the girl and the kitten: *Tiny Tiger Tea*.

Inside Grace something stirred, like the intimation of blood before menstruation, or of birth before labour begins. A wasting or a making.

CHAPTER EIGHTEEN

Once More, A Funeral

White chows, small ice-bears, were led on leashes. The horses were black with plumes like thunder clouds. The carriages tolled through the City. And behind, the women walked. She had vowed it, his mother. Women in black dresses with hats veiled black. Slender women and burly, graceful and graceless. They walked behind his hearse like the chorus in Greek tragedy.

He had been destined surely for eminence, for accolades. But his father had cast him out. The father had wanted a stable, strong son, without genius. But he had been a genius, her boy, a painter. He had loved her, the mother. She could not forget how, as a child, he had played with the curtains of her red, red hair.

Her hair was grey now, and she walked behind his coffin, her heart full of pain and ire.

Then came the cemetery, and here they gathered, black as ravens, with the dots of white, the white dogs, the lilies.

She watched, over the priest's pointless chanting, how the body of her son was let down into the earth.

Above the slopes of grass and yew, the white church under the stormy summer sky. It was like a temple in Egypt. But for her son, no special tomb.

The mother turned her head, and saw the inky women with their sombre faces, that did not care. They were thinking of the ritual. They were thinking of scandal – how the young man had courted red-haired prostitutes, to paint them. And of the cake and wine to follow this prologue of death.

Yet, at her elbow, a girl stood, straight in her black, her gold hair straying from the veil.

'Why do you cry for him?' said the mother softly and harshly. 'You did not know him.'

The girl half turned. Her eyes were heavy with tears like flowers with rain.

'To die so young—'

'Yes. But he was nothing to you. Your husband is *my* husband's kindred. So you had to come. Don't insult me with false tears.'

The golden-haired girl said quietly, 'I didn't know your son. But I knew another who died. Also without cause.'

The mother felt a moment's fury, and then her broken heart let in the other's hurt. 'Men,' she said, 'how they throw us down. They deceive us. They demean us. They die and leave us to weep.'

She and the girl leaned together like black irises. As the body of the artist was lowered into the earth.

Beyond the yews, the military male sun set with a purple flag. The night came to the churchyard. The trees stirred. Men and women raised their heads, like plants that sense water.

'I wish the world would die,' the mother said. 'I can remember him, four years of age, playing with his toys. Now there's nothing.'

'Nothing,' echoed the golden girl.

A wind came over the churchyard like a cinderous wing.

'Do you believe,' said the mother to the girl, 'those stories of a black dog?'

'No. How can they be true?'

'They say it killed my son. Oh, not the police. But a woman I have known. How else was he *old*?'

'Was it so?' asked the girl.

Clods of earth fell on the coffin of the artist. A red moon, a *redhead* moon, was rising.

'Let it *come*,' said the mother. 'I'll die.'

'Yes,' said the girl. 'Let it come.'

They clung together, and the wind moved like a black breath now, hot as a furnace, over the graves.

The white chows danced on their leashes and the horses tossed their black-plum-plumed heads.

In the sky, the evening, that might have been an evening anywhere after the sun had swiftly or slowly gone. The black banks of the City stood against it. There shone, bright as crying, one hard star.

Then they saw the dog, and it was a black cloud. They took it, a few, for an advertisement. It swelled, an artery of dread, above them all.

'Look,' said the gold-haired girl.

'I see. What is it? Is it the thing?'

Darkness swept down like a cloak.

Men screamed and women shrieked. Something rushed among them. Creatures tossed into the air—

The white chows had snapped their leashes and escaped, grunting and wheezing. The horses dropped dead, and were skins, with nothing inside them.

The mourners scattered. Felled.

The grey-haired woman and the gold-hair girl poised together. The mother said, 'Did it touch you?'

'No.'

'How strange.'

Black statues in a field of stones. Nothing upright but for the carriages. All the rest *down*. The men in their tall hats, the women who had walked, a child who had been brought to see. Flat as scythed corn. And the priest, headlong in the grave, his feet sticking up.

Had it passed, the jackal? In the deep blue sky, a blackness, fading.

The mother and the girl. Like statues.

'What shall we do?'

The older woman laughed. 'Go home and wait for bad news.'

In the parlour then, across a china service, the girl and the woman sat in the lamplit night.

They drank tea and ate little sugary things.

No other had come back, to sit with them, and in the adjacent room, the long tables were stark beneath their load of meats and pastries and ritualistic wine.

'Someone will come,' said the woman, the artist's mother, 'to tell me my husband is dead.'

'Do you care?'

'Oh no. He was nothing to me. But I loved my son.'

'I wish,' said the girl, '*my* husband had come to the funeral. But he had business affairs. So, he lives.'

The woman laughed, as before. They drank more tea. The woman said, 'Who is it that you loved?'

'Oh,' said the girl, 'a silly little crooked man. His head came under my chin. I met him at a supper. He was dark and humped and sullen.'

'What made you like him?'

'His soul blazed out of his eyes.'

'I've never seen that,' said the woman.

The girl said, proudly, 'Not all of us have souls.'

'How true. Yes, I always guessed. Not all of us.'

'But his soul,' said the girl, 'was like a piano. It wanted only to be played. And I stretched out my hand – but he was afraid. And so was I. Look at me,' said the girl. She sat, tall and golden and lovely. 'If I had been ugly, he might not have seen me. And yet, I think he would. He didn't speak. He ran away. What could I do? My father ruled me. And he, *he*—' she paused. She said, 'He thought me haughty and cold. I know. He wrote and told me so. He said: *You have never looked at me except in disdainful pity.*' The girl rose. She said, 'How *dared* he. A *man*. He thought he must understand it all. He thought, if he had been straight and tall and rich and cunning, I would have loved him. He *decided* I would not. But I did.'

The older woman said, 'How did he die?'

'Not by a black dog. He hanged himself in a clock. I read it in the newspaper. I sat for three hours reading that sentence over and over. And then I was taken to marry my husband with a wreath of roses on my hair.'

Someone knocked on the door.

The woman allowed that they might enter.

An hour later, all had been gone through. The death of her husband, the massacre of the funeral, very unexpressed and vague, for how could it be explained.

When they had washed out again, the men in their black clothes and shining eyes of buttons, they were alone again, the woman and the girl.

'What will you do?' the woman said, as if they had not been interrupted.

The girl smiled. 'Live.'

'Why?' asked the woman, gently.

'To show him, the fool, what he should have done.'

'Do you think he can see?'

The girl shook her head.

They sighed. They sat very still.

Beyond the window, the star shone bright, and the dull red moon.

At midnight, with white wine in goblets in their pale hands, they passed, the two black-clad women, through a gallery the mother had kept secret, and looked at some of the pictures the artist had made. These were very beautiful, swooning and soft, full of light and shade.

'What is love?' said the mother. 'Is it mine – or is it yours? Or both? Or neither.'

'Does it exist?' said the girl. 'Perhaps we made it up. My husband climbed on to my body and forced me on our marriage night. No one had told me what would happen. I thought he was insane. And yet, if my lover had done that, I should never have cared. If he had killed me.'

They studied the white women with russet hair who wore, or gathered, flowers, in the paintings.

'Love can do nothing,' said the mother.

'No,' said the girl. 'Love doesn't exist.'

The Time Piece struck, far off, and the girl shuddered.

'I'm a widow,' said the woman.

'And I.'

The moon sank through the window.

And in the paintings, the lovely damsels stood and sat and lay, helpless and broken, adrift on the sea of night.

CHAPTER NINETEEN

Lead Hearts and Feathers

That evening, the Society met. They arrived separately at intervals. It was not their usual observance.

Kesper North unlocked the upper door; the key had been simple to locate.

North watched the men, as they walked into the room. Judges, merchants, lawyers, lords. The clever and the not clever. The rich. The barely sufficient.

He said, standing before them, 'Anger isn't here. He's missing, gentlemen. That may be a facet of this.'

They looked at him. They waited.

A man, a rather important man, said, 'Can you explain any of it, North.'

'No. We're in a cloud. God alone knows.'

Beyond the windows of the house, the storm roiled and roared. The night was close and hot. No rain fell. The moon, when visible, had been red, but the moon was gone now.

They lit the candles, which shone into the dark table, where the sword rose, with its balance.

They sat. No man moved to don the mask of the jackal.

'Something's stirred up in the city,' said one.

'Yes,' said Kesper North.

The men sat in silence. North said, 'I think we know it all.'

Another man said firmly, 'Are we to believe it?'

North said, 'I've seen evidence.'

The largest man there, fat and sturdy, said, 'And do you credit your own eyes?'

'No.'

'You mean you think you were misled?'

'I mean that it is impossible – and yet it was.'

A thin man spoke. 'I too saw this thing.' He lowered his eyes as if abashed. He said, 'A black jackal. Anubis. It was only the size of a great dog.'

'Perhaps it *was* a dog,' said the fat man.

'Fire,' said the thin one, 'dripped from its snout.'

North rose. 'Enough of this. To speak of it gives it power. Surely all of us have seen it, if only in our dreams. What we've done – our aims and aspirations – they must cease.'

There was an outcry. One banged on the table. The sword shook and the balance swung.

'No,' said North. 'It's enough. Anger – Anger went to seek it out. But it's here, in the midst of us. And we must give it up.'

An old man said, 'What of *Angier*? What would he say?'

'He's dead,' said North.

'It's the boy,' said the old man, touching at his expensive coat, his satin waistcoat. 'He should never – who was he? A stray Angier took in.'

The fat man said, 'It should have ended with Angier.'

They put their hands on the table. Then one by one they rose and dropped into the balance, into the cup on the side farthest from the fireplace, a heart of lead. The cup dipped lower and lower. It met the table.

Outside, lightning and thunder cracked. There was a pattering like rain upon the street, but it was only the shaking of leaves in the garden of the house.

Kesper North let fall the last leaden heart. The balance stirred then. Each man stood transfixed, and stared at it.

The cup which bore the flimsy feather moved of itself, rotated, dived, and crashed down on the table. Than all the hearts of lead, the feather had become more heavy. So violent was the juxtaposition, the hearts were thrown off. They dashed about the table and the floor and men jumped back from them.

Truth had weighed more heavily than justice.

Rain lashed the windows, but it was not rain, only broken leaves, or splinters of night.

When Kesper North returned the key of the room to the desk in Anger's study, he passed once more through the conservatory, and now paused to look. Something had happened. Had he not noticed? Or had it occurred during the meeting?

The servants were lax in Anger's absence. In the summer heat, the warmth of the conservatory had been ridiculously increased. It sweltered.

North looked about. The palms were black and coiled around themselves like gigantic dead insects. Whole flower-heads lay on the walks, perfect as cups made of fine china. And there were butterflies, perched on the shrivelled leaves of things. Extraordinary wings of brilliant scarlet or sheer blue spread wide.

He went near to them, and they did not fly away. To his harsh sensible eye they looked suddenly like pretty bows that had been tied on limbs of death.

Dismayed, he touched one, and it fell. It was flightless and lifeless. The butterfly, cipher of the soul.

North caught himself, and walked smartly through into the study. He opened the compartment by a particular pressure of his fingers, and put away the key. But there the box was, which held, he knew, the Anubis ring. On the urging of some dull momentum, he drew the box out, opened it, and gazed down at the oval blackness of the ring stone.

The image of the jackal reclined, as always. Kesper North traced it over with his index finger. There was nothing to the ring, beyond its unthinkable value. No sense of force, nothing occult.

He replaced the object and shut up the desk.

Turning, he saw Anger's man, the servant, standing in the doorway, silent as only the most insignificant could be.

'Yes, what is it?'

'I thought you should know, sir.'

'Know what?'

'My master,' said the man.

North was struck, not for the first, by the awfulness of slavery. This man who must call another man 'master'.

'Do you know where he is?'

'I have some idea, sir.'

'Come in and sit down.'

The man obeyed him, sitting in the chair which was across from the desk. He seemed nervous. A servant did not sit in his 'master's' room.

North said, 'Tell me directly.'

'It was a few mornings ago. A fellow came, a rough chap from the docks. He asked for me by name. He had a letter. It was only a scrap of paper, written in watery ink, but in the master's hand.'

'You were quite sure?'

'Oh, yes, sir.'

'Well.'

'It said I must take a sum of money from this room, and give it to this man.'

'Weren't you uneasy?'

'Of course, sir. I said I must go in person. Then the fellow didn't object. He laughed. He said, "A choice place. It'll open your eyes." '

'In God's name,' said North, 'is it some whorehouse?'

The servant stared at the carpet.

'As I took it to be, an opium den, sir. In an old boat.'

A wave of pure revulsion soared through North. He had prepared himself for many things, but not for that. Not for the snuffing out of mind and spirit and reason.

'Did you see him?'

The servant hesitated. He seemed ashamed. These slaves. The smirching of the 'master' fouled them too.

'*Well?*'

'I think so, sir. Yes. I did see him. He came up into the alley. He was – he was in a filthy state. He was deathly pale. He told me to mind my own business. It – wasn't like him. It was like a stranger.'

'And you gave him the money.'

'I did, sir. I had to. It was his.'

'But you didn't wish to.'

'No, sir. It was for the drug.'

'There was no coercion? He acted freely?'

'Yes, sir.'

Kesper North sat down behind the desk. 'Very well.'

The servant got up. 'I haven't spoken of it to anyone but you, Mr North.'

'That's good.'

The servant shuffled to the door and went out.

North found a cigarette and lit it. His mind seemed full of steps, and on the highest he stood. Below he glimpsed Saul Anger, lying in the darkness, and in his hand another glowing smoking thing. But he was far away.

'The fool,' said North.

Whatever supernatural and terrible events had taken place, this cowardly escapade, irrelevant and base, disgusted him. He wished, North, to have nothing more to do with the matter. Nor need he. The Society was disbanded. An era was at an end.

For a moment then, the scene came before him again, the feather crashing down its dish, the hearts flying off.

What had they done? What recompense must they make?

North thought, still as an agate, *I have obeyed my conscience.*

It was Anger who had routed them, and Anger who paid.

North visualized the burnt-out husk his pupil, even now, became. The brain incinerated, the nature wrung like washing. Dead butterflies and palms like prehistoric ants—

He rose, Kesper North, and walked from the study, and so down through the luxuriant and pristine house, ignoring all of it. He would go now back to a chaste and careful life, devoid of vice, but for the buying and tumbling of books upon the table. He had done all he could.

His mouth like a trap, closed hard on nothing, he shut the door behind him.

In the street a curious horror assailed Kesper North. He might have been on the planet Mars. For several seconds he did not know where he was or where he might be. And all about a city hummed and sighed, and he did not know it or its name, nor any name for the blackness of the sky and air, which were night.

On the pavement before him was a huge mark, the shape of the pawprint of a hound. It had been filled with liquid – not rain – oil perhaps, or wine.

At this he gazed, seeing in it some significance which needed no logic and offered no hope.

Then the lightning flashed and the thunder rolled, and cured him. The mark was only some spillage on the road that had no form. It was the world he was in. He had nothing to fear.

CHAPTER TWENTY

Opium

No thing to fear.

A state uncommon in life.

For even in the most steady and assured, the seed of darkness loitered. Suppose . . .

The monkey leaned near, and in its hand, the glowing pipe. 'See, I've lit for you. Try, try.'

Saul Anger took the pipe. He looked at its glow. He looked some while.

'Take,' said the monkey, 'or will go out.'

'What do you care?'

'I care for your happiness.'

'Because I've paid you.'

The monkey shrugged.

Anger said to it, 'Are you a man – or a woman?'

The monkey laughed. 'Woman.'

Anger lapsed back on the cushioned ledge. He watched the creature which, even now, between the pipes, was aureoled with luminescence. 'A woman.'

'Smoke,' said the monkey.

Anger turned from her and lay prone. He put the mouthpiece between his lips. How bitter and how sweet. How had he come to this? It did not bother him. The world could wait, or fade, or die. This was so easy.

The woman walked with him along a straight narrow street. The houses were low and brightly painted, and above, the sky burned darkly blue. He thought he could see stars in it, by day. But he was a child, a baby. The woman held him, wrapped tight in bands of linen, in her arms.

Anger tried to speak, but he was too young. He was helpless.

They came down a slope, and here a terrace ran into a great malt river, which glittered under the high sun. Other women clustered on every side. All held babies, none of which cried or struggled.

Brown arms like honey stretched out. They were throwing their children, these women, into the river. Saul watched in wonder. The white bundles flew, and some fell among large jagged rocks and broke. But others threw off their wrappings in the air. White wings unfolded from their backs, and up into the blue of the sky they fluttered. Even so, things surfaced from the water. Crocodiles like brass, gaping wide their jaws, and into these some of the babies dropped, and the jaws snapped shut, and the brazen heads sank back into the river. A fish of gilt leapt into the air. It snatched a child which had already sprouted wings, and dragged it under.

Saul knew all this while the moment would come when he too would be cast out. He was not afraid. He felt only agitated, but more as if with impatience. At last he was hurled away.

He saw the sky wheel over and the river beneath, and the snapping jaws of the crocodiles. He had avoided the rocks, but wings did not burst from him. Surely he must fall. Nevertheless, he whirled on for some while, and suddenly beneath he glimpsed tall blood-dark rushes, among which purple iris grew, and it was into these that he came down, far beyond the biting things, soft among the flowers.

Two hands parted the rushes. They were white and locked with rings. Two white arms with emeralds. A pale and beautiful face with moon-white hair. Pharaoh's daughter. And she lifted him up. Her eyes were greener than the bracelets. Her breasts were bare.

He lay against her now. He was safe.

They climbed a stairway, up and up. They seemed to climb into deep blue space. He saw the stars above and below. The pillow of her breast was warm.

But at the head of the stairs they halted, and gazing up, he saw the flycycle of Ra, king of the gods, pass over, and it pulled the blazing disc of the sun. Then his mother put him down and he stood there. And it was day, and he was a man.

He rode in a golden chariot drawn by horses of coal-black iron. On every side moved others. Fringed canopies and banners massed like young trees in a forest. The ranks of spears gleamed. As they rode forward, a temple opened about them. It was incredibly high, and everywhere the shafts of pillars rose, ruby red, up into an immense ceiling studded by golden stars.

REIGNING CATS AND DOGS

Monuments loomed in the temple, obelisks and pylons, and there was the sound of cymbals, and the air was thick with incense.

Then the procession halted, and parted, and he alone rode through. The size of the temple astonished him, it was so enormous, and in its upper air, clouds drifted.

Before him he saw a plinth, and on this was seated a huge cat, with pale green fur. It looked down at him with glowing fiery eyes.

The chariot had stopped at a floor of glass, and it seemed he had left it and stood there. Towards him moved a girl in a green robe, with the diadem of a queen, but her face was veiled. Long white-blonde hair floated out beneath the spangled gauze.

Saul Anger felt neither pleasure nor unease. He knew he was to marry the girl. Yet, as she drew closer, the sheen of her green robe grew more silken and clung more, she dropped to all fours. The veil sloughed on to the floor and the royal diadem rolled away. She had changed into a green cat.

'No,' said Anger, 'I won't marry a cat.'

At his words, the whole scene crumpled and folded like a curtain, rushed into the temple roof, glinting and spinning, and was gone.

He sat alone in a stone chair in a dark vast place that dimly shone with torches.

Was he the pharaoh now? He was dressed in evening clothes, black and white, and somehow a black and white piano played by itself. Yet lions padded beyond the archways, and in a water-filled channel of the floor, crocodiles, powered now by steam, floated among the lilies.

A man in black came from the shadows.

'My lord, there are enemies massed on all your borders.'

This seemed to him foolish. It did not concern him. Yet he must pretend that it did, and say, 'The army is strong.'

'No, my lord, a terrible fever has ravaged the army and the city.'

He thought. Useless to speak of doctors, they would have only priests and magicians.

At this a magician also stepped forward. He wore gaudy garments and carried a wooden staff. This he flung down on the floor. It became a golden snake, wriggling and twisting in the torchlight.

'Dare you grasp it, lord king?'

Saul Anger rose and leaning down, picked up the snake, which instantly became stiff and straight in his hand, a staff once more.

'How courageous you are,' said the magician. 'How is it you have never learnt the wisdom of fear?'

But the other man said, 'To one who fears everything, no one thing can be more awful than another.'

The piano fell silent and instead there was the sound of little bells. A drapery blew inside, and a pale female figure walked musically into the space.

The two attendant men bowed low. The magician murmured, 'It is the king's sister.'

But Saul Anger, looking at the blonde young woman, thought, *My mother, who was to be my wife. And she is really a cat.*

Sure enough, about her silver-sandalled feet, stole four or five little spotted cats.

She was close now, and as she halted, her hair and her gown drifted lightly, like smoke.

'What shall I do?' he said.

She said, in a quiet cool voice, 'You must go into the desert and confront the great black sphinx.'

'Then I'll do it,' he said. He took a cigarette from an open case that lay by the chair, but before he could light it, it had become a glowing pipe. A monkey with a collar of blue gems patted his hand. It said, 'Smoke, smoke.'

The dark room had gone now, and Saul Anger rode towards the desert in a louring tower that was mounted on the back of some huge beast.

At first he saw the city all around, and it was black and crouching, with canted roofs and broken walls. No people were in the streets, yet all around he heard them, muttering and crying. A plague had come upon them all.

Then the curious conveyance lurched down by the river, and there he saw a miserable, horrible sight. The water had turned red, like blood, and women were going to it and drawing up this bloody water in pots and jars, and carrying it away. Palm trees grew beside the river, but their leaves were bones. In the dark sky hung a half-transparent brownish moon.

The beast marched on, and they went through a graveyard. The headstones were enormously tall, though many had fallen.

They reached the edges of the desert. It was featureless but for the shadows lying under the dunes.

The mechanical conveyance stopped, and without descending, Saul Anger found himself on the ground. He must walk forward alone into the waste. This appeared to him ludicrous and ill-advised. He foresaw no purpose in it, for the city was beyond help. He could do nothing; the scope of wickedness and distress was measureless. It was a misuse of himself to try.

Nevertheless, he began to go forward, and soon enough, under the layers of powdery sand, he felt the hard cobblestones of ancient alleyways.

The moon but not the sun moved over the sky and sank. A sort of night came, and he saw the flaming trails of flycycles cross and re-cross heaven, and once an advert flickered there, which showed only the word: *Bread*. This quickly faded.

At last a massive oblong shouldered from the sand. He knew it for a sun-dial, and as he passed below, it struck the hour of midnight.

Before him was a long valley, and in it lay three pyramids. He saw instantly by the light of the disturbed sky, that these pyramids were red on one side, black on another, and white on another. As he drew near, he became aware of activity upon them which he took at first for birds, but flashes of fire came regularly. Eventually he was close enough to see that cats ran up and down the pyramids, and their claws struck sparks from the sides. These sparks sometimes fell and nestled in the sand like red flowers.

Beyond the three pyramids, the great sphinx lay out along the earth. Its front paws were outstretched, its hindquarters gathered in. It was neither lion nor human, but a dog, a jackal of black granite, with two high ears behind which the moon, much redder now, was rising.

Anger stood and gazed up at the jackal, which seemed to him so huge and awesome as to be remote, like the sky itself.

A voice spoke, perhaps from the jackal of granite.

It said, 'You must answer my riddle.'

'Must I?' said Anger. 'Why? Where is the point?'

'There is no point. Still you must reply.'

Anger recalled some story. This thing, god or statue, would kill him if he made any mistake. But he did not care about that. He did not care about the city or the river of blood, or about himself. How should he, he had never known himself, and never *been* himself. He was a stranger. A stranger's death could mean very little.

'Tell me the riddle then,' he said, 'so that we can finish this.'

'My riddle is,' said the jackal: 'What is my riddle?'

Anger smiled. He said, 'I have no answer.'

But after this the jackal did not speak, and the moon rose higher, slowly, in a manner, Anger remembered, complementary to the rising of the moon.

Presently he saw that a child was on the sand a few feet off. Her hair was very blonde and her eyes were green. He recognized his daughter.

'Go home,' he said. 'You can't stay with me.'

'But I've come all this way,' said the child.

He thought of the perils of the desert, storms, robbers, lions. Still he said, 'Go home.'

Then the sand yawned and the child sank straight down into it, without a cry. Nothing was left of her. And when he looked beyond the spot, the jackal had become a lump of rock.

What did it matter, what had become of the child? Death was inevitable in any case, sooner or later.

Saul Anger felt deep peace. It was warm and absolute and asked nothing of him. And now it occurred to him that he had *become* nothing, or become very little, melted down among the flakes of the desert. He was only a grain of sand.

Something bent over him, and he smelled the familiar smell, the scent of the drug soaked into human flesh. He opened his eyes very slightly.

It was dark, lit with vague red glims, that shifted and became one, like a smouldering optic, then parted again and were like dull red fruits within a forest.

'Was beautiful? Three pipes. No more now. You sleep now.'

Saul Anger said, 'How long will I live?'

'Live long. Be happy. Pipes are good.'

'And what will you do with my body, toss it over the river? Or sell it to eager young doctors. Or,' he added, 'to feed dogs.'

The monkey which had told him it was a woman, drew away, and he lay, floating in the red and black atmosphere, perfectly content.

As he did so, he went over the dream. It had been as always monumental, epic, and bizarre. And the woman had been in it, which did not now concern him. Then he recollected how he had seen her last as a child, devoured by the sand. And a flicker of some feeling went through him, too real, troubling. He had known no woman. Not a mother, not a sister. No lover, no child.

And yet, the monkey was his mother, putting into his mouth the teat of comfort. He was cared for and cocooned as if within a womb. Death would be the end, not birth, that was the only difference.

CHAPTER TWENTY-ONE

Downriver

The days of Balthazar had been full of sorrow, as his God had promised him they would, and when beauty came, it startled him like the blast of a trumpet. Such a trumpet sounded now, as the door of his shop opened and the girl in the grey dress entered.

Her hair was like pale silver. Her eyes were jade.

He knew before she spoke to him, what she had come for.

'You have a green stone cat. I'd like to buy it.'

'It's to be redeemed,' he said.

She looked at him carefully. She said, 'But no one will.'

Balthazar said, 'I think not.'

Then he went into his back room and there the cat was, Pasht in jade, green as the eyes of the beautiful girl. He lifted her down slowly and bore her through, and she shone, the cat goddess, so that the shop was lighted.

'What is the price?' the girl said, after a time.

'What can you pay?'

'I've been lucky,' she said, 'and had a lot of things to sell. Whatever you think proper.'

Balthazar bethought him of the laws of balance. He said, 'For this I paid two pounds. I paid it to thieves who didn't wish to keep it.'

'Will you take three?'

'I will take two.'

From a little whore's bag she removed the money and set it before him.

The cat's glimmering had gone down, but it seemed now more than three-dimensional.

'She will guard you,' said Balthazar.

'No, it isn't for that.'

Balthazar laid out his hands, which said that he was there. They were strong hands, strong enough for murder. But they had only held a woman, and children, and animals, and other objects rent away.

'Her name is Pasht,' he said.

'I know.'

Grace touched the paws of Pasht for the first time. It was the gentle loving gesture of a woman used to cats. But the goddess who was a cat would not mind this.

'Where will you take her?' said Balthazar.

Grace said, 'Downriver, to Dogs Island.'

'Because of the black dog which haunts the City,' said Balthazar.

'There was a legend. Anubis was angry. Pasht was taken to the temple of Anubis.'

'And what do you suppose they did, cat and dog?' asked Balthazar.

'He possessed her, and became quiet.'

They stood in silence. It had not been a prurient question, nor a licentious answer.

Outside the day was overcast and hot, and sweat dripped down the windows.

Grace and Balthazar might have known each other some weeks.

'Don't go by the roads,' said Balthazar. 'You must travel by water. Down the artery of the river.'

'Yes. Who would take me?'

'I will take you. Do you trust a man and a Jew?'

Grace tilted her head. 'Of course.'

'Of course,' he said, and sighed.

When she had gone, with the supernatural in brown paper, he went into the back room, and putting the stole over his head, he prayed to his God, touching the lovely fragment of belief, but not in the way that a worshipping woman might touch a cat.

And then he went about among the sad furniture and other lost items. He said to them, 'You were better that she was here.'

Overhead the stars shone bright. Below, the river was black and plaited by motion.

A steam-boat had gone by, and after this the Time Piece smote for midnight.

Then came timelessness.

Balthazar rowed with smooth, strong actions, as if flying low above the water. The woman sat astern in her thin pale dress, a white veil cast over her hair.

The docks went by, the warehouses and the abandoned places. The City was mysterious and sombre.

Balthazar thought of how many men had rowed in this way over how many rivers. And of carrying a queen to the land in a costly carpet. Far off there stirred a singing, like the voices behind the candles in the House of God. But probably these notes emanated from the jade cat which lay in the woman's lap.

All spots were one, interchangeable both with each other and with the regions of Heaven and Hell. All gods were one God and might be given no Name.

The river curved, and reed beds opened near the shore. It seemed they must go among the reeds, and now a new peculiar sound struck him, like the thin wails of babies crying. But doubtless it was only some noise of the duck which roosted there.

Across the river from Dogs Island, upstream of the bridge, St Darks, the unfinished church, stuck its white forepaws in the water and the torches blazed. Bullock the fence had stepped down from his telescope to the pulpit, with the after-image of the star Sirius still dazzling on his eye.

The pews of the church were crowded, for Bullock had assembled a crew of dregs to partake, as he sometimes did, of a sermon.

The Bible lay open on a lectern, and from it Bullock read in his barrel-deep tones. The rows of thieves and cut-throats attended awkwardly, not knowing what to do for the best, resentful, uneasy, shamed and amused, longing to be off.

'The angel moved upon the waters,' read Bullock, 'and from every part, fishes arose.'

The thieves shifted, coughed, and picked their noses into ragged handkerchiefs and sleeves.

'Between two pillars,' Bullock read, 'the sun and the moon came up together.'

Something shivered through the church like a black breeze. Some ebb or flow had caught the oil lamps so that they blinked together: a moment of darkness.

Bullock stared at the pages of the Bible spread before him. He saw the mighty word *God*, and it had reversed itself, seemed to spell *dog*. A little patch of darkness on the columns of words, which he had taken for the trick of the faltering light, was soaking out like the stain of thin ink.

Bullock glared. Had one of the felons dared to play some game with him?

Up in the church roof the single silver star glowed as if molten.

The stones of the church hummed. This vibration, like a second's vertigo, came and went.

The thieves were startled, snuffling and cursing.

Bullock bawled them down, and they relapsed. But he could no longer read from the pages of the Bible. The stain had advanced all across them. It was in the shape of a dog's paw-print.

Bullock slapped shut the mighty book and the thud ran through the church. Men now jumped to their feet.

Then came a shock of sound that was noiseless. It rocked about St Darks. Men held their ears and groaned. Some sprawled to the floor.

Bullock stood alone on his platform in his great red boots, that seemed capable of striding by leagues.

The dreadful concussion passed. The church was still upright.

A little ratty cutpurse yelled, 'It's a collision in the river. A big boat's gone down!'

And they were scattering for the doors, to see. Bullock laid his hand upon the Bible, but did not penetrate it, nor shout.

The boat had got among the reeds, and the Island had come to hang above it, formless and whispering with huge trees. The far side of this mound of earth lay streets and fashionable houses, and a stables, on whose roof flycycles might land, guided by lamps and flags. But here the wide and unlit park was stretched, its ancient trees girdled by winding hilly paths. Its crown was the Observatory, where, clear of the City smokes, from a milk-white dome men observed the stars.

The silence was wonderful, composed of choruses of tiny lambent sounds – the clocking of the water, the snake-like sibilance of the reeds, the leafy converse of approaching oaks and beeches.

Then came a wind, hot as a fire. It beat against the boat and stopped them, the oars, the strong arms of Balthazar.

All the musics of the silence ceased, and instead came a torrid hollow clap, a thunder that made no noise.

The boat tilted up as if a beast rose from the river, some hippopotamus or crocodile, directly under it. It stood upright.

In the instant of falling, Balthazar saw the girl flung away and down, a white glimpse, into the bitumen black of the river. Saw her vanish, as night shut over her head.

Balthazar's horror was not of drowning but of losing the woman to the river.

He came up and spat the taste of it, all the corruption of the City and the dark, out of his mouth. And so he beheld Grace at once, a white nymph free of the water, which circled in rings her knees where the wet white gown sank in. She shook the water from her hair, which had come undone, like silver weed. In her hands she clasped the cat goddess. They were in the shallows.

When Balthazar turned, however, the boat was gone.

'Something upset us,' said Balthazar.

She nodded.

They began to go ashore, up the sloping steps of the reed-banks. The Jew thought that one might take off one's shoes, but it was still treacherous, and perhaps these gods did not demand such vulnerability.

The lawns of the wide park swept down, and finally they stood, Grace and Balthazar, under the trees, from which a breathing susurration came. The melody of the night had returned. Balthazar did not speculate on what had tried to prevent the landing. Some antique impulse, possibly unsure of itself, or only cruelly playful.

In the quiet, they glanced across at the farther bank. Some event went on there. A church, with lighted beacons, a vague shouting.

'St Darks,' said Balthazar, 'a thieves' shop of business.'

Grace started to climb one of the paths that led up the hill. Balthazar followed, keeping a few paces behind her.

The trees were mighty limbs, holding up gardens of foliage. An owl called across the Island.

Farther on, the park was overgrown. Rhododendrons massed bursting flowers, and a pool gleamed like a black mirror. Little summer-houses and pavilions, empty by night as forgotten shrines, echoed back the boots of Balthazar on the gravel.

Then, through these tiers of trees, the Observatory appeared like a palace, its pearl dome of astronomy, and the golden cage of plants above.

Grace paused. She held the jade cat and looked up to the light, and never had Balthazar seen a face so absolute, so much what the face of a woman might be.

How foolish was this world, to produce a girl like this, like an angel. What purpose could there be in it? For she had no wings.

The green cat did not glow. It was quiescent. Could it be that it was only a statuette, and also had no purpose?

Beyond the Observatory, a white glimmering moved on the grass between the trees.

Without undue surprise, Balthazar saw that a lioness or leopardess walked there, and little lights flared at her feet. But she was like a fallen moon.

Naturally, no man in the Observatory would see her. Their eyes were fixed on the stars. And then, any way, she vanished, might have been imagined. The scent of flowers grew very sweet.

They stood on the lawn of grass under the lighted conservatory above. Balthazar considered. The temple of the dog should be here, on the Island, but was not. This had been given to science.

Balthazar looked over his shoulder, and saw in a cameo between the trunks of the oaks, the river far below now, and across the river, St Darks again with its two paws of burning brands. Indeed, the church was like a temple of Egypt. And from it a miniature fire moved slowly out into the river.

Bullock rowed across the river to the Island. In the prow of the boat the lantern flamed. And he was full of rage, which kindled about him like the lantern light.

Behind him, the thieves and other miscreants had scattered over the dry caked mud of the shore. Bullock was not concerned with them. It was his whim, which they must obey, to hold and attend a service in St Darks. But the event had been curtailed. They had thought that he sniffed riches or opportunity, and so left him to row out on the night. But Bullock had sensed a threat – an impudence.

The skirt of the Island drew close and he drove among the reeds. The boat nosed in, and grounded.

Bullock came ashore, colossal, the lantern in his hand. He saw the way up the hill as the obvious way. He did not reason.

He strode, like a world on legs, up the slope. He noted nothing until the Observatory shone out above. A man, a Jew, was standing there, and a woman, on the grass. Bullock saw the green object which she held. He raised the lantern high, and their two faces, like clever mechanisms, turned into the light.

'Who put you up to this?' said Bullock. 'What's your game?'

REIGNING CATS AND DOGS

'You are mistaken,' said Balthazar.

'And you are a Jew. Shut your row.'

Grace held the green cat, and now Bullock circled round her. A heat came from him, more than the lantern. He was carnivorous and awful. One blow of his paw could mow them down.

'I was offered that trumpery before,' said Bullock. 'I wouldn't take it. Worthless.'

Grace said nothing. Her lids were lowered, as with a violent customer, not to annoy him further with a look.

'Take it away,' said Bullock.

'The boat was sunk,' said Balthazar.

'What, deaf as well as a Jew? I told you to be quiet. Let *her* speak, dolly here.'

Balthazar regarded Bullock with centuries-sad eyes. But the eyes saw what Bullock had become. The guardian prowled out from the temple to bar the way. They had been led up to a high place, but the god was not here. Was the god in the church across the river? The phenomenon was muddled and uncertain, because it was not truly a fact, only a sort of dream that had come halfway into the world of men. Yet even in dreams there could be logic.

The guardian should be distracted, drawn off, and they had lured him here.

Balthazar thought they were like two pillars, the gigantic bulking Bullock and himself, and Grace between them like a mote of white.

The Jew was aware of his past, the past of his race, the running and the cunning necessary to survive.

He said, 'Gentile scum. In the last days, you will go down into the fiftieth Hell.'

Bullock, arrested, glanced at him.

'Eh?'

'Eater of pigs, filth-belly. Rod in swaddling.' Balthazar stepped forward. As he straightened from his stooping he was tall. He slapped Bullock across his toad-angel's mouth.

And Bullock wheeled forward with meaty hands outstretched. For two decades or more, no man had insulted Bullock. They did as he bid, and he had been a king. This slave had made him less. He grabbed for the yellow Jew, and the Jew was gone, laughing – had Balthazar laughed for twenty years? – making clown's gestures, a creature possessed by imps.

Bullock let off his roar, which was not loud. He set down the light and ambled towards Balthazar. But Balthazar, capering now, was off, away, a boy taunting the bully; or a demon leading the unwary into the wood.

Like a hare, abruptly the Jew ran. As if released, Bullock bounded after him. They passed into the trees with a clash of twigs and branches, a boar pursuing an ape.

The green cat was so heavy now, like a stone in Grace's arms. She went down the hill, back the way she had come. Only shadows massed before her as the light faded.

The descent reminded her of something from her childhood, the night-black stairs of some house she had had to go down. She had not been afraid, although rough treatment awaited her at their foot.

The path presently curled out again upon the shore, and framed between the reeds, she saw the breadth of the river and over it, the church. Only the water, then, between her and St Darks.

Downriver stretched the bridge, but it seemed miles off and barely real. There was no other means to cross save Bullock's boat, wedged fast into the reed-bank, with two large unwieldy oars she could not have managed.

Grace stood and waited. The night ticked like a vast clock, and the torchlight of the church trembled in the river.

A shiver agitated the reeds, perhaps a breath of air.

Two dozen duck rose on clapping wings and fanned across the bank, all about her. Viridian sparks sprayed through their plumage. They curved and spread out again into the night, rayed over, and came down on the black stream.

Where they landed there was an altercation. They were no longer required to swim, but stood, clucking to each other, splashing and waddling, raising one wing after another. The river had been changed.

Grace stepped out among the duck. The water went to a depth of two inches, under this a causeway had risen. Beneath her shoes the surface was sugary, firm yet yielding, both at once. It was a ridge of sand.

Grace moved on the water. The duck, feathered with night, fluttered aside, winking their smooth nacre eyes.

The substance on which she walked might subside as swiftly as it had formed, or some tidal impulse of the river, built up unnaturally behind this sudden barrier, sweep down on her and dash her off and under. Yet all her life had been of that sort, the treading upon shifting sand, the giving of herself to night and tide. She went on steadily, the statue of Pasht heavier than a boulder.

REIGNING CATS AND DOGS

While behind her in the park, the nimble Jew nipped between the trees and towering Bullock after him, stumbling on the roots of the earth.

About the church was currently an empty waste of muck and debris. From this most of the cowed thieves of Bullock's impromptu congregation had withdrawn, although the specks and flecks of their lanterns were visible here and there, along the bank, as they searched for a sunken boat or wealthy passengers.

Grace climbed the wet steps between the torches. She came to the tall door, which stood open.

Beyond, the church, unfinished yet begun. Looking up she saw the one silver star flicker in dying lamplight. They had left a few lamps, but most were out. From ochre shade Bullock's pulpit rose, massive, like the prow of a ship.

Under this, a solitary man sat, a big fellow with a wooden leg. The leg was pushed out, as if he examined it.

As Grace moved up the aisle, where brides might have glided in silk and webby veils, Albert Ross looked round. He was lonely, for Mooley had caught the fever and hurried to explore the river's edge, and the dog was no longer there, and tonight the false leg hurt like a wounded heart.

'He's gone,' said Albert Ross, as if she had inquired. 'But I couldn't see the point of it.'

Grace smiled at him. And Albert Ross stood up, even on the throbbing pole of the leg. And felt his invisible toes fill with healing blood.

'Old sailor,' said Albert Ross. 'The river's a wretch. It swells with the sea. But it ain't. I saw a mermaid once.'

Grace halted, but the jade cat Albert Ross did not, in the vagary of the light, perceive.

'A mermaid?' asked Grace.

'Yes. We was three days out, and I was on a watch. And she danced up from the water. She was white and green, like a lily. Green hair and a green tail. She was beautiful but she frighted me. Face wasn't – like a girl's. Too lovely. Better 'an you, even. And she made a noise.'

'Did she?' asked Grace, attending to the one true tale of Albert Ross's life.

'Sang like a fish – or a whale. Like a pipe. Very thin and high, a long curling note. And then she'd gone down. And when they come and asked if I'd seen anything, I said no. But I'd seen the flip of her tail. All glittering it was. I can see it now.'

Grace said, 'How lucky you were.'

'Was I? No, I've not been that lucky. And we lost the old dog. Good old dog, he was.'

She said, 'Perhaps the dog will come back.'

Albert Ross went towards the door, striding on his two legs, one of which ended in a ball.

'I'll find Mooley. He won't get nothing. That mud's hunted out. Time to go home.'

She thought, *Home*. And what was that?

But Albert Ross pulled shut the great door behind him, and she was in St Darks, so she climbed up into the pulpit and put down the weight of the world, Pasht the goddess of joy, on Bullock's closed Bible.

As the terrible heaviness went from her, Grace poised in the pulpit, where Bullock had ranted and recounted. There was no vestige of him left. The church felt calm and still.

A mermaid. Grace felt herself, for a moment, fish and woman, slip through the shoals. Such freedom. And her loins locked, surely, since a mermaid was a fish, against the sexual act and the sexual pleas of men.

Yes, for a moment, the ocean was her hair, and she lay deep under the bellies of the ships, staring up from her green eyes, without compunction.

Then instead she looked about. Shadow was filling the church, perhaps to cover the cat of jade.

Grace folded her arms around herself and discovered her body, graceful and young, and the beating of her heart.

The face of Pasht was enigmatic. Released from her burden, Grace became aware also of her own mind and will. For although her heart had always beaten, she had not felt it until now.

It was as if she saw, as they said the drowning did, all her life rush through her brain.

First came the man, the dark prince whom she had embraced in a waltz. And love, which had been gentle within her, boiled up on fiery wings. Tears broke from her eyes, hurting her as if they had had to stab her to get out. She loved him. But he had left her, after the promise – left her in the tinsel light. She did not know his name. She had no name to cry aloud. If she were to die, on whom should she call? Another had claimed her and she had not resisted. The magic had been undone. By herself?

After this, the other things bore in, her life and her service. A thousand men who had used her, taken her healing, triumphed on her body. Back and back, a crowd of faces, leering and snarling with desire and climax, the masks of beasts. Back to the beginning in the sooty streets, the dark stairs, the descent. A child, lifted up and indecently fondled. A young girl mouthed and devoured.

Had anything been left? It seemed to her she was a shell upon a desolate beach. The wind chimed through her. Her soul was sucked dry.

Grace wept. She sobbed aloud, and the half-born church heard her and magnified her lament.

Unfinished – so she was too. She had been nothing – a dream, a ghost. She had not lived.

She beat her hands on the rail of the pulpit. Her hair showered round her. Tears like hard emeralds sprang from her emerald eyes. She reached up to tear at her own flesh – her cheeks, her throat—

And in this instant the church door was pushed open once more, a little way.

Two of Bullock's indrawing of thieves stood gazing up at a gorgeous girl raised high over them in the fitful light. They did not see tears – had never seen them.

'Come on down, pretty,' called one.

They knew she must be a whore, and had her slight price.

But the girl stepped down with a wild white face that might have risen from an ocean, and her legs were a silver-green tail, though they did not see this either.

'That's right. Come here.'

Tickled at the idea of defiling Bullock's church – for to whom else did it belong? – they rambled forward, and caught at her.

Then she spun and raked them with her nails. The whips of her hair slashed at their faces. They fell back yelping. She was a witch, a *thing*— Blood dripped down their brows.

'The bitch – where is she?'

'Gone. The bitch.'

Darkness settled on St Darks. Darkness covered the pulpit, hiding everything.

'Nothing else here,' said one of the thieves. 'She must have been Bullock's, to fight like that.'

'Little cat,' said the other.

CHAPTER TWENTY-TWO

Anoxberus the Golden

By the time the dusk came, he would lie down, the dog. He would lie by the bank of sere grass, where he had worn a sort of hollow. This now was home. He had no other.

The river lay ahead, and the City behind, both pitiless. Buskit recalled an era when there had been, if not kindness, at least connection. He had been a part – of something.

But now, the hot and overcast days, wandering along this riverine desert. A woman threw a stone at him, which had occurred before. The inn loomed above, but there was no one there. He was lost.

He starved, Buskit. The bones stood out in his terrible orange coat. He looked old now for certain. Who could like such a thing? His slender glowing life showed only dimly through his faded eyes. His race too, abused, misused.

And now, the dusk came again, with a small thin wind blowing off the stinking river, and above the bright Dog Star, like a tear on fire. He looked at it drearily, put his head on his narrow paws, much muddied, and slept.

Down he sank, his dog soul, deep into some inner confine. He mourned.

A shooting star went over, and from the depths, Buskit peered at it. It made a bridge between the sky and the earth. In his sleep, he raised his head, the dog, to stare. There was the sense of a padlock undone. Chains fell from him.

Buskit lay under the bank, but even so, he stood up. He rose and stepped clear of what he was, ravelled it up, absorbed it, and trotting to the shining bridge of the static star, Buskit leapt, and ran into heaven.

How strange it was. So big and dark and strung with sparkling lights. Where the bridge ended, he spun free, and now he sailed across space.

Never had he known such pleasure or delight. But he knew many things. He knew who he was. Large and golden, strong as a bull, sleek as cream.

His black eyes were so clear he saw to the back of the moon, saw where Venus wandered on her azure way, and the flame of Mars, and the majesty of Jupiter.

He had traversed such paths before, they were familiar to him. Stardust sprinkled, and he licked it with his long clean tongue. Hunger and thirst left him.

The dog played in the gusts of space. He knew his name now, it was Anoxberus. He was ancient and very young. His pack was huge as the world. He was all dogs and one dog. He laughed and jumped over the moon.

But on the far side, a cool black hand appeared and caught him. And Anoxberus, who was all dogs, lay tiny as a golden coin, there on that ebony palm. It was a wonderful hand. It smelled of life and shade and dreams. Shaped like the hand of a man, but Anoxberus knew quite well, it was the hand of a god.

Anubis, the Guide and Judge, supported the tiny golden god-dog, and looked down at him with the black face of a jackal, and eyes that held a million stars.

Anoxberus laughed again, he could not resist, and lolled on his back, and jumped up and wagged his tail like a comet, and kissed the black palm.

Then Anubis carried him, across the great court in space.

It was quite beautiful, like a palace of pure glass, and outside the night was, lit by planets and distant galaxies. Clouds passed, in the form of dragons and ships and towers. Among the transparent pillars walked many beings, too many to know. But then a goddess approached. She was pale like first light. She had the head of a cat. In her long eyes were seas and rivers and the moving of reeds.

They went on side by side, then, the cat and the jackal, and out on the glassy floor stood a balance made of silver.

Anoxberus lay still and waited. He did not mind what happened and had nothing to fear.

Anubis put him into one of the cups of the balance. Here Anoxberus stood, swinging back and forth. And he saw the goddess put into the other cup something white as winter snow, which was a cat.

Anoxberus barked. But the white cat only glanced at him sublimely. She swung about as he did.

Thoughts of the world went through the skull of the dog. To chase and catch. She was smaller than he.

The white cat partly closed her eyes, and lay down, with her paws under her breast.

Anoxberus also sat. The thoughts of the world, chase and catch, floated away from him, like the clouds which slipped over the palace in space. He heard the cat purr, and he thought about this instead.

So they were, each in a silver cup, and the balance hanging level, almost looking at each other, swinging mildly.

Gods moved by and observed them. Silver and golden gods, and ebony and alabaster and bronze. And eons off, unseen, tiny figures of the earth scurried to and fro.

'Here dog, what are you doing here?'

Anoxberus widened his eyes. He had come back among the little creatures, and they were once more of human size. A girl bent over him. She had a flush of brown curly hair, ugly boots, a scarf at her neck like a sin. Hyena and Calamine Mason had dragged him along the river bank. Which one of them was this?

The big golden dog raised himself and growled.

The girl caught his head in her hands and chuckled. 'What, growl at Eureka?'

Because he knew things, he knew too that Eureka Mason was dead. She had died in infancy, and never become this strapping rosy girl. Her hands felt actual and warm as the summer night. A taut breeze blew from the river now, and a steam-boat passed with a red-hot funnel.

Eureka, who had never lived to assume her discovery of a name, posed with her fists on her hips. 'Oh to be off and see the world, eh, Anoxy?'

Anoxberus, stationed now at her back, regarded her impartially. She was not a ghost but another possibility. Neither did she exude beastliness as her sisters had, but a type of clumsy freshness. She had employed a variation of his correct title.

He nosed her skirt and she squeezed at his silken coat. 'Come on, Anoxy: Better do our best.'

They paced up the shore. The wise dog squinted at buildings on either side of the river. They seemed as memory supplied them. Even a cloud – an earthly cloud – hung at the horizon, stippled with a word that dripped away: *Alone*. Anoxberus could read it. He experienced a faint concern for them, these mortal persons. Alone was not a word that could be applied to him, who was all dogs of time or place. He frisked and sensed all dogs frisking in their fur. The million stars that were their million upon million of eyes, beamed out of his, and lit up sturdy Eureka swaggering beside him.

Then they reached the sewer opening. Water trickled from it in a shiny saliva. Within, the rats were sitting like bunches of grey grapes.

'It's a shame,' said Eureka, 'to kill the poor things. But it's the law.'

Anoxberus looked into the darkness and beheld the rats like the legions of Avernus. He knew the law, and as he filled the entry with his bright body, he bowed low to the rats.

They in turn got up and hurled themselves at him like steel knives with eyes.

Anoxberus, all-dogs, pranced and whirled, rolled upon them, turned and tore out their throats. Rats flailed into the black air and fell dead. He saw the wisps of their psychic secret life go up from them like steam. He fought until a hundred or more lay dead about him, and the rest fled like leaves before a storm.

When he came from the tunnel in the bank, blood streamed down him, and when he shook himself, drops of it splashed Eureka's drab skirt, making it for a moment gaudy as her scarf.

'Brave dog,' she said. 'Da would be glad to get the use of you.'

Over the river the lonely word had washed from the cloud. Eureka Mason walked into the river and melted, as the rents closed in the hide of the dog. Above in the sky, presumably, Anubis presided over the balance.

CHAPTER TWENTY-THREE

The Black Church Terror

If she thought back, Kitty Stockings could remember another life, her early days, when she had tasted luxury and even happiness. And thinking of herself as she had been, that Kitty was another Kitty. She would say to herself, *When I was young.* The time when she had known Grace had now become also another life. Then there had seemed to be at least some chance or hope, though of what Kitty did not know. Certainly there was about it a sheen, a lightness like the music of the music box which Kitty had sold. But Grace was gone, had been gone a long while, with her gentleman. She would not return, and that was lucky for Grace. But for Kitty the shadows had crept closer, as they did before you lit the candle.

She had even seen the spectre of Grace, there in the cubicle of the attic room. Once before the green curtain, putting up her blonde hair, and once sitting on the bed at play with the white cat. But firstly it had been a shaft of sunlight, and secondly the moon.

Kitty fed the cat on scraps, when she found it, but generally the cat roamed outside. The cat did not pine for Grace. And in the Rookery sometimes they spoke of Grace slightingly, because she had left them, too good for them now. They forgot her gifts of money, how she had cured toothache and colic and burns. They called her a witch and a slut and worse. And although no one had claimed her room, soon enough now it must happen. Then even her phantom would disappear, and the white cat, doubtless, run away.

Kitty put on her little red hat and rouged her lips. So much red, and the sunset poured red in the slum outside the house. There was no sense in hanging back, for there was no Grace to go out with, and the dangers of the streets seemed inevitable, like a duty. It was true, Kitty had tried the photographer once more, but he had gone off and left only his debts. There was no other way but the custom of the alleys.

Yet tonight she felt so heavy. As if she carried some weight in her arms that might be her heart. Who could say, perhaps the religious people were right, a hell existed, and Kitty and her kind would fry there.

Death must come first, however. Was it then death that she feared tonight?

With a shudder she stood back from her broken mirror. Was it not always death that Kitty dreaded, and Grace, her talisman, absent for ever. Prey to all things now, Kitty Stockings. Why flinch at the stories of the black dog, when anything might do it, some drunken man, a blow of fist or blade, or the invisible disease, or poverty in its extremest image.

Kitty put straight the bird on her hat. It fell over at once, but she had tried. She went down jauntily to the street, humming a popular tune.

Up among the street lamps of Black Church Kitty went, and as the carriages went by her, and she saw the bustle of so many people, bright with lives, she thought perhaps she was safe, and after all there was some sense to things.

Above was a roseate comfortable cloud, with a picture thrown up on it, of a black and brown dog: *Bulldog Boot Polish*.

From Kitty's stomach something like a great smooth stone kept rising into the back of her throat. She swallowed it repeatedly, but instantly it returned.

At a corner a man in middle years stopped her. He was decently dressed. First he asked the way to some public house. Then, he said, would she accompany him for a drink. Kitty said that she would.

All light was emptying from the sky, and the boot-polish cloud was now a fiery red.

They went into a tavern and drank some gins, and the man became bold enough to ask Kitty for what he had wanted all along.

She felt pity for him. He was mild and afraid. They went arm in arm into a horrible alley, and here he looked about, all guilt, and Kitty stroked his cheek. 'It's only natural.'

He kissed her, and she in her kindness caressed him. She did not mind when he pulled up her skirts and entered her. He had bought her drinks, even if not champagne. As she murmured to him, Kitty thought of Grace. Was Grace happy? Hopefully it must be so. Kitty's client came with a sad low grunt. He flung away, and her skirts fell like the heads of autumn flowers. He gave her coins and his face was full of trouble.

REIGNING CATS AND DOGS

What a world it was, where simple desire must buy what it required or go bereft.

The gin had eased the stone in her belly and throat, but now it returned. As the man hurried away, she too felt afraid. She had not given him relief. Instead he had bought from her shame and distress. Were these the measure of her worth? Grace would have said no. But Grace was elsewhere.

As she emerged from the alley, Kitty came into one of the broad thoroughfares. The area was packed by people, and all looking up. Kitty too looked into the sky.

Certainly, this advertisement was wonderful. The little bulldog had been replaced by a vast scene, some pillared building, where women danced in floating saffron robes, with skeins of roses. Kitty, like the rest, was pleased by the display. It would be for some perfume or sachet.

Then, a disturbance spoilt the show. Transparent summer lightning flittered over the sky. The crowd exclaimed.

A woman near Kitty, obviously one of her sisterhood, cried out, 'Ooh, look at that!'

Aloft in heaven, the night had gathered all into one place. Nothing was so dark, not the sky, not the shadows between the buildings. This darkness crossed the cloud, and the cloud vanished. Only a glow persisted, which outlined one new figure. The women of the advertisement fluttered round it, minuscule by contrast, and apparently oblivious, still strewing their flowers. And below, the mass of watchers held their breath, for beside this thing was no spot to dance.

It was the dog, the black dog, the hound, the beast. It covered most of the sky, and from its eyes looked fires.

Women in the crowd screamed. And in that moment the black dog bent its head, long as a blade, and snapped up the dancers all about like flies. It bit them in half and hurled the pieces away, and these fell like fireworks and went out. The women on the ground went on screaming. There was silence above.

And then a paw of the hound extended and came down. Though a dog, and four-legged, it resembled at once a spider. The black stem descended, and went in, unmistakably in, at the roof of a tall building, some streets off.

The crowd stared, and they saw the lighted windows of that place erupt. Glass showered out like champagne bubbles and with that same faint celebratory effusion of sound. Then all the windows were black. And the building moved – it changed. Each of the watchers saw it, and Kitty too, caught in the press, stone lodged in her throat. The architecture was a cliff, massive yet without form. And down its side a slow flame trickled.

Kitty felt the crowd surge, like the same congestion that was in her neck. Men thrust and women beat with their hands. A stall went over with a rowdy noise.

The dog had turned to glance down upon them all. Its bestial visage had none of the sympathy of a beast's. No, it was not Anubis, had never been. Some human corruption of that pure symbol, overseer of justice and guide of souls – the debris of human minds had made it and now a mind doused by bitter fumes . . . But it was not even a dog. It was a thing of Nothing. Nullity, coreless and unreasonable. A huge leg and foot, dog-formed, was set in the street in a column of iron.

Kitty in the crowd, which was rotating like a drum – with the force of a thick wave it pushed her forward. She could do nothing but go with it. Away from the monstrous hound.

She could not scream, but everywhere the screaming was being seen to. After a minute, she was no longer on her feet. The tidal mass carried her, and instinctively, as she clutched at the bodies which crushed and toiled against hers, she was wrenched off, punched and buffeted, by those who did not see her, saw only what came behind.

So her life had been. She was not offended, only terrified. She counted for nothing, and would be destroyed.

The lamps were going out. Some burst with a clash of glass, which showered into the streets upon the fleeing people. Some smoked into the void as blown-out candles would.

All along the way men and women hung out of their windows calling. What had happened? Why the rush of the mob? What came on at their back?

Kitty could see nothing of the black dog now, yet she felt it, like a storm cloud poised above the roofs. When thunder sounded it was a footstep. In the extinction of the lamps, the lighted windows above burned like wild primal fires, and when the lightning fitfully shocked, she saw all about her the ghastly straining faces of the newly dead, and knew that her face was a replica of theirs.

But if it was a dog, it had lost its master and its pack. There was besides a cat in its kennel. Did fumes of opium mount into its supernatural skull?

Somewhere it had crossed the river, and banks of blue poppies had come up on the water, alongside the boats given over to the drug of opium. Deep in the recesses of one such hulk, a devotee died as the smoke turned to flowers in his throat. Not Saul Anger, of course. Anger was seeped in dreams of pyramids, of chariots, of a great jar in which a flaming stomach boiled, intestines like serpents.

The dog came into Black Church, where it always came, where once the priests had worshipped a shadow they had called for a dog, reckoning it the Devil, some old scent.

The dog, the god backwards, trod among the roads and buildings, putting its iron spider's legs deep into the cavities of life. Four legs now, or eight? One head or three? Was the tail, drooping as the tails of wretched hounds do, also headed by a jackal's mask?

Sometimes it leaned to slash at the flanks of the running crowd, or at those who plummeted out from their houses. It must lean down a long way. And sometimes it tore at creatures which had stayed transfixed in windows.

Black Church was altering. It seemed hemmed in by cliffs. The baying in the streets was an ancient noise, historic as men.

Bells had begun to ring from churches, a panic of sound. Smoke rose, now here, now there. And over all this, which union of concrete things seemed closed away from the rest of the City, a unique moon rose on the wings of a storm cloud, a moon with a gorgon's face.

The policeman, Moans, had not been unhappy. Dressed in female attire, one of the last of 'Morgrave's Girls', he stood at the bar of the Palmer's Pigeon, drinking grey gin, and admiring himself in the spotted mirrors. He had been propositioned twice, and flightily told them he must wait for his gentleman. He pursed his sticky red lips each time, and added that he was sorry. Now and then he twitched his hindquarters, and the petticoats rustled.

Morgrave would be disgraced over this affair, so it was rumoured. Nothing of the crimes had been solved, nothing stopped. The great man sat, mummy-tanned and harsh, in his elegant office, playing with toys brought from Egypt. It had come out, Morgrave consorted with whores.

Like me, thought Moans and smirked, and had his gin.

Just then the noise started to penetrate into the public house. It was not after all the intermittent drum-rolls of thunder, accompanied by a sink-green flash at stained-glass slits. Something else was up. And Moans recalled the riots there had been, the arson at a printer's, and the ransacking of a stable where a steam-driven horse was kept for a joke.

The bar was putting up its ears. Bold with booze, the drinkers were ambling into the street, to see.

Moans became aware of his duty, and with a tug at his saucy hat, he too went out into the night.

It was not dark enough. The sky above the poverty-stricken houses, which tilted on to one another like a shuffle of cards, was streaked with something red. A fire had caught somewhere. And in the roil of clouds was also something strange, tangles that looked like dismembered arms and garlands. These puzzled Moans only a moment. He heard now the roar of a crowd, and the high-pitched shrieks of women. This concerned him, and he felt in his bodice for his whistle.

Suddenly a man ran down the street. He was alone, arriving like a messenger. He flung up his arms and his face, lit by the windows of the public house, and by the careless flash of lightning, was insane, or perhaps holy.

The drinkers jested with and at him as he ran nearer. But Moans was dreadfully alerted. The policeman stepped forward, a fat harlot, and grabbed the man, who, halting, clung to him.

'What's up?'

'It's coming,' said the running, halted man.

'What is?'

'The thing. The dog.'

A silence fell. The drinkers stood, and overhead was the sensation of a vast roof of glass or vitreous, a hellish conservatory shutting them all in.

'What dog, then?' asked Moans, the jolly prostitute. Under other circumstances, his voice would have been questioned by now.

'The black dog. I seen it.' The man put his head on the padded bosom of Moans, upon the hollow breasts. 'Oh Christ.'

Moans reached into his skirts and drew out his pistol. No one among the drinkers jeered. Rather they swayed together uneasily, like trees before the updraught of the approaching storm.

Thunder swarmed. And the clouds opened high overhead, a mile above the shuffled street.

Moans saw then the head of the monster. The black snout and horned ears, the red eyes, the jaw that salivated phosphorus. And behind this was a landscape of lunar mountains from which coursed soft lethal crimson lava.

REIGNING CATS AND DOGS

The running man sprang from Moans and ran on. Tumblers smashed on the dirty vein of the street. Questions with only one answer.

All these faces, turned up like saucers to receive the rain of terror, and filled.

And after this Moans beheld the long black limb of the dog, passing over, and put down upon the lighted beacon of the Palmer's Pigeon. And the light was crushed. A smouldering heap of yellow clinker it became, and out of it crawled the ants from their broken nest.

Moans fired, point blank, up into the face of the demon.

But the bullet was like a star that fell the wrong way. And next the world turned over. A wall of bodies hit Moans, bricks of flesh and muscle. While he was heaved up and down, he stupidly noticed, drooping in the air, a woman depended from a cave. In her hat was a skeletal bird, which shot into the night, and from her body splintered a carcass, a mesh of bones that might have been a whale. But she was old and thin as string. The heart of the cave was scarlet, the mouth of the dog. She dropped dead into the street.

Somehow, via some psychic aperture, the fire-engines had got into Black Church. They poured through the avenues with their brass bells ringing, at odds with the useless tocsin of the churches.

From all the little seeds of fire, the flames now spurted, the spilled cigarettes, the over-knocked lanterns, the gas fixtures which exploded, the infernal heat of sheer horror. Or from two red eyes that glared out of the firmament.

The engines ran on steam, not to risk horses, and at their front they had the mouths of dragons. Into the cut of the river the huge tubes were hooked, and ran up now with black water pumped to spew from twenty dragon lips. Hot river rain to quench the fire. A torrent. But the air was webbed by sparks and coals, and red tenements and orange halls rose shining into the lightning-powdered sky. Black Church gleamed and was spangled. On a score of roofs, black figures cried for rescue. The earthly menace was overtaking all other stalking things. Mobs in the streets, insects which carried their homes, a million breakages, the ebb like a sea against the temple walls of churches. And on the pews, pale figures not like the black ones in the silhouette of conflagration, not raging but mewing.

Somewhere a rumble and concussion, some large masonry brought down, falling like a dinosaur, a column of soot and dust.

The moon high overhead and bleeding red.
Pandemonium, fear, fire and smoke.

Kitty, as she lay in the rubble of what might have been an avalanche, became aware of the beefy painted face which hung over her. For a second she did not know what it was, for it was female and male together. And then she saw that this fellow shipwreck was a man who had clad himself as a woman. The crowd had somehow cast them down here. But here was not definite. All around ran alleys and the sides of buildings, but these were no longer coherent, more like a damaged hillside, while above the sky was red and reeling. Thunder resonated and a thousand stones and tiles rattled. But nearer was the washing sea-song of humankind, screaming on ten dozen notes.

'Well, miss,' said Moans. He observed her abjectly. 'There was a beast. Did you see?'

'Oh, yes,' said Kitty.

Moans seemed, in the centre of chaos, a little relieved. 'Ah, you did then. You wonder. If you can credit your own eyes.'

'The City's on fire,' said Kitty, sitting up in child-like amazement, in a sort of aching dream. She had been bruised from head to foot and her stays were snapped and sticking into her. Her mind was also bruised and thoughts stabbed at it.

'Fire-engines,' said Moans. 'Good men. They'll see to this.'

Kitty sat on the mash of ruin, unable to decipher anything for sure.

But then, turning a little, she beheld against the russet sky, the black shape, so exact and positive. The world had come down, but yet *it* was. And though the clouds streamed by, she could not fail to know.

'See there,' she said.

Moans looked.

Above the tenements and burning stacks of Black Church the forehead of the dog was clearly and absurdly visible, and its two ears, tall, like those of a rabbit, humorous almost. Awful. Awful as to know that you must one day die.

'What is it?' said Moans. He fumbled against the evidence, after logic. 'Is it an advertisement?'

'For what?' asked Kitty.

The clangour and the screaming went on at a little distance, and they sat there in their gloomy island, on the rubble of something unidentifiable.

Like two prehistoric persons they were, up on their rock, draped in skins, powerless against the earth and the sky and everything, for which purpose of defence, their ancestors had invented gods.

CHAPTER TWENTY-FOUR

Green Witch

'Another pipe?'

'Not yet.'

'Will keep one ready for you.'

The interior of the boat had not changed. Above, the wooden shelf on which, probably, lay another dreamer. And beyond the small space, all darkness and glimmer. The brazier too had been lighted today, and here the monkey had resumed her seat, and opposite was posted a shadowy figure, leafing through some cards. Irrelevant, all of that.

He would want the next pipe soon, but would wait a little while. It was good to hunger when one knew one would soon be filled.

Velvet noises rumbled in Anger's ears. He smiled, listening to them. The rout of some great city, masonry falling, and the trumpeting of enraged beasts. Perhaps a storm over the river?

But the monkey turned her head, and the man with the leaves of card, he too. Outside the womb of the opium boat, shifted a shimmer of light.

'Safe here?' asked the monkey abruptly. This amused Anger. That she, the mistress of everything, should be concerned.

'Who knows,' said the shadow glumly.

'I go out and see,' said the monkey.

She crept to the opening of the boat and skittered up and away, and after a moment the other followed her, leaving his cards on the stool.

Saul Anger sat up slowly and his head rang and cleared. He was calm and not very interested. Getting to his feet he walked over to the brazier and looked down at what the man had left. In the hot light it was quickly evident, four or five pornographic photographs of young women, smiling and inviting, their hair down, their bosoms bare, wisps of veiling at their loins. Saul took them up and glanced at each one, and in his body came a sleepy stirring, but it did not offend him now, and they were only paper.

Until the last one turned over into his hand.

And here was the girl of the Egyptian dream, crowned with a snake and coiled with flowers. She did not smile or invite, but her beauty was like a welcome. Her pale hair fell about her and over her breasts like flawless fruits, luminous with the want of touching. Even through the grey and brown and white, he saw the pure green of her eyes.

It was true she was a witch, this girl. He had danced with her and she had sent him here. And now she followed him.

In the trance he had not possessed her. As a bride he had refused her, as a child he had let her die. Yet she was the sister he had taken counsel from, and the mother who bore him.

He sat on the vacated stool, and stared at her. Ordinary lust, rich as wine, tingled through his blood, and the animal at his groin was hard and strong, questing, moving about. Could he take her back again into the dream with him? He could have her in the dream.

Impatiently he looked at the monkey's abandoned stool, and the unlit pipes. He let the cards of women fall, and walked up and out of the boat, and climbed down the ladder on to the bank of the City.

The monkey was indeed out here, standing a little way off among a group of others. Before he could peremptorily summon her, Anger became aware of the vast night about him, and of the being of the night.

The ships lay nearby, slowly tossed by some motion of the river, and behind stretched the heaps of usual darkness and brickwork. But there, upstream, and inward of the river's curve, was a heart of fire.

Anger looked at this. It was a great opium pipe, smouldering in the nest of the night, its dream-smoke rising up into a maelstrom of churning cloud. Some dead blackness came and went in this, but that had the appearance only of char. Sound lifted from the centre of it all, a symphony of thunders and human crying, which, at this distance, was almost inconsequential. Even the loud booming bell of St-Davids-by-the-Meadow seemed merely to keep time. It was all upriver, separate.

'The river's full of them blue flowers,' said one of the watchers. 'They float down, half burned.'

'The fire-engines are out, the new ones with dragon mouths.'

'They'll call in the army,' said another.

Another said, 'I heard a dog started it, upset a lantern.'

'All Black Church.'

The wind passed over them, the wind out of the inferno, and brought the myriad scents of the fire, of sweet things cooked, and charcoal, and roasting, and the acrid choking purge of ashes, and enormous heat.

From the opium boat other draggled forms were stealing forth, those not lost in narcosis. They fastened their eyes on the fire, not alarmed, for they had travelled far and seen already monumental sights.

How silent this area beyond the cacophony, the ships creaking at their moorings. And now the Time Piece heartlessly struck for ten o'clock.

'It won't come here. The army'll stop it.'

The monkey came sidling back towards her boat and Saul Anger saw her, but then looked away again towards that other vaster lit pipe, which was Black Church.

She paid him no heed. He was not her child, though she had fed him with her poisonous teat.

He thought of the beautiful girl with her Nile green eyes, left lying on the stool to be fingered. It was as if she had somehow come into him, into his mind and heart, waited there in the darkness within, jade carried into shade. Her grace.

But there the fire was, the red anger his anger had made, and the Dog was there, the Dog that was not real yet *was*.

He was drawn towards this, the final burning pipe of oblivion. It could kill him also, more swiftly, and with pain. He had not deserved a gentle death.

He walked away from the boat, and someone called after him, mockingly. But then the roar from the City became much louder. And through the shapes of other things, he saw to the truth of the fire.

Had there been an end to the night, and then a day, when she had sheltered in a hut above the river? Yes, this was surely so. She was partly a creature of night, nocturnal. At daybreak she had sat on a wooden bench and smelled the oil from the river, slept a little, and in the late afternoon, gone out again, to walk the rest of the way.

She had had no plan, or nothing much to assist her. She remembered only what had been said, what he had said in Black Church, 'Up the hill. The tall house.' Possibly she could find it, some street of fine mansions, and his tall house among them. She had drawn him to her once, and might recognize his refuge. She would go to his door and knock, and doubtless they would turn her away, or he would turn her away. Yet at the idea of this such fury filled her, that she seemed on fire. She would not let him do it. She, who had never attempted to have any say, would speak now. She had not told him of her love. Had been held by, yet barely touched him. If she were to be allowed to go in, if he would take from her the one gift she might offer, then the rest of it no longer mattered. The past would have been cancelled, the wound salved.

It had seemed to her it was his rescue she assayed, but also it was her own. Pasht then had made her into this. Pasht, goddess of joy, had given her true grief and utter anger.

But, in the thrall of a goddess, Grace was humanly a little confused. As the shelter of the hut was vague, so the journey back upriver, along the streets of the outer City, seemed conducted on another plane. Here the black dwellings that surrounded her, the alleys and dirt paths and weedy desperate lots, were transformed into hallucinatory objects, the people who went by were ghosts, unless they made some foray upon her. And this had happened many times. For just as anger and passion had broken free in her, so her beauty had come undone like her hair, and streamed round her, blazing. A few this very effulgence kept off, but others, less able to perceive, were wooed by it, and came upon her eager to partake.

Then Grace, who had been since her first childhood a willing, kindly whore, cursed them and pushed them violently off, and when this was not enough, she fought them, spitting and scratching and shrieking, a fiend. Only one man was able to pin her back against a wall, threatening to kill her with a knife if she did not do as he said. At this Grace, who had already scored his brutish face with her nails, turned like a snake or fish, and bit into his hand that held the weapon. Next moment she was past him and gone, and though he blundered after her, titling her with all the hatred for ever known by some men for most women, he was not light or fleet or possessed by the spirit of a cat goddess, and he did not catch her up.

So she made her way, her mythic journey, back along the roads of the City, grounded and not upon water, elemental as her name, loosed of everything, all responsibility, all care, all thought for others or hope of others, save only one.

And by these avenues it took some time. It took the last peach-coloured hours of day, and the red hour of sunfall, when Kitty, and a thousand other women, were putting on their hats to confront the customs of the world. It took the initial darkness.

Then, ahead of her, above the slumps and slopes of houses, chimneys, bridges and burrowing lanes, Grace saw the core of the metropolis rising, as if quite proud of itself and sure, that panoply of spires and hovels,

REIGNING CATS AND DOGS

domes and tenements, the absolute emblem of the marvellously aspiring yet genuinely crippled wishes of mankind.

Grace stopped on the street, which was not busy, and looked at this, and for the first she properly knew the disgrace of it. Her innocence was no more.

Just at this instant, the storm began, birthed out of the sky with no warning.

It was a violent storm, and those others on the street hastened into their cubbies. They did not fear the rain, for plainly no rain could come down out of this lashing cauldron of dry blackness and avid lightning. Doors were slamming all around, to keep something out.

Grace stood on, her head angled up, and she recalled the supernatural cry she had heard in Black Church. Something horrible had happened. Something unspeakable had cracked the walls of the world and stepped through. Darkness, and blood.

And then in the sky she saw the jackal moving like a mountain. She was able to note every feature. And after this, the cloud boiled over and covered it from her sight.

Thunder shook all things.

Grace folded her arms about herself, as she had in the church above the river. The one she must save, and who must save her, was her enemy. She knew this now.

She walked on steadily, through the slaps and cudgels of the wind. She had always been brave but it had been easier when she was also kind.

The streets ran up and over. Had all the lights been stifled or hidden? Total black pressing down now. She moved into a valley and here the City seemed actually deserted, as if Death's Angel had gone by. She could hear no sound but the storm. But she was near to Black Church, felt it like a terror and a frenzy under her skin.

At first, the fire seemed part of the storm, as perhaps it was. Pieces of buildings and the road began to grow visible, but in such a fitful dancing manner that vision added to bewilderment, and the sense of catastrophe.

Then the clouds were blushed by red. Grace understood, as if everything had been prearranged, what had occurred.

The noise swelled next, and reached her, and with it the perfume of burning, and, most astonishing of all, the whirling detritus of the conflagration started to gush through the air about her and over her head, like a host of winged incendiary moths. Very often a spark alighted on her flesh or in her hair, and she brushed it out absently, to begin with, but in increasing agitation.

After this prelude, the doors of the whole drama crashed wide, and brought the whirlwind down on her.

It was as if an enormous mouth – the fire – blew outwards at her from the midst of Black Church. It blew heat and cinders and fiery motes, it blew screaming and shouts and the ringing of bells and the thunders of collapse. Finally it blew people.

They came running and staggering and crawling and flailing, their eyes red and insane, their lips black with smoke and profanity. Some carried things – boxes and bundles, curiosities, animals and children. The children and the animals cried, but the people who bore them along cried also. They were all children, all animals, half blind with shock and fear, running before and from the fire mouth, into the wastes of darkness.

Grace was knocked aside. She leaned against a wall. A woman tried to pull her away, and next a man. She resisted and they left her.

When the flux of bodies lessened somewhat, she went on again, picking her path between them.

'What – are you mad – not that way—' So they clamoured at her. She put them from her quite carefully now. She did not know how her impatient yet compassionate tappings healed their burns. She did not care.

It seemed to her that now she was reaching the heart of the labyrinth – but a labyrinth it was, for she could recognize nothing, or very little. Over there a spire of some church reared up, still howling with its bell. And there some street was with its lamps yet burning cheerily, in a civilized way, as the flaming ash fell into them. But all about the fire ruled, an architecture of flames. It was not the City, it was the city of Hell.

At the corner a fire-engine gouted out its water through its smart black dragon face. The gang stood sweating and black as it, with the helmets of warrior bronze upon their heads.

They watched Grace pass, white as snow, and did not stay her. Many had gone crazy. You could only do your best.

Around the corner was a fallen street. Maybe the fire had done this, or some other thing. Stark and sooty, the rubble poised against the glory of the wine-red light.

Grace did not know where she was or where she had come. She knew only that above the flames the black dog prowled through heaven. Of this alone she was certain. But of the man, the man who was her lover, nothing. He was not here.

It was then that Grace saw a whiteness which seemed like her own, billowing in the black street. White moths, unlike the moths of fire which raced over, linked by tenuous streamers, perching there.

They turned their heads, and gazed at her, and the sparks darted like fireflies over their bridal veils. So brittle, so tinderous, yet they had not caught alight. Their faces of ancient girls were fixed, fearless, about fourteen eyes the pale blue of dying gas.

The Seven Brides were in the street, awaiting her, and irresistibly Grace went towards them. She had heard of them but never seen.

Had she come to this? An ultimate omen of loss like no other.

She thought they might flutter away as she approached. In the firelight the strings of pearls, the rifts of lace which joined them, trembled and glittered. But they did not attempt to elude her. Instead, they opened like a poor dying white flower that really means to drop apart.

Flimsy as chitin, their narrow fingers settled on her wrists, her breast.

Their sadness was so awful, out of pace with the burning City, slower and deeper, worse.

She let them take her hands.

It came to her the soot and flakes had fallen on her hair and mantled it like one of their own insectile veils.

She was the Eighth Bride. Bereft of love for ever.

Grace looked into their glass dolls' eyes.

She held their hands.

'No,' she said. She leaned to kiss the first one on the mouth. The Bride shrank away, then hesitated. And the kiss was pressed home. Grace turned to the next. Their lips were like dry rose petals kept in a book, petals that should have been candied and eaten in pleasure.

Her tears fell on their papery cheeks. She kissed them all, and always she said, 'No.'

When they were done, these seven kisses, the women wafted immediately from her. Some rite had been concluded. She saw them flit between the broken walls. They did not mind the fire. Perhaps, for them, the cruel world always burned.

Grace put her hands to her hair and the cinders sloughed from it. She had no burns but must be smirched with soot. She looked behind her now, and so she saw the street had filled with a new thing, not the fire, which quivered and sprang.

Never had she seen so many cats, all together, in one spot. Had the flames driven them here? They did not seem afraid. And though the sparks scattered among them, and some miaowed a complaint, there was no dismay. Some even played, patting at the drips of fire with sudden paws. And all the while they rubbed against each other, friendly, with waving pennons of tails. Now too they rubbed against Grace, their sleek bodies gleaming in the light of Hell. Their eyes were emeralds and sapphires and topazes, and the fire lit each one also with a ruby.

Lean cats and plump cats, fat cats like cushions, cats thin as walking sticks. Cats of long fur and of short, and cats almost furless. Cats of torn ears and missing ears and ears like lilies. Cats of foolish names and wise names and no names and secret names.

They had come from gardens and high bowers. From towers and tenements and holes in alleys. Up from the docks and down from the palaces of the rich. Black and red and white and grey, blue and brown and tabby, and all mixtures.

Through the fire they had progressed, yowling with annoyance, untainted. Things crashed round them and they leapt free. They slunk beneath the wrath of chaos, and blossomed here like the froth on a wave. Their voices ascended to Grace over the roar and toll of Black Church. Cats singing their eerie hymn under the shower of embers.

The mermaid girl stood in her sea of cats, and bending to them, stroked their fur, hot as a summer day, and smelled their small cat smell of honey and vanilla, herbs and meat and magic.

All around the flames and the raw bells, all around the wickedness. And here, this; silly, pretty, sacred.

And still they came, jumping from the high places and slinking from the low places, bounding across the obstacles of the night. Cat upon cat.

But from the other end of the street, the last arrival strode, nodding to Grace not to frighten her, stepping over the furry boulders of cats that nipped his feet and pulled his tail. Tall almost as a pony, streaming his golden hair like a harvest moon, the dog from the balance of Anubis, Anoxberus, to lead the way.

CHAPTER TWENTY-FIVE

The Moon Into Blood

To enter Hell was, of course, easy. He looked at it impartially. Like the rest of his kind, he had seen epic sights, and was in a manner now accustomed to them.

The drug moved with him, and he was calm. He expected death with every moment.

The buildings rose very high, and the flame bloomed out of them. Fire-engines hurtled past him. People ran about like beetles. Only he, Saul Anger, seemed to go forward steadily, but then, he was not trying to run away.

He felt, too, childish in those streets, to begin with, as if he had become small and slight, for the fire made everything much taller, and from the gas lamps gushed up fountains of flame. In this way he remembered Guinevere and Lylch, and the houses of starvation and sodomy. There was no need for any anger, for it had been externalized, it bellowed all about him.

Then the drug commenced to change its course within him. A craving rose, like hunger or thirst. All at once the panoply through which he walked was different. It threatened not death, but loss of reason. He began to hear the screaming as it was.

Anger stopped. He could not go on, for in front of him was a great mass of people fighting with itself. Incongruous symbol of the whole, a huge man with a sideboard on his shoulders, reared up from the press, shouting. Beyond, some ant-heap burned sulphur yellow, and there on a stage, a woman swayed, clutching a bundle in her arms. This, evidently, she entreated the crowd to catch. It must be her child.

Saul Anger watched, with the acuity of bared nerves from which now all the opium was sluicing off. He saw her writhe and run about, and turning, desperate, hurl down the baby in its cloth. He saw the baby thrown through the air. And stiff as two posts, his arms went out, but he was nowhere near. The bundle revolved and dashed upon the street. As it did so, the cloth gave way. Anger beheld a child's white face and black hair. But after this the fire threw up some other jet of light. The child was blonde, with green wide eyes. There came a smashing noise. The cloth had opened to reveal a stack of plates, some heirloom china destroyed on the cobbles.

After this, the crowd parted and let him through, and so he had come up against a cart halted like a rock in a river. Things washed round it and it did not move. A woman sat alone amid a pile of furniture, and she held a real child, which screamed and cried.

Saul looked into her face. He had no protection against her, for he had clothed himself exclusively in the drug, and now it ebbed away.

Her face was all faces that fear. And the screaming, crying child was all children in pain, and so all hurt humanity.

The woman gazed at him without comprehension. He realized the child was red with fever and its skin chalked by burns. He thought of Lylch's children, starved and chained and whipped.

'He left me,' said the woman. 'He says, I'll be quicker, off without you. And he went.'

Saul did not speak, for there were no appropriate words, and he had no coldness to armour him. He hoped the fire would sweep down and have them all, the woman, the harmed child, himself. But the fire cavorted and did not come.

'Look at these burns,' said the woman. She wished to show God, but God was not there. This man of black hair and eyes, he would have to do.

The man put up his hand as if to ward her off. But instead the hand settled on the child's scorched head.

Saul Anger did not know why he touched the child. Perhaps he meant to kill it, to make it quiet. In the lurid glare of the fire, the child's colour altered. It cooled. The heat from it seemed to lift off under his hand and diminish in the air. Two pale eyes like jewels looked at him, with the tears netted on the lashes as the other tears ceased. The child murmured. It turned its head shyly into the woman's chest.

'What have you done?' asked the woman. From the child's leg, one of the chalky places flaked, and whole firm skin appeared.

Then a burly man had hold of the cart. He raised it up and began to drag it away. 'Hold tight, ma.'

The woman stared back at Saul, and the child observed him from a sleepy aquamarine eye, until they were pulled between the intervening walls.

Then a building came down close by. There was a ruff of sound and flaming shards splashed into the street. The crowd sheered off, and one clean column of crimson arched into the red sky. There for an instant, held in this spotlight, Anger saw the bulldog of the boot-polish advertisement. The mechanism of advertising was somehow still going on.

Against the thrusting of the crowd, Saul Anger moved forward. His hand, where he had touched the child, stung and was very hot, as if it had been scalded. He felt disembodied, quite ill, sick now with want and need of the drug, yet uncaring. It would be simple to advance, soon it would all be over.

He did not consider what had happened with the child. This night was lawless and had no rules.

Now he had reached the spot where the building had collapsed. He saw men digging at the rubble like dogs. Saul Anger approached and began to dig with them, pulling off the slabs of masonry and hauling aside the beams. He had never been at one with any, yet now he was, and as the rubbish was cleared, a man thanked him with a trembling voice.

Presently they were able to drag out a thin wan boy, and this being the man who had thanked Saul, clasped in his arms. The boy laughed and said, 'I saw an angel, and I thought, I've had my chance now, I'm in heaven.'

Saul walked on. People ran against him and a woman fell. He helped her up, and she bolted away.

Above, the picture of a tiny cat played with a ball, then vanished in the smoke.

An old man sat on a doorstep. The house behind was black, but its roof smouldered, coined with tiny incendiaries.

'It's the end of the world,' he said to Saul. He seemed, as Saul did, ill and calm, only a witness. He pointed into the sky, and Saul glanced and beheld now the blood moon behind the fire. Below there was no landmark, the smoke was closing like a fog. Somewhere in the heart of darkness was the jackal.

Beyond the street where the old man sat, began a void. The smoke had occluded the illumination of the fire, but there was also a strangeness, as if the City had been changed, not only by flame and destruction. Hills rose dimly, some with a rose of volcanic light. And there were distant deep primeval lakes, where waters had flooded out, or oil or beer, which shone.

Things were underfoot. The toys of children and the toys of mankind – books, shoes, shawls, even bank-notes. It was a weird area, a country before or after time, and entering it, Saul Anger knew that here after all lay nemesis, truth and death.

He walked down a stairway. The fog was very thick. It occurred to him that somehow he could breathe in this miasma, where surely another would be choked.

Even so, he moved sluggishly. His body was yearning for the other smoke, the smoke of delight. He ached, and put his hand upon something to be steady.

It was the crooked arm of a wooden sailor. The sailor, ironically, held a pipe. *He* smiled upon the carnage, all at an angle.

Saul looked about him. He had come into a pit that must be the cellar of some public house, for everywhere ranged black barrels, and from these pushed a tart fierce odour. Liquid covered the floor, which liquid burned and went out and burned again, but the flame was a vivid green. He smelled the burning gin, heated and sugary. The drunken brew seeped into his head and abruptly he laughed, grasping the slanted sailor, some figurehead.

Nearby were others. A wooden woman in a flowing dress. A mermaid. And there a pharaoh of Egypt, with a little pyramid in his hands. All leaning sideways in the fog.

Saul noticed that above, where the walls of the drinking house had presumably been flamed away, the tower of a church went up. Staring at it, this black spire in smoke, made him dizzy, and he sank against the theatre of barrels. It seemed they let him down tenderly as friends, until he lay upon the lowest ranks of them. This was the comfort of utter dependency. He had relinquished all, even the figurehead. He knew that here, in the pit, was the negation of whatever he had attempted to be. He was dead drunk from the breath of burning spirits, and dying for the gasp of opium, and useless, without control, drained of anything but the acceptance of everything which he had resisted. He had given up. He had let go. He closed his eyes. And found a sweetness forgotten since before childhood.

Because she had not yet died, Kitty had tried to stay cheerful, and in answer to a few feeble jokes from the policeman in skirts, she had laughed.

Moans, however, despite attempting to entertain her, was depressed.

He could not make out any direction, and when he took his compass from his bodice, the needle went circling round and round, unable to decide.

The smoke had condensed even while it seemed the fire had moved on. As for the terrible head of the beast in the sky, this was now hidden and might never have existed.

They climbed down with difficulty from the height, both privately wondering how they had come up there in the welter of the running mob.

Reaching a sort of abyss that might have been a street, they picked along it.

Brooding silence had folded round them and they began to realize that all the bells, of churches and rescue engines, had fallen dumb. The baying of human throats too was inaudible, though now and then a strangely silken rush betokened the descent of some edifice.

'Gas explosions,' said Moans, ponderously. 'It's been a curse, that gas. Too dangerous. Ought never to have been put in.'

High overhead, like a beautiful cloud, a far bank of light appeared, gauzily gleaming through the fog.

'Upper streets,' said Moans, 'fire's spread. Rich and poor alike.'

Kitty paused and bent down to take up a doll that had been left on the ground.

She stared at it surprised. It was magnificent, with enamelled cheeks and indigo eyes. Its pink dress was of satin. How unimportant even such wonders had become, in the race of panic.

'That's got real hair, that doll,' said Moans, inadvertently adjusting his flowery hat.

Kitty carried the doll. It was too good to throw away, even in the apocalypse.

At the street's end, the smoke was even more thick, and now they coughed convulsively. Moans waved Kitty back.

'You stay put. I'll go on and see.'

He went coughing away, barking off into the fog, leaving her there. She doubted he would return. He had done his duty, but she was an encumbrance.

Kitty talked to the doll.

'I might have had a little girl like you. Dressed her up nice, and curled her hair. And we'd go for walks on a Sunday, and she'd hold my hand.'

Kitty Stockings sighed. Why pretend. She lowered the doll and held it by its waist, trailing, the long golden locks trickling over her sooty skirt.

Bit by bit the glowing bank of the upper streets was disappearing. A red globe loured in the sky instead, the smoke moon.

Kitty looked round, and so, behind her, and glimpsed, lit by this red moon, a tattered advertisement for beer. But through the rags of it pierced two scarlet eyes, and then the muzzle of the jackal was directly above her, and she saw that the pillars of its legs had come down into the deserted desert of the street.

It was useless to deny that it was there. Foolish to believe that it was smoke or dream.

Did it see her? It seemed that it must, though perhaps essentially it searched for something else.

'God forgive me all my sins,' whispered Kitty. 'I never meant to be bad.'

One great leg moved. It slid through a wall, which showered into powder.

There was a vibration in all things, and in her bones. She was falling, was she? Or flying up? Something made her see the doll. Its hair, which was real, was turning white.

Kitty gripped the doll, and waited.

CHAPTER TWENTY-SIX

In the Pit

It was the dog that led her, and she did not resist. In any case, the tide of cats pushed her on. As the Hell light dulled and the smoke thickened, Grace did not lose sight of her guide. She began to feel a curious elation, a weightlessness. Perhaps it was the effect of the smoke.

A church was there, she thought it was a church, a temple of the City, modelled in smog.

Next came a flight of steps, up which the dog climbed and so did she, and the cats rippled around her.

There was an enormous silence now, as if they had gone into some clandestine region of the night. The cats did not sing, only the faintest patter of their footfalls sounded out like scattered leaves, and sometimes their incongruous purring, like a murmurous engine.

Below, deep below, lay the Pit. It was black and lined by coffins. A water lay on the floor of it that burned with lime-green flame. And from the depths things shouldered, eccentric figures, but not alive.

The golden dog jumped instantly down, and Grace smelled the scent of sugar cooking into toffee, and then the companionable aroma of gin.

The cats hustled her mildly, milling around her like rats, as she edged through the rubble into the Pit.

Her feet were wet, wet with gin. And on an impulse, she leant and dipped in her fingers, and licked them. But this was the memory of human commerce. She did not feel human now.

The dog stepped daintily, and around the barrels – they were not coffins – and Grace followed the dog. It was a corrupt wonderland, a cellar lined with casks. The cats frisked in the peridot fires.

Above, the tablet of the fog was riven by black.

Grace slipped by the figurehead of a sailor, and by a mermaid with hard round mammae.

The dog brushed her, and curved away; was gone. Only the cats now, rubbing and nudging against her, the acid reek of the gin and the chocolate smell of the smoke.

Along a ledge of the barrels, he lay, in a ruin of black clothes. His head was flung back. His black hair caught the glimmer of the green fires, and looked alive as some plant. But he – he seemed quite dead.

She went closer, to be sure. She stood over him. The dead are the dead, not to be touched or troubled. Her heart blazed in her, for she had come so far and abstained so long, all her life.

Was it truly the man she had danced with in the hall of glass, among the rainbow and prismatic lamps?

Yes, truly it was. But not dancing now, not tall and strong. He breathed, she could just see it.

She bent towards him, and her long hair brushed his face, and she cast it aside. An image lifted in her mind. Was it something Balthazar the Jew had told her in the boat? A goddess – and all the goddesses of Egypt were one goddess – who had journeyed over the river and the land, to find her lord, a god – and all the gods of Egypt were one god – and she found him, but he was dead, insensate, lost to her. By magical arts she had revived him. By tinctures and spells, and by her own witchcraft.

A second time Grace dipped her hand into the green and flaming water which was gin. She did not think of anything but how she had seen mothers ease the pains of their infants with this brew. Had her innocence returned? She put her finger to his pale closed lips. It did not seem to her that she insulted him, although she would have realized he drank only fine wines, this man. But neither could she tell if the sorcerous spirit had in any way helped him. He did not move. His eyes did not open.

The cats thrust all about her, purring and muttering in their cat voices.

Then she did what she wanted. She lowered her face to his face, and set her mouth on his mouth. And, this not being enough, she pressed her cat's tongue between his lips, her tongue clean and fragrant as fruit. She tasted him. She had never kissed before. Now, the first kiss. Beyond the coolness of his mouth was the fire. She held his face between her hands and searched him, the limpid inner surfaces, and sparks rose through moisture, the fiery moths, towards her.

Up in heaven, the jackal had turned. It moved a pace, possibly half a mile. Below, something white had entered into its sphere of darkness. The jackal sought, the long head casting about. And behind, the ghost of the deadly moon.

Anoxberus saw this, this horrible questing. Anoxberus braced himself and trod up two or three steps into the sky. Beneath, he glimpsed a woman lying on a street, but this was not of immediate concern. The balance was the needful thing. And to balance the black jackal Anoxberus now found that he grew suddenly light and large. The City shrank down as he himself soared upward. Gigantic he became, he towered above the tops of churches, he shone into the black air and drank of his own strength. A colossus now, Anoxberus, and in his path the other enormous dog, blacker than anything, its ruby eyes boring into his.

It should not go by him. Neither to right nor left, nor up, nor down.

Anoxberus bared his silver teeth and the other thing, a little, as if unused to such duels, as of course it was, showed only the edges of its icy fire-rimmed fangs. A low growl, massive as the thunder, issued from the throat of the golden dog.

And the jackal barked, A rusty unembodied sound.

By the river, some clock, which was the Time Piece, struck for midnight. The noise was little, the reciting of a well-taught, stupid child.

Anoxberus gathered himself. He sprang like a spear into the face of night.

He had drifted somewhere, perhaps into the outer universe. He woke and it seemed to him he was on a boat that glided down a river lilting as glass. A cat sat on his body, staring into his face with green jade eyes. Behind her head were a million stars. Out to sea, the great green sea, they would float. The moon would be their sail, and the huge temples would melt away, the City and the world.

But it was not a cat. The pale and beautiful face of a woman . . . Her mouth was on his.

She felt her kiss returned, the live warmth of him invading her. His hands slid over her. She lay against him now, and all the length of her body felt his body, the superfluity of garments, flesh and muscle and bone beneath, life and mortality together.

The woman pulled herself away. She hung above him, her face in its cascade of hair, moon in a cloud. Her eyes were savage stars. She dragged on his clothes, breaking them with her fingers, all the chainmail of coat, waistcoat, shirt, appearance, mask. To his naked body her hands came back, smooth and hurried, her hungry fingers, and her lips that were cold and warm, and her tongue hotter than fire. She was the dream.

He had no strength, save in one part of himself, that animal part. He tried to hold her but she was like a creature in the sea, darting and diving, free, securing his head above the waves and drowning him—

Her hands had also torn off from herself veils of cotton and linen. To his mouth she brought her breasts, like tight-budded flowers, and he drowned now in these, their scent of rose and mint and skin and youth and living. Under her skirt her limbs writhed in his clasp, the thrashing of the sea-thing. But the torrent of fibres rose up and he had her flesh within his hands.

Where now would they go? The boat travelled swiftly over rapids, tumbling yet sure.

It was she, she who had done all things, who drew the organ of his sex into the sweet fruit of her mouth, she, knowing and cunning, making him into the pillar that upheld the roof of the sky.

As the sea-cave wrapped him, and her petal-tongue lapped him, there began to slough from him in pieces a thousand hauntings of a thousand evils. And as her fingers, soft as silk, stroked and teased at the single male aperture into his body, some locked door gave way inside him. Open as the route into the sea, he too, and the horror washed out of him, done with, as if it had never been. The rapists in the darkness returned to shadows, the matchboxes gone back to pyramids. The sword he must not use.

The cats rushed round them, scrambling and miaowing, their purring a low and rasping roar. The perfume of lust, rising like incense, combers of cats, rolling and arching in it. And beyond, the night held back, tangled with gold in the blank dome of the smoke—

Of all things that he had ever wanted, he wanted now only one thing. Nothing else had any importance. He had forgotten who he was, his name, his history. To have this woman, to be inside this woman, in the deep of her, this basic and primordial wish was all he had become.

And for her, the knot of delirium within her stretched and craned to take him.

With the skill of her other lives, she managed it so easily. And he, adept with desire, held fast at the core of her, embarked upon that last procession, that chariot ride into light and darkness, for which only a dream had prepared him.

There was no stopping now, not even if the conclusion were death.

They danced, man and woman, meeting and almost parting, meeting more deeply, to the music of carnality, which is far louder than hate, more rhythmic than anger, more omnipotent even than love.

She above him, struggling no longer for his sake but for her own, that he should pierce her through, fill her, turn her into water or flame. He beneath her, reared against the tumult of her body, holding her to him to receive every thrust, finding his way to the centre of all questions.

And now she lifted herself up into the race of some psychic gale, her hair blown back, her eyes blinded, her throat a white bow.

And he, drowned and killed and never more alive, saw her become the demon of all storms, witch and goddess, never more beautiful or more fearful.

Out of her, or out of her womb and heart, sang a cry so desolate and pure it had no gender but instead a soul. It was a cry of something winged, and flew upwards.

From the circle of flesh and the circle of yowling, purring cats, from the sump of the City, up into new dimensions. And for a second all things stopped. They froze.

In that second a hundred ages passed. There were hurled from Saul Anger now all components of everything. In a blizzard he was refashioned, and spun, molten and total, aware only of forcing himself through the final rings, intent, mindless as an atom, into the ultimate vortex of ecstasy.

The essence of his life, his semen, burst from him, far into the vessel of flesh which held him. Full of stars too small to see, like a wave flung on a shore.

Above, the blackness recoiled from the light. A golden animal and an ebony separated.

The jackal stood and swung its head, and the flame dripped from its jaws. It seemed to listen, to no avail. Leviathan, it paused in heaven like an unwanted dog. Then bending its pointed snout, it curled in under itself and ripped out its own belly. Scarlet ichor poured across the layers of the smoke, changing everything to red, and then nothing was there but something like a heap of dying coal, some poor hearth that had not been tended and went out.

The crack that bisected the sky was more significant. It showed white, and purple veins shot off from it. Through from space itself dashed diamond galaxies. They flowered down on to the place beneath, columns of bright water, heavy as stones.

Rain like crushed masonry descended into burning Black Church. Tiles slid from the roofs and branches of trees sheered off. The cordons and ropes of flame grew magenta, bled fitfully, and sizzled, a map of fading roses.

The lightning ran away.

When the clock struck once, none heeded it, could not make it out. In the river, rain like silver knives. And in the streets, rain like vehicles. The sound of mighty waters. Who could hear, who could not hear the tone of the clock, how the night had turned over like a page?

The cats were spitting, furious, bedraggled, fur flat and colourless, made skinny as eels. In groups and troops, unlovingly they pelted for refuge.

Saul drew Grace in under the shelter of the sarcophagi of barrels. Tired as death, they did not speak. They covered their primitive nakedness against the rain, although the gods had departed.

Epilogue

At Home

All the while she walked there, through the waste, Kitty Stockings knew in her heart. Black Church was black now, burnt and strange. She trudged through avenues of skeletal lamps, and by the façades of things which had no backs. People loitered in silent gatherings, or sat, idle, or wiping the sooty faces of their children, with the remains of their possessions perched around them. It was a grim holiday. Nothing to do. Barrels had been rescued from the wreck. Beer and gin were handed out to any who asked. Kitty drank her fill. Like the rest, it was her due. And on and on the rain poured down like a fountain, as if some sluice had given way. The streets ran like rivers, and here and there still a pylon of smoke went up, vitiated but black, into the mauve sky.

The army was coming, they said, and nurses, and the rich had sent money. One might attend on that, then.

When Kitty reached Rotwalk Lane, it was no more. She had guessed as much. A black treacle, with black gapes in it. A single chimney betokened the Rookery. She gazed up at this and caught her breath at the idea of her tiny room devoured in the gusts of the fire. There she had slept and put on her rouge, and sometimes danced with Grace to the music box. And there, down in that hole, the kitchen had been, with the cosy hearth, the arguments and press of living things, tea, cards and herrings.

As she looked, Ma Crow clambered out from the defile, the sleeves rolled up her red arms. She had hold of a single chair, and this she put down on the treacle of the alley, with a grunt of satisfaction. Nearby stood Jack Black, consoling his bristly head and puffing on a pipe. Round his neck was a filthy stole of greyish fur.

'No good coming scrounging for nothing here,' said Ma Crow to Kitty.

But Jack Black, glancing about, smacked his lips and chucked Kitty under the chin. 'You're looking nice.'

'Who is it?' demanded Ma Crow.

'It's our Kitty Stockings. See here, girl, I've got your darling.'

He unhooked from his shoulders the dirty fur wrap. It was now seen to be a white cat, much tarnished, with green, clean eyes. Handed to Kitty, it purred and rubbed her face with its own. Kitty held it close, smelling its smell of Hell. She wanted to put it in the tub and scrub it white again. Neglected, the doll rolled on the black alley.

'What's that you got?' asked Ma Crow.

'Leave it,' said Jack Black, 'that's hers. Here, Kit, are you on for a go?'

Kitty shook her head. Her hat was no longer with her, and her dark hair hung loose. The white cat was snuggling into this hair. It owned her, apparently. She bent to retrieve the doll.

'Please yourself,' said Jack Black. 'Where'll you go?'

Kitty said, 'I met a gentleman.' This was a lie, but necessary, not to offend. He accepted it at once.

The cat purred against Kitty's ear, and she thought that perhaps the cat was why she had come here. The cat had belonged to Grace.

As she moved away, Kitty felt a peculiar freedom. She had nothing save a cat and a doll. And, herself.

She had not thought she would survive. The darkness had curved over her and she had experienced the darkness, brushing her body end to end. It was cold and hot at once, and she had seemed to fall and to fly, to shrink and to swell. And as this happened, oddly, she had seen a pot of flowers, left somehow intact on a burned window-sill, flare up, the plants detonating into blood and gold, a tree which met the clouds and then disintegrated and crumbled apart. But in the instant that this too must occur also with her, something hauled the dark away and out of her, painless as a razor. Kitty lay on the ground and disjointedly saw two planets fighting in the sky. They fought until a huge bell sounded, or it was the thunder. Then the sky itself was stained with red, and then smashed in fragments and coursed down.

When she got to her feet she was wet through, and in her hand was the decorously pink-dressed child-doll with a crone's hair.

Kitty had put her fingers to her own face. What had gone on with her? She only knew she was alive.

But, walking through the streets, the mirrors of other faces told her, little by little. And Jack Black told her. And Ma Crow, who had not known her.

'I wish I had a glass,' said Kitty to the cat, now, and at this moment she found herself in Drop Street, and here many of the buildings were standing, fouled by smoke, but whole. And then there was the shop of the Jew, and in its window, scrolled with gilt, her looking glass.

Kitty stared in. Her heart turned over. She wished her father had been there, to see her too. The cat purred and purred, and, from her shoulder, began to wash itself, twisting like a monkey.

The Kitty of seventeen, who had appeared thirty, she was no more. This was a Kitty of fifteen, with peach-bloom skin and gazelle gaze. Only see, she was brand new. She was, yes for sure, she was quite lovely.

Kitty tried the door imperiously, which opened. She went into the shop and set the doll on Balthazar's counter.

Balthazar came out of his inner rooms, and Kitty laughed up at him. His stoop, his sad eyes, these made her laugh, from fellow feeling and from joy. He was a good man. He would not cheat her.

'What'll you give me for this?' asked Kitty. 'Will you give me back my music box?'

'If you wish,' said Balthazar.

He is seeing now, not his dead daughter, but his young wife, wed to him beneath the holy canopy, long, long ago. And Kitty laughing at him, is seeing that he is quite old, but so too her best suitors had always seemed in the beginning, when she was so young, as now she is again.

They say some things to each other, and then they go together into the back room, and here they brew black tea and sit drinking it, while the music box is played.

The washing rain streams on, and in here there is a little tamed fire, for the great heat of the summer has perished. The white cat grooms itself, as it will so often hereafter groom itself, between these two.

And she tells him at last of the thing she saw, the beast in the sky, and how it vanished. And he tells her of leading Bullock through the woods of Dogs Island, and how they met eventually and fought, buffeting and cursing under the trees. But daybreak lit the Island, and soon they sat and made no sense of anything. He does not say that Bullock related then that his parents had been Hebrews, who broke his nose at birth, to save him from the Gentile scourge of dislike. Nor how Bullock rowed them back together to the church at the river's edge, St Darks. And Balthazar cannot tell, for he does not know, how Bullock, going into his sanctum, found its darkness full of light, and that nothing stood upon the Bible, no cat of jade, but in the roof were a dozen silver stars. Bullock had then drawn over his head a scarf, and kneeled. With the second night, he beheld the fire raging upriver. And next the tempest of stars, which was the deluge of the rain. Balthazar does not know what Bullock might do, after such portents, and Bullock does not either, but when the rain descends, Bullock positions himself to receive it. From the river, he is a giant, drenched by water. The beacons of St Darks are out.

Besides, these events, told and untold, do not finally concern the man and woman at the hearth. They are already ironically domestic, with the white cat preening between them. There will come an hour when they will remember this with amusement, and there will come an hour, too, when what they have gained will again be taken from them, as from all living things it is. However, not yet.

Grace at her crystal window watched the rain, which came down for so many days and nights. There was a beautiful garden in the rain, and beyond that, a pleasant white road which led back to the City. The house her protector had given her was elegant and sturdy. Never again in her life, which would be long, should she want. Never again must she importune, sell her body like an apple. Only one man owns her now. He knows that he must have her, for his sanity's sake.

Every night, she awaits his arrival, and he comes to her door. Across the white lace table they regard each other. Candles take them to bed. He is passionate. And after passion he makes his confession. He has begun to learn that he must unravel these errors he does not, yet, entirely admit. One day or night he will kneel before her as men do before gods. She is the teacher and he the acolyte. His way is stony and he requires her kindness, for her kindness has come back.

Who is she then, this girl of eighteen, mermaid, and cat, and flower, and priestess? It is her gift to heal, and so she does, not only her lover, but the multitude. On most days she goes out, in her charming carriage, and riding like a lady to the hospitals, those houses of horror, sweeps in wearing her cool green gowns, to lay some fruit or book upon some quaking bed. And her hands skim skin, sadistic with renewal. She spares no one. She makes them well.

She has loved. She has loved with the power of a god. But her love was the cup of her healing. Her rapture and insistence to possess one man, these were the surgical knife. And with her knife she has cut as deeply as the murderer.

All the yearning and all the anguish left her, once she had achieved her goal. Saul, drawing himself out of her body, drew away every vestige of her desire. She had loved him, she had healed him by cutting out from him the tumour of the dark. And though she saw his blood seep away, she could do no more.

In the rain they had looked at each other. For him too the seconds of desire were over. They had been intimate with each other as if they had shared one flesh. Such seizures pass. In the rain gravely they separated, not merely now body from body, but spirit from spirit. They did not ask each of the other a name.

When Grace reached a particular street, still astonishingly upright, an isle of houses among the black slag, there was her accommodation address, with all its tawdry trappings, its mirror and posted bed. And here a messenger had come to seek her with a simple directive. She need only go thence, and wait thus, and from the incoherence of everything, a carriage would appear and carry her away, like the girl in so many stories, to the home of happiness ever after.

And the rain was kissing from her the passion of the Cat, and she was Grace again. Sweet and gentle, easy, light as a feather. She did as she had been invited to, for she had grasped the reason. He had abandoned her before, but now the shadow pushed on his neck, breathing. Here, with him, she could do her work at last.

He sits by her in the rainlight, that glimmer which, catching the moon, is mercury.

'I'm to be honoured. The atrocities, you see, have been solved and prevented. A man, burned beyond recognition in an alley. I picked him at random. He is now the mad scientist, the butcher of Black Church. The rest – mob hysteria at some advertisement. The wretched area will be rebuilt, some new pious name given to it. Do you think me wicked, Grace?'

'No,' she says. She smooths the dark hair from his parchment face. 'No, Charles.'

Morgrave winces. He is half afraid that he has reclaimed her, knowing in some inner chamber of his brain that she is here to absolve him in the ultimate and most dreadful months of his life. All his jewellery she sold, and so he has been able to buy more, gems like fire and water, to dew over her petals. Her beauty less excites or bores him now than fills him with despair. But he has never known despair, and does not see who it is.

'You're a marvellous woman,' he says, her patron.

Grace smiles. She has loved. It is like the memory of some great procession, when she rode into a desert beside her lord. It was long ago. It does not hurt her. She thinks without pity, *When I was young—*

Sometimes in her dreams she dances with him still. The Seven Brides do not enter her sleep, the omen of her loss. Nor does she query Pasht, the goddess of delight, for it was not Pasht who took away the keys of heaven. In a way, Grace knows quite well, if he had come with her at the first, out of that palace of glass where they waltzed, then – then – but happiness which has never been is really impossible to envisage. They would have been one thing for ever, perhaps, even beyond life, one thing, safe in the boat of joy that sails eternally to the sea. But their union was too late to save more than the City. Even the most generous gods cannot give what will not be taken. Soft, the paw of the infinite Cat; the gods do not need to be cruel, we are so skilled in it ourselves.

In the years ahead, sometimes Grace will sit with Kitty, who has been found in the house of Balthazar, after inquiry. And Kitty will be another Kitty, with several white cats round her, and a child in her lap. The women will play cards, and sometimes rising up, they too will dance. 'Do you remember when—' Kitty will say, and they will laugh, and have a little swig of dustbin gin.

When I was young, I loved you then, and you were all the world to me.
But who can hold the world?

He fell out of heaven, the golden son of the morning, and landed in a midden.

Yelping and disgustingly snuffling, Buskit scrambled free. He recalled he had done something relevant, and forgot what it was. Probably he had killed some rats, for he felt sore and nipped and thirsty.

Nearby, the river, crocheted with rain. Surely it was by the river he had lain down? Things were not the same.

The places of his days were not as he recollected. Smoke and gloom and water all about, and straying people, but as ever the occasional thrown stone.

Buskit scratched, cocked his ungainly leg against a post that might once have been the entry to some dwelling, and turned about to see a scrawny cat mocking him from a wall.

Buskit too must lay aside his glory, and for Buskit it was not difficult. Barking with the most idiotic bravura, he rushed upon the cat, his natural enemy, and chased it down the scarecrow miles of Black Church, through the alleys and up the lanes, over piles of rubble and the vestiges of dismembered lives.

At length, a burned dead tree, and up this the cat escaped, spitting and cursing Buskit.

Below, he circled a little, howling and gurgling his wrath. So much for ritual.

But then, the night was drawing close, and loudly and without surcease the cold rain clamoured.

Perhaps he had not known the way before, but now so much had come down, it seemed no effort to detect his road. Buskit galloped towards home.

Of all the regions of Black Church, the antique parts of it, the well-made upper streets, the outer hovels had survived by far the best. Among these, the domicile of Ralph Mooley and Albert Ross crouched all intact, and within its always soot-blackened interior, that seemed to have been exposed not to one, but to a hundred conflagrations, the two men sat at their unlucky table, the boat, dismally drinking beer.

'What's to be done with it?' asked Mooley. He meant the state of things in general. 'They promise to make it better.'

'Yes, so they do,' said Albert Ross.

'All wind and woof,' decided Mooley.

Just then, through the slosh of the rain, which also fell somewhat inside the room, they heard a devilish scratching.

'Rats,' said Mooley. 'Vermin.'

'There was a ship,' said Albert Ross, 'the *Ocean Pride* was her name. They heard a scratching in the hold—'

'Hold your noise, Albatross. It's at the door.'

They peered, across their grisly den. What would come in? There had been such talk of demons.

'Leave it be,' cautioned Mooley, snatching up the bent spoon, his big head wobbling.

But the sailor went abruptly, with his hopping, listing gait, straight for the door. He did not hesitate, but threw it wide. And there in the downpour stood a rancid bundle of sticks, somehow constructed like a hound, and decorated by itchy orange hair.

'It's the old dog,' said Albert Ross, his voice as warm as the summer which had now been ended. 'It's old Buskit.'

Buskit sloped in, belly low and box face bristling, saturated as a ginger mop. He huffed and snorted, and shook himself, and the air was bright with spangles of rain.

'Useless clot,' says Mooley. The dog watches him with eyes which have seen the secrets of the upper air, but eyes which have forgotten that, and remember him instead. Buskit sneezes evilly and scratches his flanks, his thin legs ridiculous, and his mud-doused tail held high.

Mooley puts a piece of bread into the beer, and retrieving it, holds it out.

'Here, have this, you mucker.'

The dog hurries over and slavers up the bread. Buskit is home.

As the night lies close upon the City, Buskit lies in among the tarpaulin and the quilt, where Ralph Mooley and Albert Ross repose in sleep, their three legs knitted, arms fast about each other. And Buskit snores and dreams, snapping at his worrisome fleas, chasing rodents and felines over the moon.

But outside the moon is veiled in water. It is raining cats and dogs.

When the rain is ended, by then he is far off. And as the City moves, to the strokes of the Time Piece, away into another year, and so into the future, he is farther still.

The tall house had been consumed. Its black and ornate furniture, its curtains of oxblood and mulberry, its palm trees, its selective room, the balance and the sword. Even the ring is buried under those foundations, the harmless ring that portrays Anubis.

So much he discovered, the first morning, going slowly up the side of the hill. A fallen tower, and the servants on the street, as everywhere on the streets they stood, the dispossessed. He had been sorry for them. Been sorry for them all.

But Angier's money was not stored in Black Church. It was safe and ready for Angier's heir, who took it, pillaged it, and went away.

What Grace had seen, the blood which dripped out from him, he was conscious of. There was no time to waste. He had been a prisoner, shut in the confines of houses and the soul. And the world was very vast.

The opium had killed him, perhaps, as he had reckoned that it would. Or the healing of lust. Or the dog which tore itself apart. Yes, probably the dog. But when he laid his hand upon another, he felt the virtue flow out of him and into them, as when he had touched the child in the fire. He could make no check upon this. He gave to them, and every giving lessened him.

Saul travelled away into the world which he had read of. He looked at it, coolly and quietly. He took no spice with it, did not colour it over. He saw what was to be seen, the mountains and the plains, the other cities and the seas, and the men and women who were there.

He had moved slowly from the moment that he left her, the girl with jade eyes. Perhaps he had not left her altogether either. He thought of her now and then. Who had she been, that lover he had coupled with in chaos?

He thought too about Angier, the old man, and how he had died, and the carriages came in over the snow, and the jackal's head that must have been a shadow.

He resurrected his childhood, but he had no fury at it now. It seemed near to him, closer than his days and nights in the house that was a tower. He did not ever dream.

One morning then, in a foreign land, and a city as unlike the City as was possible, brown stems of clay and brick, grapes that grew wild as daisies, and this wide pewter river, dusted by mist before the pink sun rose, a river so wide it took an hour to cross.

Saul boarded the boat, and positioned himself astern, away from passengers and crew. Already there had been a blind girl at the quay, and he had put a coin into the broken guitar that was the begging receptacle, and she had caught his hand. Like unguent, the strength ran out of him and into her. He did not grudge her this. But he was weary.

He leaned at the side of the boat, and its rosy sail was spread. As they set off across the water, birds were rising from a marsh of reeds.

Saul Anger thought of how he had made the matchboxes, red and black and white. He was at peace with this, and noted only partly that the sun had begun to rise, like the birds, out of the marsh.

Something brushed by him. He looked down. A wonderful black dog was on the deck, its hide like silk. Some rich man's pet, no doubt.

Its ears pointed upward and its muzzle was long. Its legs were slender columns, and the feet delicate, precise. Two eyes like agates met his own. It had a collar of gold.

It came to Saul this was not a collar but a necklet. It was not a dog.

He held the midnight eyes and grew giddy, but that was not uncomfortable.

The symbol of the Infinite sat down upon the deck. Otherwise, beyond himself, Saul realized the boat was now empty.

He had come into the presence of the Conductor of Souls. And in such a way, he knew himself forgiven. But also there was to be justice.

Tanith Lee

Saul stayed where he was, and gazed into the cosmos of the Jackal's eyes. The riddle was, after all, answerable.

As the boat of the rosy sail docks across the morning river, they learn, the travellers, that one of their number is not to be found. A wealthy elderly man, quite handsome, yet grey as ash, his face creased and seamed, picked at by time as if it had tried to reach the bone. A face cold and exact, almost like the face of a clock.

There is some outcry and extravagance. A search is made, to no avail. Where, oh where, has he gone to? Has the river taken him? Or can it be, the sky? He has vanished without trace. As do we all.